Toward the Flame

Toward the Flame

RAY DEAN

BLUE NOTE ⚠ BOOKS
BLUE NOTE PUBLICATIONS
FLORIDA

Library of Congress Catalog Card Number: 92-075781

ISBN: 1-878398-22-9

First Edition: August 1993
Blue Note Books
a division of BLUE NOTE PUBLICATIONS, INC.
P. O. Box 510401
Melbourne Beach, Florida 32951

Printed in the United States of America

Toward the Flame is dedicated to my loving wife Celeste, who never for one minute debated whether I could write, and who also felt quite free to tell me when she thought my writing wasn't good enough. She also fully understood the sacrifices necessary in order to get this book out while I simultaneously worked a seventy-hour-a-week job.

I would like to personally acknowledge Bill Steely, a genuine psychic whom I happened to meet during a tour of my hospital. Being a skeptic, I had to be coerced into getting a "reading" by him. The first thing he told me was: "Finish your book." At the time, unknown to anyone other than my wife, I was halfway through writing my first novel. He also predicted the long-awaited birth of our first child, along with the correct month. I have since opened my mind to the possibility that such mental powers may in fact exist.

I also want to recognize my parents, Vanda and Skender Nuredini, for their tireless support and dedication to my professional success.

To Alexander Scriabin, whose music captured my soul at age fourteen and has never let go.

To Paul Maluccio, for taking a chance on a newcomer.

Lastly, I want to thank ten thousand patients: for giving me an understanding of human pain and triumph, the primary forces which motivated me to write this novel.

Toward the Flame

CHAPTER ONE

"Are you in or out, Xave?"

The questioner was the dealer, and one would not have guessed that Tom Banks was Xavier's best friend. Tom stared at him with intense countenance, a slight eagerness, and a scrutinizing gaze.

"I'm in." Xavier tried to speak without emotion; seeming either excited or anxious would give an advantage to his playing partners. He also tried to quiet his racing heart; had his playing partners put a stethoscope to Xavier's chest they would have detected a heart beating twice the rate of a normal one. Xavier tried to listen to the soft sounds of Mozart emanating from his hidden walkman through slender metal headphones. Xavier was not fond of the hard or "alternative" rock music that his companions insisted on for background music.

Xavier was holding a pair of aces, the best possible hand in this peculiar and wicked mutation of poker called

"Guts." The rules of the game were simple; the best two-card poker hand wins, but you have to first declare if you are in or out. The rub was that if you were in and lost, you had to match the pot; in other words, all losing players put the same amount of money back into the next game as the winner just took. More importantly, this meant that the pots would often grow rapidly into sums which strained the budgets of these otherwise frugal and as yet still poor medical students.

"How 'bout you, Sam?" Tom shifted his stare onto the next player, going clockwise around the table.

"Nah, not this time."

The same procedure went around the table and only three of the six decided to go in on this hand, including the dealer Tom.

"Let's show 'em, fellas, but you can get out your wallets 'cause I got a pair of aces," exulted the future Dr. Banks.

The other player in on the hand, John, threw his cards down in disgust, and the others reacted with some amazement. Tom began scooping in the pot towards himself before even looking to see what Xavier had. But then Xavier deliberately laid down the matching hand, thus making an inconceivable draw. The shock and disappointment in Tom's face was almost matched by that of Xavier's, but Tom, by nature being more emotional, leapt out of his chair and slammed his fist against the wall.

"I can't fuckin' believe it! It's never happened. It CAN'T happen! One in a million! Damn, Xavier, you suck."

Xavier knew that Tom wasn't truly angry at him; this was a standard emotional reaction in this game, particularly at three-thirty in the morning after several beers. The game had started some eight hours previously, as the group of second-year medical students was celebrating the completion of the next-to-the-last section on pathology. This series of intense studies on the physical evidence of all forms of disease was the major subject of the entire second year. Despite the toll the game would take on the participants physically, it was the perfect mental antidote to the stressful, nearly endless textbook studying that comprised the second year. All were eager to be done with it and move on to the more exciting challenges of the third year, where students actually began caring for patients and applying their knowledge. They faced one last obstacle, the section on renal pathology, a section that most found especially difficult and tedious.

There was an unspoken taboo in the second year against jumping ahead to look at the upcoming section before taking the exam for the preceding one, but Xavier had violated this tenet and paid the price for it. He found the viewing of pictures of microscopic, desiccated slices of diseased kidneys to be incredibly laborious, confusing and even intimidating. The latter feeling was an uncommon one for Xavier, for he was filled with youthful determination and confidence which bordered on arrogance. Yet even the strongest of students was worn down by this time of year, tired of memorizing endless facts and going through the periodic trauma of do-or-die examinations. Even the process of grading the exams was traumatic for a student; as you turned in your exam card, a sober-faced attendant slipped it into an automatic grading machine and you listened with horror as each "pop" emitted by the machine indicated a wrong answer. On his poorer efforts, Xavier had imagined the series of pops to be coming from a machine gun, gunning him down along with his career. Fortunately Xavier had learned that having many mistakes was common, and that the grades would be put on a curve.

The weekend poker game forestalled that other bit of

psychological trauma perpetuated by the medical school: the Monday morning posting of revised class rankings. Competition for high class rankings was intense, and the professors at the University of Florida College of Medicine did much to make this competition even more intense. Students were constantly reminded of how critical their rankings were, and threatened with poor grades as a motivational tool. Many students had been surprised at the atmosphere here; a northern-style pressure cooker that one would expect to find only at such prestigious medical schools as Harvard and Yale. But in Gainesville, Florida, formerly a small town of hog farmers and now home to the biggest "party school" in the south, the undergraduate University of Florida, a student quickly had to learn new coping skills. One of these was to form a clique of six or seven compatible colleagues who could study together and play together.

"Gimme the cards, guys, it's my deal. No blood from you, Tom, but John you gotta match up," announced a controlled Xavier.

"Tell me something I don't know, Xave," responded the lean, wizened-looking John Cerrone, the most volatile member of the group.

The pot had been growing now, due to some draws and a few other hands in which three or more people took the risk of going in. The six had played straight poker for several hours, and chips worth quarters and half-dollars had been passed back and forth. Then after the mandatory 1:00 A.M. pizza break, the game of "Guts" had been called. Once this occurred, chips were nearly forgotten as the pots reaching upwards of fifty dollars had to be matched with the "green stuff."

Xavier shuffled the cards somewhat nervously, had Tom cut them, and then dealt everyone first one card and then the other. Xavier's heart sank as he looked down at a queen and a nine. It was essentially a worthless hand, unless he wanted to bluff, but that seemed risky considering this pot had grown to about ninety-five dollars. Xavier contemplated the consequences of losing. He had strained his budget recently on buying an octagonal poker table for just these occasions. He enjoyed hosting the group in his old, one-bedroom efficiency and then being able to collapse in bed immediately after the games were over.

The worst consequence of losing big money that night would be that Xavier might have to ask his parents for money, something he despised. Not that they didn't have it, for indeed they had an abundance of it. Xavier was born Xavier Alexander Howell, second son of Marie and Charles Edward Howell III. The Howells were a fourth generation family in Charleston, South Carolina, relative newcomers, but had managed to escalate themselves into the downtown upper class known as the "bluebloods." They also lived "South of Broad," which was a mark of distinction. Broad Street was an historic, brick-paved street which sectioned off the remaining land facing the Atlantic Ocean. The barrier to the sea was known as the "the battery," which also was used to denote this special area. The entire area south of Broad Street was filled with gorgeous, variously colored antebellum homes, all one hundred years old or older.

The fact that Charles Howell III was accepted by the old-money bluebloods was something of a miracle in Charleston, and it had certainly not been easy. A man of uncommon determination, he had parlayed a knack for clever real estate dealings into a fortune. Becoming rich wasn't by itself enough to be accepted by the bluebloods, but Charles had also gotten many of them to invest in the development of the nearby barrier islands and make a lot of money in the process. Further, he had adopted the proper Charlestonian customs and the attitude that Charleston was the center of the universe where foreigners were unwelcome, except as tourists.

Charles had also helped his standing immensely by marrying a true blueblood, Marie Ashley Ravenel, the only daughter of the longstanding Ravenels who lived on the battery. Charles and Marie had two sons, Charles Zachariah, who preferred "Zack," and Xavier Alexander. Both were expected to follow in their father's footsteps—first, in carrying on the family business, and then, in continuing to nurture the growing prominence of the Howell family in this elite community.

Zack had accepted this expectation seemingly without reservations, but Xavier had trouble with it from the start. He disliked being told not only what to do but also what and whom to like. He did not like real estate, he did not like the stuffy atmosphere in downtown Charleston, and he especially did not like being scrutinized to see if he was going out with a "proper" girl. Xavier truly did not seek or thrive on conflict; he just found himself enmeshed in it due to the rigidity of his family and the discordance in their personalities. So just by trying to follow his heart, he soon was deemed "the rebel," and was continuously chided and even chastised for his "bad choices."

One of these choices was to quit a "proper" school, the College of Charleston, and transfer all the way down to Florida State University in Tallahassee. It was bad enough that Xavier had expressed a desire to study premed, and not join Zack in Father's business; but to leave Charleston and go out of state was something approaching blasphemy. The family did not reject him, but simply hoped he would "get over this phase" and return to Charleston, even if to study medicine there at the Medical University of South Carolina, or "MUSC," downtown. When he did not, and matriculated into the University of Florida College of Medicine, this had created a rift. For Xavier to ask his parents for money would resume his dependence on them and prove that their negative evaluation of him was correct.

Xavier's momentary musings on the consequences of a failed bluff soon convinced him that going in on a Queen/nine was out of the question. However, as the in or out question circled the room, oddly, everyone declared out. Xavier, being dealer, would be last to declare; and if he declared in, the others would get another chance to get in. Xavier began reconsidering whether he should declare in or out, as it appeared no one had a strong hand and the large pot was probably scaring them off, too. Xavier's courage rose as did his heartbeat, and throwing out all the logical arguments he had just considered, he declared himself in. He did it forcefully and quickly, trying to give off an air of confidence that he indeed had a good hand and that challenging him would be foolish. His declaration was met with a barrage of various reactions, including "Ah, he's full of it, guys!" and "Somebody take him on, I got a four and a deuce!" This latter comment, made by Jimmy Roddenberry, would usually be considered out of line, but this time nobody cared.

"All right guys, anybody going to try?" Xavier tried not to overdo it by saying, "I'm ready to take my money," for this might have given away the semi-bluff. The final go around began with John, who angrily threw his cards down. "Fuck this game!" he hissed as he stormed off, indicating that he was obviously out. Jimmy also let himself out, followed by Lenny and Ken with disgruntled proclamations of being unable to challenge. That left Tom Banks, and it seemed fitting that it was left to him to challenge Xavier after the fluke of the last hand.

"Xavier Howell, I know you ain't got shit. You got the biggest balls of anyone here, but I ain't buying it. I'm in, baby!"

The air was so ripe with tension and electricity that it was cruelly ironic that just as the two warriors were about to flip their cards and decide the outcome, the light above went out.

"Goddamn it! Somebody turn on the kitchen light or something, Jesus!" screamed Tom.

Xavier immediately said, "Nobody move. The kitchen light ain't enough to play cards on. But I got a spare bulb. I'll get it, but nobody touches anything!"

Despite the fact that these six medical students were friends, the high stakes and their mental states had created a temporary atmosphere of hostility and even mistrust. Xavier quickly scurried towards the kitchen, bumping into the edge of the counter painfully as he was not accustomed to total darkness. It was eerily dark, since even the usual moonlight coming through the one window was blocked by cloudy weather. Xavier stumbled around some more until finally finding the object of his desire and made his way back to the table.

"All right, guys, I'm going to have to stand on this table to reach the light. Hold it steady." Xavier climbed aboard, deliberately standing on top of the large pile of money while he began reaching for the socket. The cord of the still-playing walkman stretched across his face and he readjusted it. He then found the bulb, unscrewed it, and handed it down to one of the others. He proceeded to reach up with his right hand, trying to find the socket with the end of the new bulb. The socket was not too high, as Xavier's six-foot-four frame made it easy to reach the ceiling. Frustrated by his failure to locate the socket with the bulb, he reached up with his left hand to grasp the outside of the socket so he could direct the bulb into it. The instant he did, there was light in the room.

It was caused by the sickening passage of electricity down Xavier's arm and throughout his body. He stood, transfixed but convulsing violently, as the gathered friends watched in horror. An arc of voltage seemed to emanate from Xavier's headphones and set his hair on fire. The sight of flames jarred Tom out of his momentary paralysis and he bear-hugged Xavier away from the evil grasp of the malfunctioning socket. The electricity still in Xavier's body transferred into Tom, knocking him away and throwing him to the floor in a heap.

Xavier lay on the table, his body still twitching slightly, his scalp still on fire and the pot money ironically burning in a pile right next to Xavier's chest. John was the next to respond, yelling "Call 911!" and running over to try to smother the flames covering Xavier's limp head. Jimmy frantically began searching to find the phone, while the others were still wildly shouting or ironically paralyzed in mute horror. John tried to feel Xavier's pulse but instead felt a very mild electrical shock as well as burned skin.   Indeed, in the resumed darkness, the greatest sensory input came from the sickening stench of electrocuted flesh, along with the ongoing cries of fear and confusion amongst the remaining.

"I can't feel a pulse, dammit! He isn't breathing either! Somebody help me do CPR and somebody check on Tom."

"Xave's fried, man, he's a goner," offered an immobile Lenny.

"Shut up, you fat fuck! Ken, you breathe him and I'll pump the heart. Come on, move it!"

And so the two worked on Xavier furiously for several minutes, alternating duties as the "pumper" grew fatigued and the "breather" light-headed. Their efforts met with no success, and despite trying to pound on Xavier's chest with his massive fist, John could not get the electrocuted heart to restart. Just as he paused for the first time since trying to revive Xavier, flashing red lights outside the window announced the arrival of the 911 emergency vehicle. A team of technicians bolted through the door. Having been already apprised of the situation by Jimmy, they ran to the table and carefully transferred

Xavier to a stretcher. Once secured, they eagerly but cautiously loaded him onto the ambulance. John and Ken lifted Tom, who was alive but unconscious, and helped load him onto a stretcher and into the ambulance, also. The ambulance sped off, lights blinking and siren blaring into the dark night.

The remaining four collectively slumped to the floor, sitting in utter dejection and horror. They silently contemplated the reality which appeared forced upon them: the reality that Xavier Howell was dead.

CHAPTER TWO

The sound was gentle and rhythmic, like the chirping of a songbird, but clearly more mechanical and lifeless. It droned on and on, accompanied by another repetitive sound in a different key, though clearly not designed to make harmony with the other. This "chamber orchestra" of beeping life-support machines had been serenading Xavier for three days, but only now did he first become conscious of it. His foggy mind struggled to come to alertness, as if the auditory input had served only to tickle Xavier's higher functions. As he grew aware of the beeping sound, Xavier opened his eyes for the first time since the accident. Initially he saw an unfocused blur and struggled desperately to make sense of his environment. He was further brought into consciousness by the squeezing of his left hand, accompanied by the exhilarated voice of Mrs. Howell.

"Xavier! Xavier! It's me, your mother! Oh, I wish

your father and brother were here, I told them I had a hunch today would be the day! They'll be back later today. You're going to be fine, Xavier, you're safe in the hospital here."

Xavier's intellectual functions returned more quickly, but the few facts he had to ponder made no sense to him whatsoever. Hospital? Why? And why was his mother here? He began his first attempt at speech.

"What. . . hap . . .pened?" Xavier was puzzled at the lack of fluency that he displayed.

"You've had an accident, Xavier, but you are going to be just fine. You suffered some burns on your left arm, but they'll heal."

"What . . . acc. . . accident?" Xavier's eyesight was improving and he could now make out the rough outline of a face leaning over him.

"You got your hand burned when you tried to put a light bulb into an apparently defective socket. You are in the burn unit right now and they'll take care of you."

"You're hold. . . ing something. . . back. Why. . . is my speech. . . so difficult?"

"Xavier, the doctors will be here soon to tell you whatever you want to know. You got temporarily knocked out by the jolt. The doctors said that it was normal to expect some slurred speech and blurry vision when you awaken." Mrs. Howell didn't have the heart to tell Xavier that he had been revived only with cardiac drugs and electroshock. She also couldn't tell him that he had been in a coma for three days with uncertain prognosis.

The first visitor, in fact, was not a doctor but a nurse who seemed genuinely pleased to see that Xavier was conscious. She checked Xavier's vital signs and checked to see if all the intravenous lines were working well. She told Xavier that all was in order and that she would inform the doctor of his status. She asked if he needed anything, and after he shook his head "no," she departed. It surprised Xavier that the slight movement of his head was extremely painful.

"What. . . the hell. . . is wrong with my. . . head?"

"You suffered some minor burns there, also. The doctor said those were not as bad as your arm, and your face is totally unburned."

"Are there. . . any other burned areas you're. . . not telling me about?"

"No, Xavier, that's all except for two small spots on your feet. You need to rest and try to relax."

Xavier did not want to relax. He wanted answers, explanations, details, and prognoses, not pacification by his well-meaning but insufferable mother. He found himself having waves of nausea and sleepiness. These interfered with his efforts to extract more information from his mother and also to check out his motor functions one by one. He discovered that although his lower extremities were in good working order, his left arm was not only heavily bandaged but also strapped down, immovable. His right arm had an intravenous line in it and was sore in several places, including the wrist, apparently from needle jabs. As Xavier slowly continued his exploration, the next visitor approached, a man wearing the same kind of drab green scrubs, face mask and gloves that both his mother and nurse had worn. The man stood only about five foot seven, but was robust in build and walked with an aggressive, purposeful stride.

"Welcome back, Xavier. I'm Dr. Johnson, the Burn Unit director. I hear you're a student here at Shands, so not only will you get the best, but I'll make sure they don't stick any med students on you to practice. Well, let's take a look at you."

The doctor made a quick check of Xavier's pupils, listened to his heart and lungs, and checked to see how fresh the bandages were. He explained, "The burns we'll look at later; they just treated and wrapped you a couple hours ago. How do you feel?"

"Like I've been clobbered. . . over the head by a two by four. What's with the nausea?" Xavier's speech was starting to flow more easily, and his eyes now could focus to perhaps ninety percent of their normal capacity.

"Well, those burns can really hurt, so you're getting some I. V. Morphine to take away the bite. Morphine can be sedating and produce some nausea, as you may well know. You have third degree burns on your left hand and arm, second degree burns on your scalp, and relatively minor burns on the bottom of both feet where you have what we call exit wounds."

"OK, I can deal with the. . . burns. Why was I out so long and why can't I . . . remember anything?"

"With any kind of electrical shock leading to unconsciousness, it is common to have no recollection of the event. At my request, you've been followed by Dr. Bream, the neurologist. He'll be in a little later to discuss that aspect of your accident with you. Try and be patient, and enjoy the break from medical school."

With that, Dr. Johnson wheeled around and exited, before Xavier could say "Thank You" or actually what he was really thinking. Xavier didn't like the last comment Dr. Johnson made, because the last thing he wanted was to fall behind in medical school, where it was hard enough just to stay caught up.

"Mother. . . have you heard from any of my friends here?"

"Why of course, dear. They've stopped by, many of them, and as you can see there are lots of cards and flowers. Two in particular, Tom and Ken, seemed particularly interested and asked that they be paged or called as soon as you were up. Would you like to see them now?"

"Yes, please call. . . wait, what time is it?"

"It's 7:45 in the morning."

"OK, they'll be just dragging in to path lecture. Have the nurse page them and they'll come."

Mrs. Howell departed quickly and Xavier chuckled to himself: there he was, giving orders to his mother. Before the third wave of nausea was quite over, the familiar figures of Tom Banks and Ken Larraia appeared at the doorway.

"Xave, Xave, the man is up and ready to play some more poker!" shouted an exuberant Tom.

"We'll even drag your table up here so you don't have to move!" added an equally excited Ken.

"Hey guys, what the hell happened to me? I don't remember. . . a thing."

Tom leaned forward. "The best way I can figure it is that you were sitting on a weak hand and when I called your bluff, you decided to stage this accident to avoid matching that big pot."

"Come on, Tom, I honestly don't remember anything. The last thing I remember is studying for. . . cardiac path."

"You passed that cardiac pathology exam with flying colors, Xave. But you were seriously bummed out by renal path so you decided to try a little homemade shock therapy."

Mrs. Howell was offended at this remark and replied "Really, boys, this is not a joking matter."

"Mom, relax; if Tom wasn't kidding with me, then I'd be really worried something was seriously wrong with me."

"Who's kidding? You really did have a weak hand in that last game of "Guts," 'cause I cleaned up the mess and your Queen/nine was still there, face down at your chair."

"How big was the pot and what did you have?" asked an intent Xavier.

"At least a hundred bucks and I had a King/four."

The trio of part-time low-rollers continued to discuss the highlights of that evening, especially the double ace draw, but they were interrupted when a large, imposing figure strode into the room.   It was Dr. Bream, the chairman of the Neurology department.

"Good morning, students. If you would, allow me to examine the patient."

The request was unnecessary, since Tom and Ken had already retreated away from the bed, giving Dr. Bream plenty of room. Dr. Bream was known as a brilliant but tough-as-nails doctor who cut medical students no slack whatsoever. He wore a bow tie, a heavily starched, pure white doctor's coat, and a stern countenance. He had a nasty habit of reminding medical students that they were not doctors yet.

"Mr. Howell, how are you feeling this morning?"

"Like I dove into a pool with no water."

"Speech is fairly fluent, good. Let me examine you again." He went through the process of reflex testing, motor strength testing, and pupil testing, nodding his head with each completed task.

"You appear to be making a full recovery."

"Recovery from what, other than my burns?"

"You sustained an electrical shock sufficient to temporarily cause cerebral anoxia and further produce some cerebral edema. The edema was mostly non-focal but did cause you to remain comatose for three days. Your CAT scan and MRI were otherwise normal, and although the test was difficult due to your scalp burns, the EEG was essentially unremarkable. Your cognitive functions should return to full capacity within a few days."

Xavier paused, stunned by the news that he had actually been shocked into a coma. He fully understood the medical jargon of Dr. Bream, and now knew that essentially his brain had temporarily been shut down and was now swollen. He pulled himself together when he recalled that Dr. Bream absolutely never sugar-coated a patient's condition.

"What about memory loss?"

"Some retrograde amnesia is expected, and you may even have some difficulty retaining memory of the events of the next few days. Other than that, I expect no further sequelae, but we can never be absolutely sure."

"I guess there's no point, then, in me studying for renal path, yet." Tom and Ken stifled their amusement, but Dr. Bream surprisingly raised the right corner of his mouth in a wry smile.

He replied, "I'll follow you up in the clinic," and abruptly departed.

Tom and Ken congratulated Xavier on his success in amusing Dr. Bream, and departed for their med school duties. As if on cue, the nurse came back in to perform her duties. When she left, the next in the procession of visitors were Mr. Howell and Zack.

"You missed all the action, guys" announced Xavier. "There were even dancing girls in here a minute ago."

His father and older brother hurried up to the bedside, expressing their excuses and well-wishes. Zack had a present for Xavier, and it was actually quite appropriate; a new Sony Discman portable CD player.

"I heard your walkman was ruined. Dad and I also got you some Mozart and Beethoven CD's to listen to."

Xavier was truly pleased and thanked them. They chit-chatted for over an hour and then paused for lunch. Xavier was fed his first real meal but discovered with dismay that he was looking at what they called a "soft diet," mostly mashed potatoes and jello. Not that it mattered, as Xavier's appetite was still impaired by the medication. Mother insisted that the three elder Howells go out to eat a long lunch and allow Xavier a chance to nap. Xavier indeed agreed, but first asked that Zack put on Beethoven's "Pastoral Symphony" on his new Discman and affix the headphones. Zack could barely put on the headphones since the bandages covered most of Xavier's ears, but it didn't matter as Xavier was soon asleep.

The next thing he knew, he was looking at his family again. "How long have I been sleeping?"

Mr. Howell stepped forward. "Oh, about three hours. You had a busy morning. How do you feel?"

"Better, actually. But there's one question I didn't get answered this morning, and that's how long would I be out of commission?"

"That's an important question. As the doctors have informed us, your neurological injury appears to be clearing nicely and won't require any treatment. Your burns, however, will require several weeks of treatment on a burn unit."

"Several weeks in the hospital?" asked an incredulous Xavier.

"Yes, and the complete healing much longer than that. That's what they told us, and I asked for a second opinion and got the same answer."

Xavier wryly noted the typical tactic of Charles Howell III, getting a second opinion on everything. Xavier's mind, however, shifted to the overwhelming consequences this accident would have on his medical school course.

"Xavier, I know what you're thinking. You're wondering about missing med school. You can't avoid it, you will have to miss some of it. The family all would very much like you to come to Charleston to receive your treatments and convalesce."

"No," Xavier stated in a controlled and somewhat angry voice. "I can get great treatment here with the best doctors in the state, I have my friends, and I can study while I'm convalescing."

"Xavier, you heard Dr. Bream. Your memory won't be totally up to snuff for awhile. More importantly, I checked on your status during lunch; you have been put on the "disabled list" temporarily, and taken off the third year rotation schedule."

"What!? No! I can't believe it! They can't do that! Who did you talk to?"

"Several people, including the dean. They feel that until you have totally rehabilitated, it would be unfair to subject you to the rigors of medical school."

"I have handled 'the rigors of medical school' just fine so far, and a burn to my non-writing hand isn't going to slow me down that much! We need to fight them on this!"

"I checked with all the authorities; this is also the recommendation of your physicians."

"Shit! I can't believe it. So I'm screwed."

Mr. Howell paused and glanced at his wife before speaking.

"Not quite. There is another option. I have spoken with the dean at MUSC in Charleston, you know, my friend Ed Hastings. He has spoken with his people, who spoke with the people down here, and have come up with an interesting proposal. Your third year rotations start in two weeks. You will be well enough to learn, but will still be needing intensive burn treatments. The Burn Unit Director at MUSC is willing to have you come aboard as both a patient and a student, getting credit for a rotation while you are convalescing. All you have to do is help the other students learn what it's really like to be a burn patient, plus attend rounds and take your exams. Once you are healed, you can return here to Shands and rejoin your peers."

Xavier sat in silence for several moments, trying to digest this scenario. He felt waves of different emotions coursing through him, including some anger and resentment, puzzlement, and a thread of optimism. Then he grew angrier as he thought how this sounded like a typical Charles Howell manipulation to get what he wanted. Xavier also realized his father's offer might be a good opportunity, but the anger pushed through and Xavier erupted. "This sounds like more of your crap, Dad, more scheming to get me back to the business!"

Mr. Howell bristled at this, but was surprisingly mute. Mrs. Howell stepped in front of him to handle the situation.

"Xavier, you are correct that Charles used his connections and influence to arrange this. But it is only to please you and best serve your needs. We know how much medical school means to you. We also want to give you the support that only a family can give in times of struggle. You have our word that we will not try to persuade you to give up your medical career or stay in Charleston."

With that, Xavier's rage subsided, for whatever else she was, Marie Howell was not a liar. Xavier pondered the situation a good while longer, but it was inescapably dawning on him that this was an offer he couldn't refuse.

CHAPTER THREE

The view was impressive despite its familiarity. There, in the distance, overlooking the ancient and majestic oak trees which lined the battery, was Fort Sumter. More to the left, one could see the edges of the Sullivan's Island barrier. To the right was James Island, still fairly well-wooded and inviting. And in Charleston Harbor itself, one could see several fishing boats going out for their morning expeditions. As Xavier looked to each side, he could see the old, historic houses near which he had grown up. He noted with amazement again how well they had stood up to the ravages of Hurricane Hugo a couple of years ago. Of course he knew there had been reconstruction and much money put into re-beautifying the area, and no doubt Charles and Zachariah Howell had much to do with that. How symbolic it seemed, Xavier mused, since Charles Howell III thrived on turning disaster into opportunity.

Xavier had spent a couple of days recuperating in Shands hospital before he was flown by private jet back to Charleston with his family. He would still have to spend the major part of each day in the hospital for some time, but due in part to another aggressive campaign by his father, he would be allowed to spend evenings and early mornings with his family. Mr. Howell had hired a burn-specialist nurse to handle any needs Xavier might have, and arranged for her to be available 24 hours a day. She also happened to be tall, red-headed and attractive, a description which could be applied to Xavier's mother as well.

Xavier was sitting on what was known in Charleston as a widow's walk, an outside deck built adjacent to the top of the house. In bygone days, the wives of sailors supposedly would wait there, anguishing over whether their husbands would return from sea or not. The air was not crisp, despite the early morning hour. In Charleston in late June, the weather was oppressively hot and humid, sometimes much worse than that in Florida. Xavier reclined his long, lean frame against the sturdy oak chair which had survived the years, not unlike the historic oaks out in front of the house. He adjusted his left arm uncomfortably, and despite the heavy bandages there was indeed no comfortable position for it. Soon after he had gotten himself re-acclimated to the setting, he was joined by his mother, bringing him some breakfast. Xavier smiled his own wry smile when his saw that he was being served shrimp and grits. This awkward food combination was a Charleston specialty which Xavier actually had grown to like but didn't cherish as passionately as did his family. It was certainly an improvement from the "soft diet" that he had endured over the past several days. Mother not unreasonably expected both "thank you" and some conversation for the meal, although the latter could sometimes be tiring.

"You can hardly tell Hugo was here, can you, Xavier?"

"No, I can't. In fact, it looks like they've been busy building more than just new houses." Xavier pointed off to the right where construction of a bridge over to James Island was under way.

"Yes, the James Island connector was controversial for the downtown people, but you should have seen the controversy over the Isle of Palms connector. My word, I thought we had another civil war on our hands."

Mrs. Howell rambled on with the story of the Isle of Palms bridge for several minutes; and Xavier appeared to be listening, but his mind drifted far away. In fact only a loud car's horn brought him back to his situation and saved him some embarrassment. He reacted with a slight jerk of his body and then turned to face his mother.

"Mother, could you get the nurse? I think I need my medication."

"Why, certainly, Xavier. Are you feeling OK?"

"Yes, just pain, lots of pain."

Having successfully wrested himself from his momentary daze, Xavier pondered how many other visitors he would have had to entertain today, were it not for his need to go to the hospital in an hour or so for his health care. The list could have been endless: aunts, cousins, and probably half a dozen of their kids. He had endured many a Christmas or Thanksgiving gathering at which he had to say at least a few sentences to each family member present. Sometimes this could take several hours, and heaven forbid anyone was missed. If so, one would be chastised on their lack of "proper consideration."

Xavier craned his head to better scan the vista ahead and had to admit to himself that indeed there was much to consider beautiful in Charleston, especially here on the battery. The interplay of historic buildings, indomitable trees, massive sculptures, and the picturesque ocean scene, complete with boats, ships, sea gulls, and barrier islands in the distance, was something to behold. One could go inland just a mile or so and see poverty at its worst, but for those with the money and proper blood-lines, downtown Charleston was certainly a gorgeous place to live.

"Forgotten how beautiful it is?"

Xavier looked up to discover the likewise good-looking and tall figure of his brother Zack. Xavier paused for a minute, contemplating how everyone in his imme-diate family seemed to possess some slight ability to guess each other's thoughts. This was either through intuition or smart guessing, he had figured. Xavier had done it to others as well, although he had often assumed he was experiencing "just a hunch."

"To be honest, Zack, yes. But remember the last time I saw it was when I came up here shortly after Hugo."

"Yes, that was an ugly scene, to say the least, not to mention the noise. My God, I'll never forget the sound of a symphony of a thousand chain saws screaming all day long. You know we made a killing in repossessions and reconstructions afterward. But you don't want to hear about that; I'm just curious about how you're feeling."

Suddenly, Xavier felt a wave of disquieting emotions and thoughts surge through him. He quickly replied, "I'm fine," but then tried to sort out in his mind what he was feeling. It came to him; he seemed to sense that Zack had an unspoken mixture of admiration and jealousy for him, along with a genuine desire to be friends. Being friends with Zack when they were growing up had been difficult, partly because Zack was three years older and associated with a different peer group, but also because Zack and he were of two radically dissimilar mindsets. Neither of them was any more or less rebellious than most other children, but Zack always seemed to end up making the "proper choices" while Xavier often did not. Zack never seemed to mind when the influence of his family was used to further his progress or get him out of jams. Xavier remembered resenting this as early as second grade, when his mother rushed to school to scold a teacher for falsely accusing Xavier of stealing. Xavier had in fact stolen some candy from a girl, something he was not proud to remember. But he remembered feeling even worse that after he told his mother the lie, she went to school the next day and informed this teacher that she simply "must be mistaken, for a Howell has no need to steal."

"You look like you've been to the Persian Gulf war," offered Zack to get the conversation rolling.

"Yeah, well I actually just burned myself so I could get sent back before the fighting broke out."

Neither laughed at the other's sarcastic jokes. Xavier was still having the strong feelings about Zack, but it was different than before. He had always suspected that Zack had a silent respect for him, along with the usual sibling rivalry, but now he knew it. It was as if he could see it as clearly as he saw Zack's wavy black hair.

"Xave, I know we haven't talked much in the past couple years, since you left for college. I wanted to take this chance to let you know that I respect your decision to go to medical school, and I know you work very hard at it."

"Thanks. I'm sure you don't just play tennis and golf all day either."

"No, I've tried hard to establish myself as a worthy business partner to Dad. The business is going extremely well, despite the bad economy right now. Whatever business there is to be done in this town, it gets done only by the most stable, reputable firms like ours. People aren't willing to gamble with an unknown in this recession."

"I understand. I'm glad to hear it's going well for

you," Xavier replied after another somewhat lengthy pause.

"Look, Xavier, part of what I'm driving at is that the door is still open for you to join us. You could get to work immediately learning the ropes, and take it at whatever pace your health or heart dictated. You could even apply your medical knowledge to getting into the medical-office building sector, for that's still a wide open field in this town."

Xavier normally would be somewhat offended by this offer, considering all that had transpired in the past. Usually he would simply decline, and not bring up unnecessary hard feelings. But today he felt a surge of anger far beyond what he expected to feel; and before he could even consider it, he exploded: "Go to hell, Zack! Will you ever quit trying to `get me to see the light?' I'm going to be a doctor, but even if I changed my mind tomorrow, I would not change it for a position as your second in command!"

"Well, to hell with you, then! I come in here trying to make peace and extend an offer without pressure, and you blow up. Maybe your head did get damaged in the accident, or maybe it was damaged a long time ago. Well, I'll never make the mistake of trying to be nice to you again." And with that Zack stormed off, and Xavier almost called for him to return but did not. He tried to contemplate their brief and hostile interaction, but found his mind wandering off again, to some distant place far away from the conflicts of family. Xavier had always been fond of daydreaming, imagining and fantasy, but he always felt it was a totally voluntary indulgence. Today, twice already, he had felt his mind go elsewhere, either spontaneously or as an escape from an unwanted situation.

As he pondered this a bit more, he felt the presence of yet another visitor next to him, and he turned abruptly to see who it was and to perhaps insist they leave. However it was his nurse, Rachel, showing her attractive face to greater advantage by wearing a bright big smile.

"Good morning, Dr. Howell." The somewhat premature use of the title "Doctor" did not go unnoticed.

"I guess it can still be a good morning."

"Anything the matter, Dr. Howell? Are the burns hurting badly?"

"No, pain of a different kind."

"Oh? Do you have some nausea or other discomfort?"

Xavier looked up at her pretty face. He could see that her expression was genuinely caring and that she had no idea what complaint he was referring to. Nevertheless, she was the first person this morning who didn't evoke a visceral and mental turmoil inside him.

"Oh, it's nothing really. Is it time to go to the hospital?"

"Yes, sir. It's 8:50. If we leave right now we'll be there on time. I didn't want to interrupt your visits with your family."

"I wish you had, my dear. I wish you had."

CHAPTER FOUR

Screams of agony were heard not so far away. The smell of disease was everywhere, only partially hidden by the smell of antiseptics and other alcohol or ammonia products. To the right, there was an odd collection of metallic devices, most of them hanging menacingly from a hanger-filled wall. To the left, there was a sinister series of chambers with numbers overhead and drapes hiding the inhabitants. There was tension in the air, and white-garbed, totally covered-up people were scurrying around.

Xavier was escorted into this new frontier, for him, and was immediately put ill at ease, sensing it to be some sort of modern-day torture chamber. Worse than even his own apprehension of the treatments he was about to receive, was a peculiar sense of horror he felt for the unseen inhabitants of the draped rooms. Xavier had been to a burn unit the last couple of days back in Gainesville, but for some reason either he didn't remember it at all or

29

it was a much more benign environment there. He vaguely remembered being heavily medicated prior to going into that forgotten unit.

Xavier was still accompanied by Rachel, who introduced him to Steve, a relatively short man with piercing blue eyes but otherwise mostly unknown features due to the facemask all wore in the Burn Intensive Care Unit. Rachel excused herself, and bade Xavier have her paged when it was time for him to return home in the evening.

"Welcome to the Burn Unit, Mr. Howell. We've been expecting you. Let's go into the side room there and sit down and talk."

Xavier silently complied and the two settled into a small, sparsely decorated room with a table and eight chairs around it.

"Mr. Howell, the records I have, which were sent to me from Gainesville, indicate fifteen percent total body burns with third degree's on the left upper extremity and second's on the scalp. Is that your understanding of it?"

"Yes." Xavier was not offended by the totally business-like attitude of the technician, as he was used to it from medical school; but he found it strangely disconcerting now that he was the patient.

"I understand that you are a medical student, and that somehow you will be continuing your education here while you are recuperating. How much training have you had with burns?"

"Not much, just a small section in pathology where we covered superficial burns."

"Wonderful. Well then, you really will get an education while you are here. Let me tell you a few things you need to know and then we'll take a look around."

Xavier sensed that although this man clearly wanted to help, he did not possess a genuine caring and empathy. Or perhaps it was just covered up by the years of witnessing trauma and tragedy. They talked for quite some time, explaining the process of debridement and other necessary burn treatments, how often and when the doctors would examine him, precautions against infection, proper fluid intake and nutritional support, and much more. Having briefed him, Steve led Xavier back out into the unit and guided him around the relatively small unit. As he led him by the series of small chambers, some of the drapes were parted enough to witness the unfortunates inside. Several were charred or bandaged over a majority of their bodies, and all of them lay immobile and perhaps even unconscious. They were all hooked up to a variety of lines and monitors, even more than Xavier vaguely recalled he was hooked up to in Gainesville. Even worse than the charred skin that still was exposed on several of them was a horrendous bloating, some of them with faces the size of volleyballs and arms the size of small tree trunks. Xavier knew the medical reasons why this might occur but was totally unprepared to witness it; the sight caused him to shudder momentarily. After going through the nursing center where there was an array of monitors, knobs and switches looking much like a NASA control room, Xavier was led into the treatment area. Here was where the metal apparatus and some bath-like structures were, and Xavier was here to do more than look at them.

Steve began the process of treatments by unwrapping Xavier's arm. Although Xavier had seen it exposed two days ago, he was still sickened at the sight of his reddened, disfigured remnant of a once lean and muscular arm. Steve applied various solutions to it, and then began removing some of the dead skin, which caused Xavier to howl in pain. Steve demanded, "Hold still!" but when he continued the process Xavier flew into a rage, shouting at him.

"Wait a fucking minute! You're hurting me like hell, and I'm not sure you know what you're doing!"

Steve immediately became defensive and the two got into a heated argument. Another white-garbed figure approached and introduced himself as Dr. Robertson, medical director of the burn unit. He quickly deescalated the argument and subsequently sent Steve away. He listened to Xavier's complaints and then suggested that he simply needed to have some analgesics prior to treatment, and if necessary some tranquilizers.

"Burn treatments do hurt like hell. It takes some time to become mentally toughened to face them without fear or apprehension. You'll get there, but perhaps Steve assumed you were already medicated and used to treatments. Here, let me finish your treatments for today."

Xavier felt reassured, and liked Dr. Robertson immediately. He felt that the doctor had an innate caring and understanding of the emotional aspects of being burned, almost as if he or one of his family had been burned. He couldn't resist asking.

"Dr. Robertson, did you or one of your family suffer serious burns?"

"Why yes, my brother. He. . . unfortunately was horribly burned when his car burst into flames after a traffic accident. He struggled to stay alive in a burn unit for weeks before finally succumbing. How did you guess that something like that had happened?"

"I didn't guess, I just felt that you understood burns from a personal angle, not just an academic interest."

As they spoke, Dr. Robertson was just finishing putting the dressing and bandages on Xavier's arm. He commented that he agreed with the doctors at Shands, that there would likely be full return of function to the arm and hand. He then began removing the bandages from Xavier's head, and Xavier saw his reflection in a nearby wall mirror actually for the first time without his scalp bandaged. He was taken aback far worse than when he first saw his arm, for here he was, without a strand of hair on his head. The skin on top did not appear as charred and angry red as that on his arm, but that didn't help matters much.

"Where is my hair!!?"

"This must be the first time you saw yourself completely. I know it can be quite a shock. The electrical current running up and out your scalp obviously burned off all your hair."

"Will it grow back?"

"To be honest with you, possibly not. Time will tell."

Xavier detected much more pessimism in Dr. Robertson than his statements indicated. The prospect of being bald was in many ways far more disconcerting than the eventual result of having very noticeable scars all over his left arm. Xavier had turned his face away, but braced himself to look again.

"What are those scarred areas on the front of my head?"

"Exit wounds. It's pretty common in shock victims, especially with lightning. But I must admit, I've never seen two perfectly symmetrical exit wounds like this. They are both a couple inches above your temples and equidistant from the midline of your scalp. Were you wearing a cap with some metal on it?"

"No. . . but I don't remember anything about the evening so I can't be positive. I am fond of wearing a headphone, however. Does it matter?"

"Not really. I read your neurologicals and you checked out as fine, so I wouldn't worry about some minor sequelae to your shock. The scars should fade somewhat anyway, and either your hair will cover them up or a hairpiece would."

As the doctor was finishing his statement, Xavier somehow knew that he had lost his hair for good. He actually felt he could tolerate the baldness, for he was nearly bald back in his FSU swim team days, and people had commented on how well-formed his head was. Nevertheless, it would be more difficult if the burned scalp did not heal very well. The doctor continued treating the scalp area, and then finished wrapping it.

"Dr. Robertson, I would like to be able to do my own treatments as soon as you feel that I am ready to do so."

"Very well; that will be part of your education. But not quite yet. As you have seen, it is not a procedure to be taken lightly. But you can learn more by tagging along with Steve, and you can also come on rounds with me until your third year rotation begins next week. I haven't checked the roster, so I don't know if you'll be on my service or not. Follow me; it's time for my rounds."

Xavier followed compliantly, and the two soon approached a gathering of about five other garbed figures. Xavier suspected that they were residents and medical students on their final few days of their last third year rotation. *What a wonderful feeling,* he mused to himself. Dr. Robertson briefly introduced Xavier, and then quickly proceeded to begin his morning patient rounds, room by room.

"OK, let's start. How is Mr. Jenkins doing, ah. . wait. Who of the students is following Mr. Jenkins?"

A thin, somewhat angular-looking young woman named Charlotte Sanders stepped forward. "I am, sir."

"Well, Ms. Sanders, present Mr. Jenkins to our guest."

"OK. Mr. Jenkins is a 47 year old white male construction worker three days status post 38% total body burns incurred during an attempted rescue of a co-worker caught in an industrial fire. His burns include second and third degree burns to both upper extremities, face, and much of his thorax."

"Well done, Charlotte. How is he doing today?"

"He is still awake only on and off. His vital signs are moderately stable, with slightly elevated pulse at 110 and blood. . . "

Charlotte was abruptly interrupted by a loud proclamation from down the hall.

"CODE IN FIVE! CODE IN FIVE! CODE IN FIVE!"

Immediately everyone in the gathering began running toward room five, and Xavier seemed totally lost and out of place. He followed, much less manically, and arrived to see Dr. Robertson spearheading an all-out attempt to save a dying soul. Xavier stood, motionless, with both amazement and horror as he witnessed the group's collective efforts to save the nearly unrecognizable ash of humanity lying on the bed. Dr. Robertson barked out a series of orders for different intravenous or intramuscular medications, and then, still seeing a "flat line," removed the resident who was doing CPR on the patient, proclaiming, "We need to shock him." Dr. Robertson was intense, animated, but totally in control. The shock paddles were quickly placed and the procedure begun. No success. They tried it again. Again no success. Xavier had witnessed this scene as had most people in various movies or on television, but never in person. This time it didn't look quite like in the movies, for the patient was not responding. The gathered clinicians tried furiously for another ten minutes or so, trying new drugs, different voltages of shock, etc., but all to no avail. The hunk of charred flesh was truly now nothing more, save for perhaps his soul.

He was "pronounced" at 10:46, meaning that was the official time of his death. Suddenly all of that frantic activity ceased, and everyone began dispersing except the unfortunate medical student who had followed this patient since admission.

Nearby, Xavier Howell was still standing in the exact spot he had settled into when the code began, and he was weeping uncontrollably.

CHAPTER FIVE

Over the next several days Xavier tagged along with Dr. Robertson during his rounds but learned that he would get a different attending physician when he formally began his third year rotation. The treatments continued unmercifully, although Xavier began trying to put himself in a trance-like state prior to them in order to minimize the pain and make them go by quicker. Xavier had always been quite adept at self-hypnosis, training himself in order that he could study better for college. By the time he had reached medical school, he was able to concentrate totally on his studies without extraneous thoughts intruding. Over time, however, he learned that his trance was easier to maintain, and more enjoyable, with the music he loved being played over and over again on his walkman. The music could not be so unfamiliar that it would draw his attention to it; Xavier would listen to this music just for fun. Xavier took pride in knowing that, although he was smart, what set him apart from most of the others was his ability to maximize the mental capacities that he did possess. He had known others with greater pure intellect: nineteen year old first-year med students with IQ's in the Mensa range. But few could match Xavier for his ability to study twenty hours in a row and retain a high degree of the information, and to do it without fifteen No-Doz pills or even amphetamines, as many students used. Perhaps even more impressive than his hypnotic abilities was the fact that Xavier seemed to possess nearly perfect control of his emotions, allowing the joy, anger or sadness to come out when appropriate or completely make it vanish if the situation demanded it.

Thus it was with chagrin and confusion that Xavier had found himself more emotional as of late. The weeping spell he suffered after witnessing the unsuccessful code several days ago was not an isolated incident. He had found himself struggling with waves of different feelings surging through him like gusts of wind in a Charleston March. He rationalized that he most certainly must be having some expected post-accident adjustment difficulties and that he would soon get over it, particularly as his burns healed.

Although Dr. Robertson remained caring, and checked on Xavier periodically, Xavier could tell that the novelty of his situation had worn off and that this was a very busy man who had many other things to attend to. Xavier picked up a few pointers every day from rounds, and felt reasonably good about starting his third year rotation.

So on the morning of July first, the day most medical students trembled with apprehension, Xavier Howell felt he was going to start with a good attitude and a reasonably tolerable situation. He arrived at MUSC's Burn Unit, as usual accompanied by Rachel, and joined a group of young, eager faces standing nervously together near the nursing station. As he approached, they all turned to stare at him with inquisitive eyes. Xavier introduced himself, and he immediately discovered that these students had not been informed that he was to join them on their rotation. In addition to three medical students, there were two residents, both of whom were ignorant of Xavier's prearranged deal. When he told the saga of the accident to all of them, they were very intrigued. However, when he explained that he would actually be a student along with them but carrying no patient load, the older residents seemed dubious. More than seemed, Xavier noted to himself, as again he could read the feeling as if reading a book. He sensed that they considered this an almost unacceptable softening of the usual and expected third year toil. Xavier remembered that the Howell name was well known; he even thought that they might have guessed that leverage was used to concoct this arrangement. But that much he could not quite be sure of.

One of the students, Samuel Ravenell, was Charleston-born like Xavier. The two immediately recognized each other's blue-blood twang, distinct even from the typical Charleston drawl, and an early bond was formed. Sam also was quite sociable and seemed particularly interested in Xavier's situation. They chatted for a while, with Sam eagerly trying to hear Xavier's entire story. But the oldest resident, a Dr. McHenry, who more properly was known as a "fellow" specializing in burn management, announced that he wanted their attention.

"Hi, I'm Reg McHenry. Let me prepare you for what you are about to experience. Dr. Mitchell will be our attending; and he is known for being a real son of a bitch to medical students. He will grill you frequently with some of the most esoteric questions he can dream up, just to keep you studying like mad so as to not be embarrassed. You should know by now that this type of interrogation is called `pimping,' and Dr. Mitchell has refined the art. For if he pimps you and you have no clue, he will embarrass you.   John here, your front line resident, will keep tabs on you and your patients.   I will not be around as much, but will assist you in those situations requiring some expertise or specialized knowledge on burns.   John?"

Dr. John Perkins stepped forward, and the younger resident at least seemed outwardly to be less stiff and formal than did Dr. McHenry. He began explaining what he expected as well, but stopped dead in mid-sentence, and then whispered, "Everyone look sharp; here comes Dr. Mitchell."

In strode an imposing figure, a man of nearly Xavier's height but weighing one hundred pounds more or so. He, like everyone else in the ICU, was covered with the usual garb, but through it one could see intense, even glaring eyes.   He resembled a ravished grisly bear searching for fresh meat.

"Good morning, doctors and students.   I am Dr. Mitchell, your attending for this rotation.   I will either enable you to greatly progress on your paths to becoming practicing physicians, or help you realize that medicine is not for you.   The Burn Unit is one of the most intense and demanding places in which we attempt to preserve human life, and I will accept only total dedication while you are on this rotation. I will expect to begin my rounds at eight a.m. sharp each morning, unless I am occupied in an emergency.   Please introduce yourselves."

The introductions proceeded in a circle, ending with Xavier.

Dr. Mitchell proceeded: "Mr. Howell, you have a most unique situation here, which I consented to by personal request of the dean. In many ways you will be getting an easier deal, yet I expect you to take from this rotation no less knowledge than the others.   You will present yourself as a patient each day and report on your progress. You will learn to manage your own wounds and also report to the others what it actually feels like to be a burn patient. In case the others have not yet heard, present yourself."

"Yes, sir. I am Xavier Howell, and a couple of weeks ago I was electrocuted when I reached up to screw in a light bulb. I apparently was unconscious for three days. . ."

"Mr. Howell! You will have to learn proper presenting technique! I have studied your case, and you should present as follows. `Xavier Howell is a 25 year old white male two weeks status post electrical shock to the cranium and left upper extremity. The electrocution, incurred while touching a light socket, produced immediate cardiac arrest necessitating advanced cardiac life support. The patient remained comatose for three days, but has regained normal mental status and has had negative MRI and EEG. The remaining sequelae are limited to the second degree cranial burns and third degree burns to the left hand and arm, and are healing at expected pace.' This is how I expect all of you to present. Dr. Perkins, I will allow you to divide up the patient load. Today, you will present the current ICU patients to the group on rounds. Let us commence."

The group ambled over to the first ICU bed and Dr. Perkins presented the case amid silent tension. The patient, a young black woman, was horribly burned over her entire lower body and her legs were bloated and oozing. Dr. Mitchell allowed the entire presentation to proceed without interruption, and then asked only one question.

"Dr. Perkins, what do you think this patient's prognosis is?"

"I'm afraid not too good, due to the significant percentage of burns, plus she appears to be getting septic.

"Dr. Perkins, if you lose this patient it will be negligence on your part, for if she dies of sepsis it will be because you didn't detect it soon enough or treat it effectively. Fortunately, I believe she will make it. Next patient."

The group ambled over to the second ICU bed chamber, and Dr. Perkins presented Mr. Jackson, a thirty-two year old, well-built man with burns over both of his hands and part of his neck and lower face. Again Dr. Mitchell allowed an uninterrupted presentation, and again asked the same question.

"Dr. Perkins, in case you didn't notice I expect some estimate of prognosis with each presentation."

"I understand, sir. Mr. Jackson should stabilize within one week and have reasonably good functional recovery, although he will probably require cosmetic procedures."

"Dr. Perkins, this man has only fourteen percent total body burns. I want him stabilized and off ICU in two days. We need this bed for sicker patients."

As these rounds progressed, everyone except the two principals had remained silent. Even the advanced-level fellow knew better than to enter the discussions unsolicited. It was thus all the more shocking when one Xavier Howell saw fit to abruptly interject.

"Excuse me, sir, but I fear this man's prognosis is far worse than expected. I question whether he has the will to live." Inside, Xavier felt even more strongly than his stated words about the patient's weakened character and hopeless mental state.

"Oh do you, Mr. Howell! And on what evidence do you base this fascinating prediction? Did you read his horoscope? Or did you read his palm?"

Xavier felt a surge of anger at the insult, but suppressed it as he quickly realized he had put himself in a predicament. He knew he had to rationalize the unexplainable feelings he had inside. "Sir, I note that although he has only fourteen percent burns, I noticed that the location of the burns may be psychologically intolerable for a man who has obviously taken pains to sculpt such a muscular body."

"Rubbish!" Dr. Mitchell turned his shoulder to Xavier, and addressed the others. "It appears Mr. Howell feels he can perform psychiatric evaluations without even talking to the patient. Anybody else want to hazard a guess about Mr. Jackson? Perhaps the lack of a wedding ring on his burned left hand leads us to believe that he will soon fall in love with his ICU nurse, marry her and live happily ever after."

Dr. Mitchell glared briefly at the still mute group of very anxious students, and then stormed off to the next ICU bed. The remainder of rounds took only another twenty minutes and no one dared challenge Dr. Mitchell again. After rounds were over, a flush-faced John Perkins took Xavier aside.

"What do you have, a death wish or something? You do NOT challenge Dr. Mitchell, especially as a new student!"

"I'm sorry, but I felt it was important."

"Let me decide what's important and what's not. As a student, you've got to trust your residents, and acknowledge your lack of knowledge. I've got to admit, you sure must have guts, but if you want to succeed as a medical student here, you've got to learn protocol."

"I understand."

Dr. Perkins then took the students and divided the patients up among them. Each student only had to follow two or three patients, and Mr. Jackson was assigned to Sam Ravenell. The students then dispersed and began the task of learning about their new patients as well as their new responsibilities. Xavier tagged along with Sam at Sam's insistence, and the two went to the cafeteria for a quick lunch together. Sam bemoaned over lunch that he was the unlucky student to get the first night's call. Xavier detected a genuine fear, but felt also that Sam was bright enough and strong enough to handle the pressure. Xavier then invited Sam to come with him to observe his burn treatments, which he did. Sam seemed more taken aback to see the damaged flesh on his new-found friend than the far more hideous-looking burns on the other patients. Xavier was impressed with Sam's concern, and tried to lighten his worry by making a joke about how he would "save a lot of money by not needing shampoo and conditioner anymore."

Xavier was picked up by Rachel as usual at about five in the afternoon: he introduced her to Sam. Xavier and Rachel departed and retired to the Howell home again, as had become routine. Xavier found himself more tired than usual and went to sleep a good hour earlier than he had been recently. Sleep took him quickly, even before the sedating effects of his nighttime medication did.

*   *   *

The next morning, he arrived at the Burn Unit with the events of the previous day practically forgotten. He was accosted by a haggard, weary and distressed Sam Ravenell.

"Xavier! My god, you were right!   Mr. Jackson `coded' last night and we couldn't save him."

CHAPTER SIX

"What do you have, Xave?"

Xavier was intently staring at two cards, and not two of the best, either. Just as he was about to show, the lights went out!

"I can't fuckin' believe it!" stated the one next to Xavier, who then replied, "Nobody move, I'll get a bulb."

Somehow Xavier knew this was a risky adventure, but he proceeded to get the bulb and attempt to screw it in.

A bolt of electricity descended from above like a thunderbolt from Zeus and electrified Xavier's body from head to toe. The bolt caused Xavier to convulse malevolently, and shocked him out of his sweaty nightmare and into the darkness of his bedroom.

"Goddammit, not again!" Xavier cried out into the night. Rachel came running in.

"Oh, Xavier, not the dream again?"

"Yes. The same. Every night now for a week."

"Look at you, you poor thing, you're covered with sweat. Let me get a cold compress."

As Rachel fetched the wet towel, Xavier was struggling uncomfortably, not with residual terror from the dream, but anger at having had it again. Rachel returned and leaned over the bed to wipe Xavier's brow. As she did, Xavier took note of the shapely form in front of him, tightly wrapped in a white nurse's uniform. The trim waist was inviting, and Xavier placed his unburned hand on the small of it. He then slowly worked his way up the curvy outline leading to her not overly large but well-formed bosom, and gently ran his hand across her breasts, following their contours. Rachel simply reached down and casually removed Xavier's hand, remaining nonchalant and still focused on the task of toweling Xavier's perspiring brow. Xavier tried again, but with a slightly different tactic. He leaned forward, reached out to put his arm around Rachel's lower back, and pulled her against his chest in a firm embrace.

"Rachel, I find you very attractive, and I believe that your feelings for me are strong, too. Give in to them; don't question them. I can feel the hurt inside of you from having had several men, some of them doctors and med students, who have taken advantage of you. I won't add to that hurt, but rather help you to heal it. Give in to me if your heart tells you to."

Rachel backed off slightly but, after only a brief pause, began peeling off the snug-fitting nurse's uniform, and the slip underneath. Her shapely, even statuesque form, silhouetted by the moonlight coming through the window, was not a surprise to Xavier as he already surmised as much. She came forward, and still mindful of the burns, approached from the right side of the bed. She leaned forward as if to kiss Xavier, but continued leaning so that what Xavier encountered on his expectant lips was a succulent breast instead. He lifted his "good" hand up and cradled the pale white breast while he kissed her already erect nipple. His hand paused only briefly at the breast, continuing down her smooth abdomen until reaching down to between her legs. The foreplay was brief, however, and soon Xavier was satisfying his long dormant lust. With Rachel quietly and cautiously riding on top of him, both of them struggled to suppress their moans of joy for fear of waking the family. Despite the constraints against making noise, there was no lack of passion between them. Indeed to Xavier, it was more of a "healing" to him than Rachel, both because he had relatively few sexual encounters in his life and because his life recently had been filled mostly with pain. Upon completion of their love-making, Rachel seemed to want to quickly revert back into the role of nurse, rapidly getting dressed and then toweling off other parts of Xavier besides his brow. Xavier barely took notice of the cool towel descending down his body, as he was enraptured in a luxuriant afterglow which soon progressed into sleep. Rachel adjusted her uniform and briefly ran her hands through her hair; not that it mattered at one a.m. in the dark, but it somehow made her feel better. She smiled one last time at Xavier, and returned to her bed next door. She would not really sleep, but lie awake, sometimes reading, just awaiting any problems that might arise for Xavier. The days in which she might be needed for a genuine medical emergency were probably already passed, but nobody minded her presence and Xavier definitely enjoyed it.

Xavier was permitted the joy of blissful sleep for perhaps only thirty minutes before he started shaking violently in bed. His upper body jerked upright and consciousness returned, bringing with it the incredibly distressing reality that he had experienced the same dream again. He lurched out of bed, literally screaming

"Not again!" and experienced a wave of anger so intense that he was unable to control it. He began pacing the room, lashing out with both arms at everything in sight, breaking vases, lamps, even chairs. He was oblivious to the pain and added damage he was wreaking on his left arm, not to mention the commotion he was causing. The family came running in, joining Rachel only seconds after she got there. Rachel, however, had been standing immobile, watching Xavier vent his considerable rage, and feeling powerless to intervene. But when the family arrived, it shocked her into action. She screamed out, "Xavier, STOP!" and was soon joined by a chorus of similar exhortations by the family. Xavier's rage soon dissipated, at least to the point that he stopped demolishing things, and stood in the middle of the room, trembling and holding both fists tightly clenched. The awareness of what he had wrought upon the room, including damaging or ruining several priceless family heirlooms, struck Xavier much like a slap in the face, and he actually began to weep. In between sobs, he tried to explain that he had experienced "the nightmare" again, twice in one night no less. The family had been unaware of the nightmare entirely, as Rachel had been sworn to secrecy. But now that Xavier had informed them, she expounded on it, stating how it had tormented him and caused him to arise from a restless sleep sweating and shaking. Mr. Howell stepped forth.

"Why didn't you tell us?"

Mrs. Howell grabbed her husband's elbow and softly scolded, "Charles, we need to support him, not interrogate him."

"OK, OK. Xavier, don't worry about the damage; I didn't really like some of those old vases anyway. It's certainly not worth crying over."

Xavier's weeping slowed to a sob. He felt remorse for his destructive behavior, but he was more shaken by the uncontrollable nature of his rage attack and the sudden weeping, both unheard of for Xavier Howell prior to the accident.

"I'm sorry. . . for what I have done. But I'm worried about my emotions, which seem more out of control due to this recurring nightmare."

"Well, son, we need to get you off to a specialist. Your mother sees Dr. Burana, a neurologist, for her migraines and occasional insomnia. In fact, why don't you try one of mother's Restorils; they'll knock you out and fix those bad dreams."

Xavier instinctively bristled at this, feeling once again that his father was attempting to "fix" things for a somehow defective Xavier, and the anger started welling up inside him. He fought to suppress it, but this time his mind seemed to shift into another world, a world without his family, Charleston, or for that matter, medical school. It was a world of fantasy, filled with blue, sunny skies, and an ocean nearby with its muffled roar. It was a world of peace, and Xavier did not merely see himself in it but felt he was actually, physically there. It was a good place, a place he could stay for a while. . .

"Xavier! Xavier!" It was more than just the voice of his father bringing him back to their shared reality, but also the strong hands firmly grasping his shoulders. "Xavier. You looked like you were blacking out on us or something. Has this happened before? You really do need to talk to Dr. Burana."

Xavier stood, motionless and silent.

Mrs. Howell, as usual, tried her different approach when Mr. Howell's failed. "Xavier, I agree with your father, but more so because I know Dr. Burana, who is a very smart man, and I think he could help you with your nightmare problem. Do it for yourself, not for us."

Mother's plea registered more with Xavier, and he seemed to come fully back to awareness of the situation he was in. "OK, I'll go. I'm sure this problem will pass. I figure it's something like the war vets get after they come back from battle, but in my case it was only one accident, not a war full of forced violence. I'm sure it would go away by itself but, in the interest of protecting your furniture, I'll try one of those tranquilizers tonight and I'll see the doctor tomorrow."

Xavier's mother hugged him, and father and brother patted him on the back before departing. Mother returned with the sleeping pill, and then wished him a good remainder of the night. Rachel came in to "tuck him in" and asked if he was truly OK.

"Probably, but I'm a little perplexed about something. It appears I forgot some of the conversation. I remember talking to Dad, being angry with him, and the next thing I remember is agreeing with both Mom and Dad about going to see that doctor. What happened?"

"It looked like you just tried to avoid getting real angry again. You were silent and glassy eyed, but only for about thirty seconds or so. I wouldn't get too worried about it; it's not like you had a seizure. Besides, you had a negative EEG, if I recall."

Xavier smiled to himself at how easily and naturally this woman shifted from lover back to nurse. He smiled even more as he pulled her in to him, beginning to shift her back to lover. This time there was no resistance at all, and the two reunited in quiet, cautious but still very passionate lovemaking.

CHAPTER SEVEN

Xavier arrived at the Burn Unit the next morning at eight o'clock, two hours later than the other medical students who were fortunate enough to not be on call the previous night. The one who was, Laura, a frail, serious and slightly older student, was scurrying around appearing none the worse for wear after her night up. The group gathered for rounds, and when Xavier's turn came to present his own progress as far as his burn care, he reported how "many things can get in the way of successful healing, such as accidents." He unwrapped his arm and stated that he had tripped on the steep steps leading up to the Howell mansion and hit his hand and arm badly. Xavier had never been one to lie, but as he told this relatively "white" lie he felt inside a remorse and discomfort inside stronger than he expected. It seemed most of his feelings lately were amplified or distorted in some way. He then realized part of what he was

51

struggling with was a mixture of embarrassment for his loss of control last night, and amazement at his lustful adventures with Rachel.

Rounds progressed more uneventfully today, and Xavier found it marginally easier to keep himself from interjecting unsolicited comments or "predictions," as his peers chided him. His mind was elsewhere, mostly thinking of his need to check in with the neurologist plus seeing what needed to be done with the worsened condition of his arm. After the preliminary rounds were completed, Dr. Mitchell arrived for attending rounds. When Xavier's condition came up, Dr. Mitchell made a point to state that "accidents are usually the consequences of being either unprepared, not cautious, or just plain foolish." Xavier smartly let this one pass without rebuttal. Saying something in his defense would truly be foolish, especially since he didn't tell them what really happened.

The attending rounds were mercifully brief, allowing Xavier sufficient time to go to the third floor, where the neurology department was. He went directly to Dr. Burana's secretary, and told her who he was and that he needed to see the doctor as soon as possible. Dr. Burana was chief of the neurology department, and "as soon as possible" usually meant five or six weeks later. However, the secretary looked on her book and saw a note written by the doctor to "Fit the Howell boy in today," and told Xavier to come back at one and he would be seen. Xavier was pleased to get the early time, but his old resentments about parental influence surfaced and he walked away with a frown on his face. He proceeded back to the Burn Unit, this time for treatments. Xavier showed his newly damaged arm to Steve, who showed more dismay than compassion.

"Oh, brother, this doesn't look too good. You might need skin grafts because of this; it's hard to suture this fragile new skin. Let's check with Dr. Robertson."

They did, and fortunately Dr. Robertson felt that with some careful dressing and padding Xavier could get by without grafting. Xavier did not whisper one ounce of protest about allowing someone else to do the dressing, and he sat patiently while Dr. Robertson did it. It was painful, as usual, but Xavier was finding it progressively easier to mentally block out the pain. After the treatment, he grabbed a quick lunch with Sam and was then off to the neurology department. After a brief wait, a man of medium stature but sagacious appearance, including the stereotypical glasses and balding pate, came out of his office.

"Xavier Howell, I presume."

"Yes, sir."

"Come in to my office and have a seat."

Xavier complied, and proceeded to present himself, this time in formal, "proper" style. He then added that his real reason for coming was due to the distressing nightmares he was having and that he wondered if some medication might help him with that. Dr. Burana nodded often while Xavier was speaking, in part because he had reviewed Xavier's medical records from Gainesville, courtesy of Charles Howell III. He was quite interested in Xavier's case, and asked him several questions about sleep and appetite patterns, relative strength, and, curiously, if he was having difficulties with anger control or sadness.

With the last question, Xavier could tell that although Dr. Burana was genuinely interested in the case, he felt that Xavier's nightmare problem was probably psychological in origin. In fact, Xavier could feel all this within the first couple of minutes with him. Dr. Burana paused only briefly before giving his recommendations.

"Mr. Howell, I feel that it is quite common to have this type of sequelae to a traumatic event, both because you suffered an insult to your brain and had an emotional reaction to dealing with your burns afterward. I feel this will be a time-limited phenomenon, but I cannot predict how long it will take to dissipate, if left to its natural course. Sometimes it is days, sometimes months. Therefore, I do recommend use of some medication to induce a deeper sleep. I would choose Sinequan, an antidepressant, over Restoril. Sinequan can help suppress the sleep stage in which you are having the dreams. Besides, it is not habit-forming. Beyond that, I would recommend a repeat neurological work-up, including an enhanced MRI and a sleep-deprived EEG this time. I will have my secretary schedule both of them for tomorrow, so stay up all night tonight. You can drink coffee if you must, but don't eat after midnight."

Xavier was not thrilled to hear this, but it dawned on him that nightmares due to a psychological after-effect of his accident would probably be a more acceptable cause than a neurological one. The latter might not be so easily treated, or clear as completely, as he expected a psychological one would. He felt the doctor had been quite reasonable, and asked him only one question. "Dr. Burana, do you feel that I need a psychiatric evaluation as well?"

Dr. Burana was slightly taken aback by this question, acting as if he had just been caught lying, even though he hadn't been.

"Well, I feel that if indeed your nightmares are solely due to the emotional adjustment to the trauma, you are coping very well. With the use of medication to help the one symptom which really bothers you, you probably don't need a psychiatrist's help."

"OK, but if my tests tomorrow are negative, will you get me one anyway? My next rotation is psychiatry anyway and I'd like to go through one for that reason too."

"Very well, I'll see about getting you in with Dr. Findlay in the Institute."

Xavier shook Dr. Burana's hand and departed. After a couple of hours studying and checking on some things in the unit, he returned home with Rachel as usual at dinnertime. He announced to his family the results of his meeting with Dr. Burana, and the news of Xavier having to stay up all night was treated like a cause to have a special event. Mrs. Howell in particular got excited, stating that they were going to play some trivial pursuit and other games to help stay awake. Mr. Howell spoke of getting the coffee pot brewing and Zack ran off to see if he could rent some action-packed thriller movies to help entertain Xavier. Xavier thought all of this was far too much commotion for a simple night up and explained to his family that his peers on the Burn Unit have to stay up all night every third night as it is.

Nevertheless, he didn't want to be a party pooper and played along with his family. As he expected anyway, his parents gave out at about one a.m., and his brother at about three. Rachel was very used to sleep deprivation, being in the medical field, and was left alone with him after that. Xavier looked at her, smiled and simply said, "finally." One of the many intensified feelings Xavier noticed he was having was lust, although he thought it quite reasonable, considering how attractive and seductively caring Rachel was. Xavier and Rachel spent the remainder of the night exploring each other's bodies, sharing past experiences, and keeping each other gloriously awake.

By eight o'clock Xavier arrived at the hospital for his tests, and underwent them without difficulty. Some found having an MRI an unnerving experience, as the hour's worth of being enclosed in a tomb-like, noisy apparatus produced a sense of claustrophobia. Xavier, however, put himself into a trance-like state and easily tolerated the procedure.

The EEG turned out to be a far more fascinating experience. Xavier was comatose when the first one was done, so he wasn't entirely sure what to expect. His head had healed enough that the electrodes could be placed on the scalp, although with extreme care and special creams. As soon as the test began, Xavier decided to put himself into his trance-like state to see what would happen.

The technician doing the test was shocked to see the marked shift in brain wave activity.

"Mr. Howell, you just went from beta activity to pure alpha. Can you hear me?"

Xavier did hear him, at some level, but did not respond immediately. He came back out of his trance and asked, "Did you say something?"

"Yes. Did you deliberately put yourself in some kind of meditative state or trance?"

"Yes I did. Could you tell by the test?"

"Could I tell?! You just did what I didn't think was possible, changing brain wave patterns instantly at will. Can you do it again?"

Xavier complied, and again the same change in the machine graphs showed up.

"This is amazing. I've heard that some gurus or Yoga masters could do this, but I've never seen it before. Dr. Burana will certainly enjoy this. I will need you to go to sleep now so we can see your sleep and REM patterns."

Xavier again did as instructed. Far faster than the tech could believe, the brain wave patterns shifted into the theta and delta, or sleep, stages. He continued the tracing uneventfully for several minutes, but then noticed some increased signal strength on the machine. Xavier became jumpy and agitated, then jerked upright, tearing the electrodes off his scalp in the process. He screamed out, immediately becoming alert and then realizing he had again had his nightmare. He started to become angry, but the tech grabbed him gently by the shoulder and stated, "Put yourself in that trance-like state."

Xavier tried and was successful, albeit with difficulty at first, as the anger seemed to have a life of its own. He asked the tech if the test was complete, and the tech said they had what they needed and dismissed him. Xavier treated and re-wrapped his head bandages and put on the cap he had become fond of wearing. It was a golf cap Tom had sent him, and had the golf club's name, Serenity, written on the front in white letters on a sky-blue background. He was leaving the neurology department when the secretary hailed him.

"Mr. Howell! I have a message for you. You have an appointment with Dr. Findlay at eleven-thirty."

That gave Xavier just enough time to catch rounds and report on his experiences to his colleagues. He decided not to report all the details of the EEG experience.

Rounds progressed laboriously, with Dr. Mitchell being more annoying and insulting than usual. Xavier was not spared the abuse, as he was pimped on several esoteric questions that he basically had no clue on. He did figure out the answer to one of his own questions. He sensed that Dr. Mitchell was feeling tremendous anger at some ongoing source of frustration, something to do with his career not going where he wanted it to. Xavier knew better than to breathe a word of this, and was very glad when rounds ended at eleven-fifteen, with barely enough time to get over to the Institute.

The Institute of Psychiatry in Charleston was a free-standing building adjacent to the main hospital. It was a sturdy, impressive three-story building with modern architecture coupled with traditional Charlestonian columns. It was the jewel of the Medical Complex, along with the equally new and impressive Children's Hospital. Xavier strode in and was immediately struck with a peculiar feeling, as if he had entered a foreign world. He came to a locked door, and realized that this must be the psychiatric inpatient unit, and that the clinic must be elsewhere. A few left turns and he found a secretary, who informed him that Dr. Findlay was up on the third floor. He found his way there and announced his presence to Dr. Findlay's personal receptionist. She stated that the doctor would be about ten minutes late and to please have a seat. He sat down next to a woman of about thirty, not attractive and looking as though she had lived a hard life. Xavier felt waves of pain coming from her, intense searing pain as if he was being stabbed. He tried to suppress it, and found that he could, but after several minutes could not resist speaking to her.

"Forgive my bluntness, but how can you live with such anguish?"

The woman shed a small tear from eyes which had shed gallons already. "What did you say?"

"I said, how can you live with such anguish?"

"Dr. Findlay helps, and so does the medica. . . wait! How can you tell I'm in pain?"

"I just can. I feel your conflict; you feel some need to escape, to follow your dreams, but are tied down by a sense of duty. You need to follow your heart."

The woman burst out into a veritable flood of tears, but was smiling. She jumped up and fled down the hallway. The receptionist called her back, but to no avail. At that moment Dr. Findlay came out of his office, accompanied by a patient, an elderly man. The receptionist went up to Dr. Findlay and whispered something in his ear, and then he took Xavier into his office.

Xavier sat in a normal, comfortable chair adjacent to the large one Dr. Findlay sat in across the desk. It was not the "couch" he somehow suspected he might get.

"Well then, Mr. Howell, have a seat. Before we get started, I'd like to ask you what you said to that lady sitting outside with you."

"Nothing much, just wondered if she was here to see you too."

Xavier chose to lie, for he feared the doctor would not yet believe him if he told the truth.

"That's odd. Sure there was nothing else? You weren't rude, were you?"

"No, sir, I was definitely not rude."

"Well then, I understand that you have had an unfortunate accident and are having some disturbing nightmares. Can you describe the nightmare to me?"

Xavier repeated the details. Dr. Findlay asked several more questions, getting a lot of background history, even his family's history. Xavier actually found himself growing fatigued, seeing the process as a very inefficient and imprecise way of understanding a person. This view was a new one, strengthened by Xavier's growing ability to somehow understand others' feelings via some form of telepathy or intuition. Indeed, he understood Dr. Findlay better than Dr. Findlay understood him. Xavier decided to have some fun with the well-intentioned doctor.

When Dr. Findlay asked if Xavier had struggled with any anxiety, Xavier answered: "No, but I understand that you have been plagued by panic attacks for many years."

The well-trained psychiatrist did not display his shock externally, but Xavier felt the response in him, much like a splash of cold water in the face. Dr. Findlay's right eyebrow did rise up high on his forehead, and after several seconds' pause he replied:

"That is certainly an interesting statement. Why did you make it?"

"For the same reason I would make any other observation, like the fact that you thrive on control and power yet are troubled by the ethical sacrifices involved in obtaining it."

"Mr. Howell, my personal life is not at issue here. Besides, do you feel you can read minds?"

"Not exactly that. But I can feel the threat I have just become to you; I can feel the tension in your heart and the amazement in your mind. I can feel and understand the conflicts which trouble people when they seem obvious to me, much like reading a book. I am sorry for troubling you with my observations. I really did come here wanting your opinion on whether my nightmares or other symptoms are part of the actual brain insult I had, or an emotional condition following it."

"You certainly are an interesting individual. I think that the nightmares are a typical symptom of a Post-Traumatic Stress Disorder, and I agree with Dr. Burana's recommendation of a trial of Sinequan. You may also be experiencing some common sequelae to head injury, however, such as mood lability and subtle personality change. Good day, Mr. Howell."

The curt ending made it even more obvious that Xavier's comments had greatly unnerved the doctor. Xavier quietly departed and began walking down the hall to leave. After he exited the Institute, he saw the woman he had sat next to in Dr. Findlay's office. She was turned, facing the Institute and showing a face glowing with a mixture of exhilaration and some regret. As Xavier approached, she ran up to him and hugged him with an embrace that didn't want to end. "You understood my conflict, yet you don't even know me! Nobody else could figure it out, but you did, without even getting to know me! You have saved my life! What is your name?"

"Xavier."

CHAPTER EIGHT

Xavier pondered his reflection in the antique mirror positioned prominently in the great home's foyer. His bald pate had healed nicely, so that except in direct sunlight, he was not forced to wear bandages or a hat anymore. Two prominent scars still remained over both temples, a constant reminder to Xavier that electricity had passed through his brain. His left arm was still bandaged, and would require much more treatment, as the burns there had been fairly severe. It was Sunday, the day after Xavier had completed his one-month Burn Unit rotation at MUSC. He had done reasonably well there, he thought, grading out high on his exams and learning not to challenge Dr. Mitchell anymore. He had become something of a medical phenomenon to his peers, who had seen him reach inside the minds of even the comatose patients, not to mention the peers themselves. The university had put a hush-hush on Xavier, however, after recommendations by Doctors Findlay and Burana to the dean. Xavier's prowess was kept a well-guarded secret. Xavier didn't mind, for inside he knew his future did not lie in Charleston anyway. In fact, he was leaving today to return to Gainesville, after a ceremonial traditional Sunday with family. That included going to church at the First Baptist Church, followed by a dinner at one o'clock at home. Xavier used to resent the expected Sunday activities, feeling it used up too much of his precious weekend time, but on this occasion he didn't mind that much. Xavier had never been very religious, but as of late, he had taken to more spiritual and philosophical musings, and wondered how the old Baptist Church's service would be for him now.

"Xavier, don't you look nice in your Sunday suit." The voice was Mother's, and the refrain one he had heard before.

"Thank you."

"Well, let's go, we don't want to be late for Pastor Cooper's service. Let's get your father and brother."

Xavier knew Mother relished every second of this, despite her heart being torn since she knew it was just for a day. Xavier knew this without using any special powers; it was just the way Mother was.

The group finally arrived at the church, and as was the custom there was some socializing at the front of the church. Many people came to wish Xavier well, and he often was faced with feeling their genuine caring coupled with pity, which he found distasteful. Not soon enough the service began, and within minutes Xavier began feeling peculiar.

The next thing he knew, he was not looking at Pastor Cooper, but at an open, mystical vista with mountains in the distance. There was a haze in the air, and although there was a road ahead, directed towards the mountains, it soon became more indistinct from its surroundings the further one looked. The sun was just peeking out from behind the mountains, and its orange-yellow glow creeped out over the hilltops and painted the entire vista with its distinctive hue. Xavier found himself setting out on a journey down the unclear path ahead, but felt a sense of purpose and excitement. As he began his travel, he passed by several odd, vague forms which resembled people but were distorted in some fashion, either excessively large, small, or mis-shapen. The mountains seemed never to grow closer. The sun continued its ascent into the sky, brightening the vista with its sparkling rays. As he moved forward, the path itself grew unsteady and undefined, and Xavier felt a sense of growing panic. Soon there was no path, and although the mountain-framed sun still shone brightly ahead, he felt his journey had become impossible. The distress this caused jolted him, and almost instantly there was no vista. There was, however, the recognition of a hand on his shoulder, shaking him.

"Stand up, Xavier. Didn't you hear the preacher?"

Xavier needed several seconds to collect himself, and arose. His daydream seemed so real that he questioned if that was the reality and this church scene the dream. The congregation began singing a hymn, and Xavier's mother held the hymnal halfway between herself and Xavier, hoping he would join in. He did not, still reeling from his powerful experience and trying to sort it out. Soon after they sat down, Xavier again felt an odd sensation come over him while the preacher continued the service. Again his reality changed, now with a new horizon in front of him. He found himself in a wide open field, and felt the presence of bodies all around him, even pressing against him. There was great electricity in the air, and Xavier soon could grasp that there were thousands of people, all faceless but wearing white robes. No, Xavier reconsidered, not white robes, but rather patient gowns. The throng pressed forward, and carried Xavier along with them. All appeared intent on observing some distant figure, standing on a platform of some kind in the near distance. It was hard to see this figure, as the sun again took prominence directly behind him, making it difficult to look ahead for long. Xavier then felt a lightness come over him, so much so that he seemed to lose all weight and float upwards. Indeed it felt not so much like flying but rather more like a leaf carried by a gust of wind. He drifted along, heading in the direction of the main figure. He struggled to see the figure, but the closer he got, the more transparent the figure became until, ultimately, it was gone.

Again Xavier was accosted by the violating hand of his mother, shaking him out of his trance.

"Xavier, what is the matter with you today? You've slept through most of the service. Here, at least listen to the benediction," she whispered.

Xavier did not defend his actions, but pretended as if he was complying with mother's request. In reality his mind was still far away, but this time he was simply trying to analyze his own daydreams. They did not make any apparent sense to him so far. The closest connection he could make was that perhaps being in church precipitated the scene involving a throng of worshipers. Perhaps the figure was Jesus. As Xavier pondered these questions, the service ended. Everyone soon was leaving the church, but slowly, pausing at the door to greet Pastor Cooper and say a few words. When the Howells arrived, Charles eagerly shook the preacher's hand and told him what a good service it was. But when Xavier's turn came, he became instantly uncomfortable. The preacher shook his hand and stated: "Xavier, good to see you again. Hope the words of the Lord will help complete your healing."

Xavier recoiled from these benign words instead, as

if they were daggers poking him. Without aforethought, he blurted out:

"Pastor, that would be fine; however, I feel that you yourself have doubts about the `words of the Lord,' or at least the Baptist version of them."

It was as if Xavier had spit on the Pope. Shock came over the faces of the three other Howells, and the preacher himself was caught totally off guard. Before he could even mount a response, Mrs. Howell intervened. "Xavier! What is the matter with you? Forgive his comments, Pastor Cooper; he has been ill, you know."

Immediately Xavier lost awareness of his immediate surroundings and again found himself in a new vista. There were no people in it, this time only snow-covered mountains shadowed by angry thunderclouds. The clouds were swirling much faster than possible in reality, and Xavier's head seemed to spin as he followed their swirling maelstrom.

"I . . . understand, Mrs. Howell. But Xavier, what did you mean by it?"

The vista vanished as he heard his name, but he had not heard the question.

"Excuse me, pastor, what did you say?"

"I said, what did you mean by what you said?"

"I can feel your doubts about the words you preach. I know you mean well, but it amazes me that you still struggle with your belief after all of these years of being a preacher."

The other Howells found this equally intolerable and Charles grabbed Xavier by the arm and pulled him away. Charles, Marie and Zack progressively launched into him.

"What the hell's wrong with you? Are you trying to disgrace our friend, and a holy man at that?"

"You were asleep for most of the service anyway, so where do you get the idea you can judge him?"

"You can be a real jerk sometimes, you know that?"

The disgruntled family of four moved forward down the steps of the church, continuing their incredulity. In an afterthought, Charles turned and quickly walked back to the preacher.

"John, I apologize for my son."

"It's OK, Charles. Don't let it ruin the Sabbath for your family."

The words were kind, and as Charles walked away he thought about how John had always shown them kindness. But Charles couldn't help wondering about something. There were tears in Pastor John Cooper's eyes, and his expression held something approaching guilt. Charles announced: "All right, let's go home. John's words were to not let this ruin our last Sunday, so let's say nothing more of it."

With that, the four piled back into their car and drove home in relative silence save for the idle chit-chat Mother tried to make to break the tension. Once home, they set about the task of preparing dinner, a feast of Southern home cooking including okra soup, black-eyed peas, honey-baked ham, potato salad, roast beef, cornbread, and baked beans, followed up by a special cake known as "Red Velvet Cake." It was part of the tradition for everyone to pitch in with the preparation of the meal, but Xavier was excused due to his lack of use of one hand. Xavier used this time to say good-bye to Rachel, who was in her bedroom packing her things. Xavier found her in tears, and put his arm around her.

"I understand. You have been more than helpful, you have been a part of me for these several weeks. You have comforted me in times of panic, consoled me in times of despair. You have accommodated my unbridled lust for you. You have cared for me as if I was your brother, with devotion and yes, love. I share strong feelings, but it is difficult for me to differentiate between the gratitude I feel and the genuine passion I have felt for you. I must now go my way, however, and you have your life here in Charleston. You of all people must understand that I have a journey to make, perhaps far beyond what I myself have envisioned. I will miss you and I will not forget you."

Rachel, normally adept at words, remained silent. She wrapped both her arms around Xavier and hugged him as if to never let him go. There was no discussion of Xavier's words, as Rachel accepted the veracity of them and knew that she must allow him to leave. She had even considered doing the unthinkable, leaving her roots and family to join Xavier in his journey. However, she somehow knew that other things lay in store for Xavier, and that he would outgrow his need for her. She held her grasp of him for several minutes before relinquishing him.

"Good-bye, Xavier. I will be hearing of you."

"Good-bye, Rachel."

With that, Xavier returned to the dining room as the final dishes were being brought to the table. They all gathered around and were about to say grace, but Xavier interrupted, asking that Rachel be allowed to join in their family dinner. Although this was usually considered taboo, the family was comfortable with it, as all of them had grown fond of her. Xavier fetched her and she graciously thanked the Howells for their hospitality.

Xavier hoped for a stress-free, conflict-free final dinner, with none of the negative comments or verbal jousts that were taken for granted at these family functions. In addition, he hoped that there would be no last minute requests for Xavier to reconsider and stay in Charleston. He got neither wish.

"Xavier, I got word from Dean Hastings that you were given an A on your first medicine rotation. He also informed me that you could continue as a student at

MUSC, provided you remain cautious about your comments and intuitions."

"I knew you would try. No. No. Never. Understand?"

Zack angrily interjected, "Don't talk to Dad like that. Have you lost all respect?"

Several more comments were volleyed at Xavier, but he was finding his mind flooding with anger and threatening to overwhelm him. He truly began to fear he would erupt in violence, but instead discovered a new way to discharge it. He focused some of the angry energy on Charles, causing him to jerk his fist out and in the process knock over his glass of ice tea. Surprised at the result, he tried again with Zack, focusing on actually causing him to mash his hand into the platter of butter in front of him. He then mentally turned to his mother, and caused her to flick the forkful of food she still held up right into her face. Rachel, who had been sitting quietly throughout this and totally ignored by the Howells, reached up to grasp Xavier's shoulder and whispered: "Xavier, please, stop. It's time for you to leave."

And without another word, he did.

CHAPTER NINE

The sign for the Archer Road exit finally came into sight, signifying the turnoff for Gainesville, and Xavier sighed with relief. He had not enjoyed his six-hour drive from Charleston, feeling his emotions swirling around like eddies and currents in an angry brook. He recognized that, for all intents and purposes, he had broken off relations with his parents, at least for a while. Although Xavier was not normally given to great expressions of varied emotions, he had found himself alternately crying, laughing, and fuming with anger at various points along the trip.

He pulled into the tight confines of his apartment complex's parking lot, and eagerly got out of his car. He was greeted at the door by his roommate Tom.

"The main man, Xave! Jeez, you still look like the white man's answer to Michael Jordan."

"I've missed your sweet compliments, Tom. But you

just don't know how good it feels to be back."

"Yeah, welcome back to the joy of hundred-hour weeks with every third night call."

"Well, you sound beat. What did you just get off of, surgery?"

"Yeah, cardio-thoracic surgery. It was brutal. I really enjoyed holding a retractor for seven hours in a row every day."

"Sounds like fun. What are you going into next?"

"Pediatrics, thank God. What about you?"

"Psych."

"That'll be cush. Who knows, you might even like being a shrink."

"Yeah, right."

Actually, with Xavier's recent discoveries of his enhanced mental abilities, he had already thought about how much of an advantage he would have in this specialty. He was now eager to see how psychiatry would be for him, which was a change from his earlier opinions about what specialties he might like. Also among his early considerations were anesthesiology, or just plain internal medicine. Psychiatry had not been a field he would have pictured himself in, not to mention the clamor he would receive from family were he to choose it. Family, hah! What difference did it make now, anyway?

Xavier and Tom debriefed each other in depth about their respective experiences for several hours, and were interrupted occasionally by friends dropping by. Xavier was saddened to hear that one of his peers, a William Samford, had dropped out of medical school after three weeks on the neurosurgery rotation. He asked if people had wondered about him, and Tom replied, "Yes, but not so much anymore, they've all just gotten so busy." They both hit the sack fairly early so they could be rested on their first day of the new rotation.

Xavier arrived on the eighth floor of Shands Hospital at eight sharp, wearing the cap Tom had given him. His return would cause enough notoriety as it was; he didn't need his bald head to attract more. Soon after he arrived, he was greeted by his fellow med students starting this rotation. There were three of them, two of whom were young ladies. One of the girls was Sara, a friend and fellow PIMS grad from FSU. The other female, Sherry, was a renowned bitch and was known for her fierce ambition and competitiveness. The last, Melvin, was a nerdy unknown who, most of the time, was quiet and reserved.

The three bombarded Xavier with questions, particularly Sara, but Xavier was surprised to see that even Sherry was interested in his story. In fact, there seemed to be a pulse of electricity between them as she observed his altered appearance. There were also two residents who came over while Xavier was retelling his story for the hundredth time. The residents seemed more friendly and easygoing than Xavier's Burn Unit residents, and he was clearly relieved about that. They informed everyone that their attending, Dr. Hobari, was considered "benign," but that he liked the patients already assigned and seen by his ten o'clock rounds.

Thus they got going quickly, and Xavier was assigned two patients. The first, Amy, was a nineteen year old bulimic, and the second, Mrs. Jefferson, a somewhat older lady afflicted with psychosis. Xavier met Amy first, a just barely overweight, fairly attractive brunette with a cherubic face. Amy had struggled with her binge-purge compulsion for over a year and, despite the efforts of several prominent psychiatrists and multiple others, had failed to get control over her illness. She was presented in the final chart notes of the previous student as "the classic victim of a perfectionistic, overcontrolling family, who had been refractory to all medications and therapeutic interventions." Xavier spent about thirty minutes with her, trying to follow the format of questioning that had just been given to him, including systematically tracking back the history of the problem, frequency of bingeing and purging, quality of sleep, energy, etc. He noticed as he was doing this, the girl was answering in a monotone voice, instantly answering the questions almost before Xavier could finish his sentences. Xavier paused, then stated: "You have done this so often it bores you, doesn't it?"

"Brilliant deduction."

Xavier then sat in silence for several moments, tying to reach inside of her, to get beyond the proposed theories and truly understand the young woman's conflicts. He mumbled, "No. No, they've had it all wrong."

"What did you say?"

"It's not your family's current perfectionistic expectations driving your eating disorder. The family therapists themselves note that they are puzzled at how much the family has relaxed their expectations as well as shown considerable caring and understanding. It's far older than that. I feel that your parents, who now spend an inordinate amount of time and money on you, do so more out of guilt than love. Your father was absent when you were a young child and truly needed him, and your mother was emotionally absent. You apparently have forgotten this. I feel the hunger of a child in you, an emptiness and void which you continually try to fill by gorging yourself, but it cannot replace what you never received in the first place. All I know about your father is that he is a wealthy man; perhaps he was too busy earning his fortune, or maybe he just had too many responsibilities. As for your mother, from what I understand she was very young when you were born, and was probably not emotionally prepared at the time to give you what you needed. Regardless, you will need to put aside your fury at them and forgive, or you will always feel the hunger."

The previously disinterested patient came to life, as if switched on, but was soon overwhelmed with feelings and burst into a shower of happy tears. She leapt forward and wrapped her arms around Xavier, causing him to wince slightly at the still tender arm she unknowingly was pressing against. She whispered in his ear, "You are right. Somehow you must be right. It will end," and then released him.   She jumped up and ran off, hardly touching the ground as she went.

Xavier was pleased with himself, and proceeded on to his next patient.   Mrs. Jefferson was what medical students euphemistically called a "train wreck:" a severely disturbed patient with multiple problems and bad prognosis. She was a thirty-eight year old woman who had gotten intermittently psychotic over the past several years, going in and out of hospitals frequently. Xavier was presented that she was "incurable, but could be stabilized to baseline with anti-psychotic medication and transferred out of the hospital." This was apparently a desired outcome, as this patient also tended to be extremely demanding and difficult on staff.

Xavier approached more cautiously than he had with Amy. Even if he wanted to, this woman would not have complied with a long laundry list of psychiatric questions. Xavier simply introduced himself and asked if she would give him a chance to help. This approach surprised this woman, who often sat in glassy-eyed oblivion, and she made eye contact with Xavier. Xavier reached out to hold her hand and continued the silence. As he was becoming ever more able to do, he felt deep conflicts inside of her. Xavier was able to differentiate the patient with uncorrectable neurological impairment from those with conflict-based mental difficulties. With the former, he could sense the absence of activity in areas of the person's mind, as if whatever damage they had sustained had killed off some of the signals emanating from them. With this woman, he did not feel this at all, and was encouraged.

"Mrs. Jefferson, I sense tremendous fear in you. I don't yet fully comprehend it, but it seems that you have a conflict with your husband which is mentally paralyzing you."

The patient seemed to spring to life, eyes widening and posture coming erect. She uttered, "How do you know?"

"I have a good sense of. . . intuition. Why do you resent him; is it his wealth?"

With that, the woman grew angry and hostile, essentially throwing Xavier out of the room. Xavier was surprised at this, but felt as he left that he must have struck a nerve. He wandered over to the nursing station, and had some twenty minutes to kill before rounds since he was the first student done with their preliminary interviews. He looked through Mrs. Jefferson's old chart for details on her family life and background. Xavier had simply assumed Mr. Jefferson was wealthy, since he could afford years of psychiatric help for his wife. He discovered that in fact he was a CEO of a large business firm in town. He could not find any data on her early background, as the notes repeatedly read "Patient unable to provide older background history."

It was time for rounds and Dr. Hobari arrived. He was a slightly built, well-dressed Indian psychiatrist who introduced himself with a smile and a comment. It was his desire that "no matter what specialty each of you students might eventually go into, this rotation should serve to teach you not only what psychiatry is, but to respect it. For psychiatry as a field is on the cutting edge of research and will be one of the most exciting areas of medicine for several decades to come."

Having given this brief speech, Dr. Hobari wanted the students to present their cases. Sherry went first, detailing her first two patients with the precision borne of ambition and zeal. Sara followed, doing an adequate job on such short notice. Melvin went next, and he awkwardly stumbled through his two patients, getting the main facts out but without any fluidity or organization.

Then it was Xavier's turn. "Sir, my first patient is Amy Butler, a nineteen year old white female who has carried a diagnosis of bulimia for the past year. She has been tried on multiple medications, including tricyclics, Prozac, Trazodone, Xanax, and Tegretol, all without success. In my session with her today, I feel I have discovered the underlying conflict driving her eating disorder. I believe that Amy's father was predominantly absent during the critical years of her childhood, and the memory of the resentment and emptiness she felt then has long been lost. Yet the hunger for his love has remained, and has created a bottomless pit that she tries to fill with food. Providing her with this interpretation produced an immediate affective response, and she asked me, 'How did you know?'"

The small gathering of doctors and students sat, stunned. Dr. Hobari then responded: "Mr. Howell, that is an extremely interesting theory. How did you arrive at it?"

Xavier realized that once again he had managed to get into a self-imposed trap, and tried to be creative with his response. "First, I assumed that the presumed formulation, that her perfectionistic, overcontrolled family was the main etiological factor in her bulimia, was incorrect, since repeated work on this theme has yielded no improvement. So I probed deeper, exploring her earlier memories and uncovering previously unconscious resentment and yearning. Again assuming that the father was frequently gone due to his early dedication to his company, which I found in the chart, I put two and two together and presented this to the patient."

"And you did all of this, this morning?"

"Why yes, sir. "It's my first day, like everyone else here."

"Well, if you are trying to impress me, you have certainly done a good job. However, making quick and powerful dynamic formulations can be very damaging to a patient not prepared to hear them. Even if your formulation is correct, and it quite possibly is, there is no possible way you could have established sufficient rapport with the patient to risk hitting her with that deep and far-reaching a supposition. Please learn this very important lesson, and that goes for all of you students."

Xavier bit his tongue, as he was dying to say "But what if it works?" He was sure he was correct, but he realized once again there was such a thing as protocol and proper procedure. When he was asked to present Mrs. Jefferson, he withheld any deep ideas he had about her pathology and simply presented the case in "proper" form. This relieved the tension in the air that everyone felt, albeit Xavier most acutely.

In what had become a familiar experience, he was taken aside by the chief resident after attending rounds and instructed as to "why he was wrong" in what he had done. It took all Xavier had to keep from exploding, as he found himself unable to tolerate hearing this same refrain. He told the resident he "understood" and then abruptly went to the bathroom, where he found himself uncontrollably pummeling the wall with his fists. The more intense pain of his left fist shocked him out of his fugue state, and it served as a literally painful reminder that he had to squeeze burn treatments into his schedule.

*   *   *

The following day, as Xavier arrived onto the unit, he was eagerly approached by Amy, who seemed deliriously happy. "Dr. Howell! Dr. Howell! It has been twenty-four hours and I haven't had even the slightest urge to binge or purge. You truly must have cured me, for even on those rare days in the past year when I didn't binge, I at least had the craving to. You can't know how grateful I am."

"Actually, I do. But remember, although you have the understanding and explanation you always needed, you also have been living a certain way for over a year, and the bad habits you learned may threaten to come back. Fight them."

Xavier was borne out to be correct overall, as in the following week Amy had total remission of her bulimia and was discharged. Xavier also had secretly figured out the underlying conflict Mrs. Jefferson had; her poor upbringing had influenced her to marry money. However, her husband was physically and emotionally abusive to her. Thus, her fear of living poor again so frightened her that she was paralyzed into not divorcing him. So the only way she could stay married and stay safe was to stay sick. Xavier worked with her to face this, and have the strength to report the abuse to the police and file for divorce. Her psychosis cleared completely.

And so it went for Xavier, going through several patients in just the first two weeks because he was curing them so quickly. The residents were jealous and resentful, as were the students. The chief resident assigned Xavier a chronic schizophrenic; he knew that this patient had no intrapsychic conflict causing his disorder, but instead a condition now known to be a neurochemical disease. Xavier indeed could not cure this man, but helped him nonetheless by daily sessions in which Xavier found he could improve the man's sense of reality. He was not sure how he was doing this. He also found it a bit frightening, because he came to understand the fears one has when one is truly crazy.

Xavier's peers soon came to realize that Xavier did unquestionably possess special abilities they did not, and Sara and Melvin responded to him with a mixture of awe and envy. Sherry was not so gracious; she was tormented by her perceived relative inferiority to him, as well as by the unthinkable thought that she found him attractive due to his power and growing charisma. She was rude and sarcastic to him at every opportunity, and made obvious efforts to discredit his successes. Xavier understood, but had more important things to consider than how Sherry was feeling or behaving. He was becoming ever more consumed in discerning the nature of his enhanced mental capacities as well as refining them.

*   *   *

Several days later, Xavier was in the psychiatry library late one evening, reading about anecdotal reports of people possessing telepathy or telekinesis, and was dissatisfied in what he was finding. It seemed to be a poorly regarded group of phenomena in the scientific world, mostly due to lack of verifiable evidence. As he poured through one journal and book after another, he heard the footsteps of someone behind him.

It was Sherry, in her scrubs, indicating that she was on call that evening. One could have told that she was on call without the scrubs, however, because she had that frazzled, exhausted look distinctive of students who have suffered through a difficult night. With a tense voice, she attempted to seize Xavier's attention. "I thought you already knew it all."

Xavier naturally found this remark offensive, but chose to ignore it and did not turn to face her. Sherry screamed, "You will not ignore me!" and began to lose control, flailing at Xavier's back with her fists. Xavier wheeled around, grabbed her wrists and uttered, "I understand. I find you very attractive also." He pulled her close to him, feeling her heaving bosom press up against his chest. Amongst the treatises and hallowed books, many of which ironically focused on the importance of sexual drive, Xavier and Sherry began their first passionate encounter. Xavier kissed her forcefully, running his hands up and down her with abandon. Sherry responded in turn, and aggressively pushed Xavier back against the wall as they kissed. Xavier became even more forward, grabbing her cheek with his better hand, and whispered, "I know that you feel the same desire that I do."

But an indignant Sherry whipped back her head as if shocked out of a trance, and pushed Xavier away from her. She stormed out of the room, shrieking, "You arrogant son of a bitch!"

CHAPTER TEN

Another week passed and Xavier continued on with his incredible success at helping psychiatric patients. More importantly for him was his growing understanding of what, precisely, he was able to do. He had learned through his studies of available literature that he did not exactly fit into any of the presumed extra-sensory perception categories. It appeared he had the ability to alter his brain waves to match or resonate with those of another person, and somehow thus experience their internal thoughts and feelings. This was different from telepathy per se, different from empathy, and certainly didn't fall into the magical categories of psychics and telekinetics. Xavier couldn't predict a single calamity nor move even a penny with his mind. Yet what he could do was amazing. He had refined his abilities to the point that he could more quickly "read" a person's psyche, often only asking a few questions. He found he could not only read another's psyche, but just as he could alter his own brain waves to produce altered states, he could effect the same changes in others. He followed a solitary journey of discovery, for he had found that discussion of his growing capabilities made everyone very uncomfortable, produced skepticism and even ridicule. Nevertheless, in the three weeks that he had been on the psychiatry rotation, he had enabled twelve patients to improve dramatically and be discharged. The other students were each still working with their original two.

Despite Xavier's attempts to keep his efforts on a low profile, news of his exploits began spreading throughout the department and even beyond. The head of the Psychiatry department, Dr. Thanatos, inquired about Xavier after hearing the rumors, and Dr. Hobari reluctantly confirmed Xavier's success stories and presumed superior abilities. Dr. Thanatos then stated he wished a grand rounds presentation with a live interview by Xavier. The "show" was staged within days and the most difficult patient selected.

It happened to be one Darlene Meadows, the daughter of a VIP in the community, the president of the College of Dentistry. Miss Meadows had a multiple personality disorder, and had been to all of the best psychiatrists and hospitals in the country which specialized in that disorder, including Sheppard-Pratt and the Menninger Institute. None had been able to help this unfortunate young lady, who shifted into different personalities uncontrollably, rendering her non-functional in society. All modalities had been tried with this patient, including shock therapy, but to no avail. The chairman of the department had also stipulated that everyone, especially Xavier, be uninformed of who the patient would be, so that he had no a priori advantage.

The time for the event arrived, and the auditorium, normally accustomed to holding maybe fifty people or so, was crowded with all the psychiatrists and psychologists in the department. Also on hand were dozens of students, residents and others from different departments such as neurology. Xavier normally would have been quite nervous at seeing such a gathering of intelligentsia, but he simply put himself in his useful trance state and quietly waited for the grand rounds to begin. He was introduced by Dr. Hobari, who presented Xavier in a credible fashion, although doubt was still present in his voice. Xavier came in and sat down in one of the two chairs positioned at the front of the stage. Miss Meadows was escorted in, and a collective gasp rattled through the audience, as her identity and disorder were well known to many of those gathered.

She sat down and glanced both at Xavier and the crowd, before lowering her gaze towards the floor. She was a reasonably attractive woman of twenty-six, but her face and hair bore the look of a troubled soul. She seemed lifeless, with almost no emotion evident in her face. Xavier introduced himself simply as "Xavier" and then waited.

She gave no reply. He then continued to sit in silence, a deathly silence which went on for nearly a minute before the patient spoke: "Well, aren't you going to ask me any of the usual questions?"

"No. Do you wish to tell your usual story?"

"Not if I don't have to."

"Good."

Several more moments went by, and actually some life entered the face of the patient, who then looked at Xavier. "Well, what are we going to do here then? I was told this was another interview."

Xavier paused again, closed his eyes and momentarily placed his hand over his brow, deep in concentration. He found her psyche difficult to read, finding many barriers. "I feel in you a need to present an artificial exterior to the world, to hide something intolerable inside."

The patient responded to this by slowly curling up into a sitting fetal position, and there were murmurs in the audience about how Xavier may have precipitated a personality switch. Xavier reached out and grabbed her hand, squeezed it gently, then said:

"Do not give in to the lie; it is making you truly crazy, and your father remains unchanged."

The woman snapped out of her fetal position, jerked her head to look directly into Xavier's eyes. She stared intently for several seconds, then burst into tears. She then jumped up and ran off the stage.

Immediate pandemonium broke out in the audience. There were exclamations of "bravo!" but even more of "Charlatan!" and other derogatory statements. The chairman stood up from his front row seat and turned to the audience, asking for quiet and getting it after an interminably long wait.

"Mr. Howell, I believe your actions demand an explanation."

Xavier stood up, thus towering over the chairman standing below the raised stage. He addressed the audience with controlled confidence. "First of all, I could tell by the audience reaction when the patient came in that she was a famous, or rather infamous patient known to most of you, no doubt chosen due to her being extremely refractory to treatment. Secondly, she obviously had been interviewed dozens if not hundreds of times previously, judging both by her attitude and brief comments. These two observations could have been made by anyone. What I did then, however, was to reach inside of her to try to understand her conflicts, her torment, or her neurosis if you will. Her attempt to switch into a childlike state has probably led to diagnoses of multiple personality disorder or dissociative disorder, but I interpreted it somewhat differently. I detected an unconscious drive in her to manufacture altered states in order to be special and unique, all done in a bizarre and desperate attempt to gain the love of her unloving father. Unfortunately for this young woman, however, her ploy succeeded only in gradually making her truly believe she was destined to a life of psychiatric illness. Further, she had to face the more overwhelming realization that her father remained unloving. Indeed the sicker she became, the more money he must have had to spend in order to continue her expensive health care, probably intensifying his resentment."

A great clamor arose, with again greatly divided sentiments. The chairman asked for order, and for perhaps the first time in his illustrious career did not immediately get it. He took off his shoe, and ala Khrushchev banged it on the stage, yelling for order this time. This time he got it, and stated there would be discussion and questions only if order were maintained.

The first one in the audience to raise his hand asked: "How do you propose that you can detect this woman's unconscious drives without speaking to her? Do you claim to be a mind-reader?"

Xavier paused briefly before answering. "In one sense of the word, yes, although I would not use that term due to the derogatory connotations usually ascribed to it. I am not precisely sure what my special abilities are, but I have a plausible explanation for part of what I can do. Since having survived electrocution, I have discovered profound changes in my mental functioning. This is not unprecedented, as all of you know, since with shock therapy, electricity can cure depression and affect memory. I have found that I possess an increasing ability to alter my brain waves, as has been proven by the EEG done on me. I have further found that I can mentally reach inside another person's mind to comprehend their conflicts, or neuroses, if you will. I have demonstrated this by my unprecedented successful treatments with twelve difficult patients during the first three weeks of my psychiatry rotation. What I do not know is the exact mechanism by which I can 'read' a patient's psyche; but based on my enhanced abilities in brain wave control, coupled with my native gift for intuition, I propose that I can momentarily mentally reconstruct or simulate the patient's entire brain wave configuration, and thereby directly experience both their cognitions and their feelings."

This brought more groans from the audience, and several people got up, yelled "quack" and departed. Others seemed very intensely interested, and the questioning continued. One distinguished professor arose and announced: "The ability to alter brain wave patterns is nothing new; meditation and hypnosis can do this. But to then presume that because you were fortunate with a handful of psychiatric patients is a quantum leap of arrogance. Can you 'read' my psyche, Mr. Howell?"

Xavier quelled a quick surge in anger, then replied, "Yes, to a degree. It is obvious that you are highly threatened by my abilities, and do not want to believe what you actually feel is plausible. Oh, by the way, I also feel that you still are troubled by the affair you recently had; at least you have a conscience."

The reaction of the crowd drowned out the professor's parting comments, which were grumbled references to not standing for these "insults from a boy." The audience then became a mass of confusion, with many running up to shout criticisms out at Xavier while a small section of students were actually chanting "Xavier knows! Xavier knows! Xavier knows!" When Xavier had heard himself called a charlatan for about the tenth time, he really became furious and began losing control. He kicked the interview chair off the stage into the audience near the offending spectators. He began shouting back at them, yelling that they were all too afraid to understand. Three or four of Xavier's fellow medical students came running up to the stage and carried him off, still kicking and screaming.

*   *   *

The word of this drama spread rapidly, going all over the hospital by day's end and into the next morning's newspaper. Headlines read "Super-Shrink Med Student Battles Colleagues" and "Whiz-Kid Cures Patients, Fights Psychiatrists." Xavier returned to his rotation, trying to get on with his business, but reporters started calling. He put them off for the most part, stating that he had "no magic, just a strong intuition which was controversial." He was going to elaborate further but he was summoned by the dean of the medical college and given the message not to speak with anyone further until he had spoken with him.

Later that day, Xavier entered the dean's office, and observed the somber, worried look on Dean Burke's face.

"Dr. Howell, please have a seat. It has come to my attention that you are a gifted student with a flair for the theatrical. I am pleased that you have recovered from your accident, and that you may well have much to offer in the future as a physician. However, we will not tolerate any more of the turmoil, insults and chaos you created yesterday. You are jeopardizing your own medical career, as well as threatening to disrupt everyone else's. If you wish to remain a student in my college, you will keep your controversial talents at a non-public, very low profile. Do you understand?"

Xavier simply smiled and nodded his head "yes," then stood and turned to walk away. As he left, the dean had an unfortunate accident, spilling a bottle of ink all over his desk.

CHAPTER ELEVEN

What power, what beauty, what. . . sense, Xavier thought
to himself, as he listened to the new music he had
purchased recently. The composer of the music was
Scriabin, a relatively obscure Russian who had lived
around the turn of the century. The piece Xavier was
listening to was the Fifth Sonata, and it demonstrated that
composer's unique style of blending mystical and even
bizarre harmonies with intense, passionate rhythms.
Since buying the Scriabin CD about three weeks ago,
Xavier had been fixated on it, listening to it hundreds of
times. He had also taken to listening to other composers
who were contemporaries of Scriabin's, including
Rachmaninoff, Mahler, and Prokofiev. All of them in
their own way displayed turmoil mixed with beauty, all
painted with a broad palette on majestic canvasses.
These now were the composers who captured Xavier's
soul, not the composers he had cherished for the past ten

years or so. Mozart now seemed downright boring to him, and even Beethoven's passionate works no longer stirred Xavier's heart. Their harmonies were too simple, too constrained by the requirements of the era. Now he knew he must find new order among the chaos in his life and in his mind, and of all of them, Scriabin came the closest to musically expressing the intellectual and emotional struggle which mirrored Xavier's own.

Xavier's preoccupation with Scriabin and the others had two negative consequences. First, his endless listening before and after working hours had decreased the amount of studying he had done for his psychiatry rotation, as the only intensive reading he had done was in researching special mental capabilities. Second, his roommate Tom found endless Scriabin intolerable and, despite their continued friendship, he decided to leave and room with another of their poker buddies. Xavier had even declined their continued pleas for another game of poker, as several of them had comparatively easier rotations this month and felt it was a good chance. It had occurred to Xavier that, with his new-found abilities, he could probably clean house at poker; but he steadfastly declined, stating he "was busy." In fact he was busy, not with medical studies, but in continuing his serious listening sessions.

Xavier had found the Fifth Sonata relatively easy to grasp and appreciate, but he found the Ninth and Tenth, Scriabin's last two sonatas, considerably more dissonant and mystical. They ebbed and flowed unpredictably instead of cutting and articulating with power and purpose, as did the Fifth. Xavier was especially intrigued upon listening to another CD of Scriabin's that he had more recently purchased, containing a symphonic work entitled "Prometheus." Xavier put it on again, and began to try to make sense of this even more bizarre and cosmic piece. The work had no discernible structure, but rambled on with Scriabin's very idiosyncratic vision of a kaleidoscopic universe embodied in music. Xavier wished he could have met this unheralded genius, to "read" his psyche directly, but instead had to do it the substantially more time-consuming and indirect way of trying to comprehend the spirit and message of his music. There was something there which had relevance to Xavier, some searching for a greater understanding of the world and an enhanced comprehension of its evolution and destiny.

As Xavier opened his eyes following the close of hearing "Prometheus" again, a ray of sunlight came in through the window and startled him. He was late for rounds! He frantically got ready and bolted out the door. He covered the half mile trek to Shands in record time, and as he arrived, breathless, Dr. Hobari turned to address him.

"No need to rush, Mr. Howell. We all figured you were reading the morning newspaper over a few times. Besides, you are excused from rounds today because the chairman of the department wants to see you."

"When?"

"Now."

Xavier was quite puzzled by all of this, particularly since he had kept the "low profile" yesterday as demanded by the dean. He went to Dr. Thanatos' office, and the secretary told him to go ahead in. Xavier found the European, graying and distinguished chairman sitting in his massive leather chair, reading the newspaper.

"Good morning, Dr. Howell. Please have a seat. Have you read today's paper, perchance?"

"No, sir, I haven't."

"Interesting article on the front page here. Says something about a "modest genius whose special powers are being kept hush-hush by the medical school, and how no psychiatrist would even offer comment about him." It seems that even an attempt to keep this out of the media is media news anyway. I did not want you here to criticize you for this article, as I believe you kept to the dean's recommendations. I wanted you here to explain that the performance you put on two days ago was obviously both highly stimulating and highly disruptive to our department. I am temporarily pulling you off your psych rotation, even though I know there are only a few days to go. You will get an A regardless, due to your exemplary work with the patients. But besides avoiding further immediate backlash from the grand rounds, I wanted you off rotation so that you could be studied by our department and the neurology department to evaluate your proposed special abilities as well as your overall mental status."

"Sir, I have already had a CT, two MRI's, two EEG's, and neuro and psych consults. Why do I need more?"

"I'm not going to beat around the bush with you. You represent a threat to the stability of our hospital, and whether or not your powers are valid, your story and charisma alone could make you a media personality quite easily. I want two questions answered. First, what is going on inside your brain, and second, do you still want to be a physician?"

As Xavier rushed to reply "I do" to the latter question, something in the back of his mind told him that perhaps that might not be his destiny after all. But there was no point in burning bridges now.

"Do you have certain physicians you want me to see?"

"Yes, I have coordinated a team of psychiatrists, neurologists, and psychologists who will work with you over the next couple of days. The entire battery of tests and interviews should be completed by next week, thus not affecting the start of your next rotation."

"I will. . . comply with this."

"That is good, although I didn't say it was an option.

Good day, Dr. Howell."

Xavier walked out of the office with a peculiar mixture of anger and bewilderment. Evidently nothing made sense anymore. His unswerving dedication to becoming a physician had been altered by recent developments, and his growing feelings of having a higher purpose or destiny left him wanting for answers. This latter problem was enough of a concern that he was not against the exhaustive evaluation; however, he felt inside that the answer, if there was one, was not to be found in Rorschachs or PET scans.

He reported to the neurology department first, and again he went through an EEG, this time with special electrodes stuck up his nose and with a computer attached that diagramed pretty color pictures of composite brain wave patterns. He enjoyed this one more than the one he had in Charleston, despite the painful leads in his nose, because he could alter not just the squiggly lines on a graph as in a regular EEG, but could alter colors on this "BEAM" machine. Xavier had become fascinated with colors recently, since he had discovered that Scriabin himself had postulated a link between color and music. Scriabin felt that each tone of the musical scale corresponded to a distinct color, and had even tried to project these synchronized colors on a screen while his music was played. This was in 1910! How far ahead of his time he was! But Scriabin had wondered if there was a greater meaning in all of this; that color, music, smells, all sensory input possessed some cosmic connection which held within it the answers to the mysteries of the universe. Xavier toyed with the BEAM, producing in succession the colors of the visible spectrum in proper order, i.e. red, orange, yellow, etc. Xavier did not enjoy the other tests, however, including the painful spinal tap, the annoying enhanced MRI, and the tedious BAERS and VERS tests. He was then flown to Washington to get a

PET scan, the latest in high-tech brain imaging. Upon returning, he was given a series of psychological tests including IQ and personality tests. The next day he was subjected to several more hours of questioning by a series of psychiatrists, behavioral neurologists and even an endocrinologist. During these interviews, Xavier would tire at certain times, and to give himself a few moments to rest, he would put the questioner's mind in a trance. At other times, he experimented with trying to answer questions while simultaneously contemplating some-thing else, a true duality of cognition that he found exciting. Further, it gave him more of an opportunity to continue trying to unravel the mysteries which plagued him, including Scriabin's visions and his own destiny.

Finally, on Saturday, the heads of all the departments gathered to discuss the findings of their evaluations and then met with Xavier. Among the gathered was Dr. Greene, chairman of Neurology, who began.

"Dr. Howell, you have been most patient with our intense evaluation of you, and simultaneously have kept your silence to the media during this process, which was critical. We have some findings to share with you. From a neurological standpoint, you have in fact proven that you possess a remarkable ability to alter your brain wave patterns, to our understanding beyond that of any known human being. Most of our tests failed to discern areas of trauma or disease in your brain; however, we did have some interesting findings from the PET scan and the BEAM. Both tests indicated increased neuronal activity in the limbic area of your brain. As you should know from your studies, this area is thought to be involved in the processing or expression of strong feelings, such as rage or sexual drive. It has also been postulated that this area may represent the potential source for other capacities such as empathy and intuition. Thus it is theoretically possible that somehow the electrical shock stimulated latent areas in your brain to function more actively, even to supra-normal levels. This may represent a sort of stereotactic electroconvulsive therapy effect to areas of the brain we do not stimulate with normal ECT. Or perhaps, it is more a function of the tremendous voltage involved in your case. Nevertheless, the trauma is more likely to explain your recent history of increased rage and loss of impulse control, as well as increased libido, according to anonymous report."

This brief latter comment actually caught Xavier off guard. He struggled to fight off a blush while also wondering which of the women he had been involved with had leaked this "anonymous report."

The neurologist then turned over the debriefing to the chief psychiatrist, Dr. Thanatos.

"While we are intrigued by the findings of the neurologists, or in some ways the lack of them, we are much more impressed that a psychiatric process is at work here. Despite your demonstrated increased mental abilities, psychological testing reveals that your IQ has not increased. It is still at superior levels, as it was when you were tested prior to medical school, but certainly not in the genius category. Yet what you have been claiming to be doing must certainly necessitate genius, genius beyond that of our greatest thinkers. This, along with the neurologists' findings of limbic area irregularities, inclines us to believe that you are experiencing a Bipolar, or Manic-Depressive Disorder, coupled with a mild to moderate Post-Traumatic Stress Disorder. The latter condition is resolving nicely with the healing of your burns and the improvements in your sleep, but the former condition appears to be getting worse, with more lability and grandiosity."

At this point, Xavier had begun to become angry, for what this was beginning to sound like was a replay of his worst childhood experience, being told what was "wrong"

with him. He found his mind slipping away, almost to
a different world, but then caught himself. He still could
not bear to hear more of the psychiatrist's diatribe, so he
put himself in that practiced duality of mind that he had
learned during his testing. He registered the words of the
psychiatrist, but was actively thinking of other things.
His mind went back to Scriabin's "Prometheus," and the
importance of colors. He replayed the piece in his mind,
as best he could, and tried to envision which colors of
Scriabin's color scheme would be prominent in the piece.
He imagined that there would be vivid reds and yellows,
as the theme of the importance of fire was central to the
myth.   But he also pictured passionate purples and
violets, angry crimsons, and orgasmic pinks. While he
was enjoying his speculations, the psychiatrist and the
neurologist got into a disagreement about which treatment Xavier should begin, with the former advocating
Lithium and the latter Carbamazepine. This argument
brought Xavier back into full awareness of his setting, as
now he rather enjoyed the spectacle of department chiefs
bickering over what was the "right drug" for Xavier.
Xavier decided to handle this situation diplomatically.
He thanked the doctors for their expert opinions, and
stated that he would consider the options presented. The
doctors pressed him a bit for a more certain commitment
to treatment, but Xavier again maintained that he needed
time to consider his options, and then excused himself.

Xavier rushed out of the hospital and headed straight
for the mall. He was in hot pursuit of more Scriabin, for
he was convinced that Scriabin was a kindred spirit and
had similarly wrestled with unknown and preternatural
forces. In some way Scriabin must have been seeking the
answer through artistic expression, and in his music
Xavier could trace the development of his thinking. From
the CD's Xavier possessed, he had detected that Scriabin
was heavily influenced in his early years by other com-

posers, particularly Chopin. But as Scriabin grew older he became progressively more mystical and powerful, a progression Xavier felt he was likewise experiencing. He tried not to run through the mall to get to the music store, the one in town with the greatest selection of classical music. He feverishly thumbed through the file on Scriabin and struck gold, finding a CD of Scriabin piano pieces which he had not yet heard. To make matters even better, the pianist was the great Horowitz, who had met Scriabin himself at the age of eleven.

Xavier flew home, staring ahead intently to spot any police cars. He made it home unmolested and eagerly played the CD. The CD was a collection spanning Scriabin's career, and Xavier enjoyed it, but he was not satisfied after hearing many of the earlier pieces. The Tenth sonata, Scriabin's last, intrigued him, but Xavier felt no special message or meaning upon first hearing. The CD closed with a piece written shortly before Scriabin's premature death called "Vers La Flamme," translated as "Toward The Flame" in English. The piece was a pyrotechnical display of gradually ascending power and energy, written with Scriabin's most idiosyncratic harmonies. Xavier sat, stunned, and knew he had found what he was looking for. "Toward the Flame" must have coordinated with the Promethean theme of fire. Fire! Fire represented power, truth, finality and purity. Scriabin was reaching for it, somehow, in his quest for knowledge, nirvana, or purification. But how? How to strive for it? How to comprehend it? How to move toward it? How?

CHAPTER TWELVE

It was four-thirty in the morning, and Xavier Howell could not sleep. This normally would not be earth-shattering news, but ever since Xavier had learned to manipulate his brain wave patterns, he could cause himself to sleep well. On this night, the mystery which captured his soul indeed felt like a pressure surrounding his heart. It caused him to have no peace, nor even want it until he could figure out the answer to his dilemma. He decided not to suffer in bed any more, and got up and dressed. He was quite the sight in his white doctor scrubs, with his bald head and still-bandaged left arm. He went into his apartment's living room and resumed listening to Scriabin. He played the piece "Toward The Flame" over and over again, each time feeling his pulse and emotions surge as the frenzied majesty of this piece escalated into its final statement. Xavier continued to labor with this, becoming so furious at one point that he pounded his unburned fist on the coffee table, cracking it and sending the books and glasses on it flying. He got up and frantically ran to destroy some other unfortunate object in the room. He grabbed the first available, which was a chair at his treasured poker table. He hurled it against the wall, and a few of the splintered pieces of wood ricochetted back onto him, jolting him out of his fury. He resumed his listening position in his favorite chair and tried again.

Flame must mean fire, he thought, or perhaps it was an analogy, or a metaphor for something else. Flame meaning the fire of spirit and ambition? The fire of life, which burns brightly and then dies, just like the torch or the matchstick? Perhaps it was related to colors again, fire meaning red. Red? Communism? Communist Party? Oh no, thank God it was not that, nothing so mundane as a political statement! He had remembered that Scriabin died in 1915, before the Communist revolution and subsequent regime started. Just before, though, and the thought that he might have had some connection with the movement was unsettling. If this was the answer to the mystery, it was going to be one colossal disappointment. What meaning could moving towards communism have for Xavier, particularly since communism had recently failed as a political and philosophical movement. Could it have been a prediction of its demise? No, it had to be something else, something totally different, something more cosmic, yet somehow more personal. Red meaning anger? Reaching for the rage inside of us all and releasing it to become pure? It was a good concept, but not original and certainly not cosmic. Xavier paused in his rambling thoughts for a minute, frustrated beyond words and feeling defeated. For the first time, a wisp of doubt entered his mind, questioning his purpose and even his sanity. Just then, the first morning rays of the sun shone through the living room window and struck Xavier in the face.

"The sun! The SUN! Of course, why didn't I see it?! Flame meaning the ultimate fire, the brightest fire, the source of life, the giver of light, the sun! This had to be it! Toward the sun, toward the sun, toward the sun. But why? It was unreachable, save for hijacking a space shuttle and flying towards it until burning up. No, it had to be something else, reaching for the sun. . . "

Suddenly, the light of recognition dawned upon Xavier, and he unabruptly but purposefully arose and strode outside. He stared directly at the morning sun, now just emerging from the horizon which moments before had hidden it. He continued to stare, unwavering, and he didn't even notice the gradually increasing, searing pain in his eyes. He remained resolute and continued to gaze, first witnessing a whiting out of the object of his gaze, followed by blackness. Darkness. Blindness. Xavier was enraptured, for he felt he had unraveled the mystery that he had shared with Scriabin. For now he could truly see! It all made sense now. He could now see with the "mind's eye," totally undistracted by the illusions of shape and color. Scriabin had abandoned color in the end, anyway! It was a clue, a symbol for all of the world's physical variables which interfered with true vision, the kind of vision Xavier had been granted the gift of ever since his accident. Or maybe he always had it, and the electrocution simply brought it out.

But that didn't matter now. Now he could truly see, see inside people, read their innermost thoughts and feelings, read their souls! This was his special purpose, this was why he had the gift, now he could use it more acutely, refine it, not unlike how blind people heighten their hearing abilities. He would use it to help mankind, to show them a new way, to help free them from their paralyzing neuroses and disabling intrapsychic conflicts. He felt his life now made more sense, much more than just a rebellion from constrictive parents, more even than just another physician. Now he could really help people, which was the one thing which coursed through his identity ever since he was a child. Xavier felt true joy, filled with the euphoria of enlightenment and conquest.

As he turned and began walking back into his apartment, Xavier became instantly aware of his new limitations, for he was truly blind to the physical, to the inanimate. He stumbled and probed to find his way back, slowly but eventually making it back to his room. He stumbled further just trying to find his favorite chair, and sat down. He contemplated his actions and his fate, and although he remained steadfast in the correctness of his actions, a different reality came over him. He began to weep, for he was compelled to mourn the death of Xavier Howell as he had known him. The tears were bittersweet at worst, however, for a new Xavier had been born.

CHAPTER THIRTEEN

Tom, Ken and Lenny had been concerned by not seeing Xavier in the hospital that day. As they were walking home together, all three considered themselves fortunate to be on rotations that ended "early" at about six, unlike some of the more brutal rotations such as medical ICU and surgery. But they could not rejoice, as they nervously speculated on where Xavier was, or what was happening to him. Medical students simply did not call in "sick." They knew what had transpired recently, including the evaluation and interrogation by the medical school's top brass, but they also knew he was supposed to be back on rotation today. They decided to stop by his room and check on him.

"Xave! Xavier! Are you in there?" they loudly inquired, after knocking on the door initially had met with no response. They grew worried, especially Tom, and they could hear the sound of music being played inside.

"He's in there, man, and I can hear his damn Scriabin playing, the stuff that drove me nuts!" cried Tom.

"Well, let's get the manager and get him to let us in," offered Ken.

"Screw that! We're going in, now!" The volatile Tom kicked the door with all his might. The wood all around the lock shattered and the door wildly swung open, barely clinging to its hinges. They stormed in, finding Xavier sitting peacefully in his favorite chair, seemingly at first oblivious but then turning his head to face the intruders.

"Xavier, what the hell's going on? Where were you today? Why didn't you answer the door?"

Xavier calmly spoke in the direction of the inquisitor, Tom. "I'm fine, Tom. Hello, guys."

"What do you mean, fine? What have you been doing, sitting here all day listening to that mystical crap?"

"Actually, yes, I have been listening, most of the day. Did you know that in the Tenth Sonata there were clues that I totally missed? The sense of yearning, climaxing to understanding but never quite concluding?"

"What the hell are you talking about?"

"I have finally understood the message; my struggles are over whereas my journey has just begun."

The words were worrisome enough to Tom, but it was only as he moved over a few feet to get closer to Xavier that he noticed a difference in his eyes. Xavier had moved his eyes back in Tom's direction, but slowly, only in response to feeling his presence shift position.

"Xavier! What is the matter with your eyes?"

"Please don't worry, Tom. I am fine. You will understand, in time."

Xavier's words did absolutely nothing to assuage Tom's fears, and he shoved a fist towards Xavier's face, deliberately stopping only inches short.

"Jesus Christ, he's blind! He's blind! Look at him, he can't see a damn thing! Ken, call 911! Jesus, what happened, Xavier?"

"Please, Tom, relax. I am fine. My eyesight is gone, but now I can truly see. I can see Ken going over to the phone, and can see the confusion and panic he feels. I can see the incredible turmoil in your heart, Tom, and bewilderment. Let me calm you."

With that, Xavier began affecting Tom's mental status by helping him attain a more alpha-rhythm brain wave state.

But Tom resisted. "I don't want to be calm, dammit! I want to know what the hell happened. How did you get blind?"

"I finally understood. To reach my higher purpose, I had to reach toward the flame, toward the sun. Vers La Flamme. Now I will be fully able to fulfill my ultimate capacities and explore the unknown."

"My god, you stared at the sun?! Come on, guys, we got to get Xavier to the ER, maybe there is something they can do before it's too late."

"I can feel your misunderstanding coupled with genuine concern. But please leave me in peace, I am perfectly fine."

"Fine like hell! Not only are you blind, but you did it on purpose! You're coming with us to the ER, now."

Without further cue, the other two friends joined Tom in moving toward Xavier to escort him out. As they reached out to grab him, he pushed back and asserted, "I said, leave me in peace."

The three then tried much more aggressively to grab Xavier, but he was able to deflect their efforts, sensing each of their presences by the desperation in their hearts, and pushing out in that direction. He managed to have his open palm find their faces, quite forcefully too, causing Lenny to recoil in screams, claiming his nose had been broken. The three redoubled their efforts, getting Xavier off the chair, but little more, as now Xavier had become enraged far worse than his would-be friends. He now venomously attacked them, not in defense, but in total offensive fury. The three stunned medical students ran out the door, and Tom ran next door to call the police. They sent Lenny running to the ER himself to get his nose attended to. Both Tom and Ken were hurting as well, in several different places, but knew they needed to wait for the police to explain the situation.

The police finally arrived, only minutes later but seemingly hours, and approached the scene.   They interviewed the two waiting medical students, and first doubted the entire story but agreed to investigate. They knocked on the damaged and partially open door. Xavier of course did not respond. Tom grew impatient with this police protocol and pushed the door fully open himself. He decided to tell a white lie, stating, "This is my apartment, too, so come in for my sake!"

As the two policemen entered, Xavier did not turn to face them, as he was busy trying to regain his composure. He was finding it difficult to suppress the rage and fury which had overcome him minutes ago.   Xavier was troubled by this difficulty, and not sure what his next move would be.

"Are you Xavier Howell?"

Xavier turned to face the questioning officer. "Yes."

"Do you know these two individuals here?"

"Yes, they are fellow medical students."

"They claim you have purposefully blinded yourself."

"That is inaccurate, officer. I suffered a momentary decrease in vision when a small fire erupted in my kitchen, but I still can see quite well."

Tom burst forward. "He's lying! Look at his eyes! Check him!"

The police officer was beginning to grow weary of Tom's exuberance and silently pushed him back out of the way.

"OK, Mr. Howell, I want you to tell me how many fingers I hold up. Here." The officer held up two fingers, and Xavier easily read the number from his mind.

"Two."

"OK, how about now?"

"Four."

The officer tried it about three more times, with Xavier reading the correct response every time.

Tom grew even more impatient. "Dammit, give him something written to read."

The officer told Tom that he'd better back off or he would be in big trouble. Nevertheless, the cop then pulled out his wallet and told Xavier to read the name and number off his driver's license.

Xavier again read the information from the policeman's mind, successfully giving the name, but he had difficulty on the last couple of digits on the number. Apparently the policeman didn't have the entire number memorized, and Xavier had no choice but to guess on the last two digits.

"Something's funny going on here; you got them all except the next to last number. Considering your eyes look odd and you claim to have suffered an accident affecting your vision, I think you should at least go to the emergency room to get your eyes checked out. We will take you there."

Xavier knew he had to go. Although he didn't think his bluff had been called, he knew that if pressed further, such as having to read from one of his textbooks, he would be totally discovered. His limitations became more obvious to the policemen as they led Xavier to their patrol car, since they saw him walk with uncertainty, taking small false steps here and there.

They arrived at the ER minutes later, and Tom and Ken were following behind on foot. When they arrived, they helped escort Xavier in. Several of the ER staff stared at them with great interest, but not surprise, as Lenny had informed them that Xavier would be coming. The internist covering the ER took Xavier into an exam room, but turned his head back to the policemen and silently mouthed the words, "Stay here." Xavier again told the story of a flash flame temporarily blinding him, but he could sense the physician's doubt. After a quick look at Xavier's eyes with an ophthalmoscope, he informed Xavier that he thought there had been some retinal damage but he wanted to consult the ophthalmologist on call.

Fortunately, one was in house and came quickly to the ER. After thoroughly examining Xavier, he reluctantly informed him that he was totally, permanently blind and that this could only have happened by prolonged staring at something like a welding torch or the sun. Xavier again denied that, knowing the consequences could be very bad for him if he acknowledged it in this setting. They would simply not understand. The ophthalmologist went outside the examination room and conferred with the first physician that had examined Xavier. They were joined by the psychiatrist on call, who was already familiar with Xavier's story, and the three determined that there was no alternative but to have Xavier admitted to the psychiatric unit for self-protection and evaluation of this self-injurious behavior. The three approached Xavier together, and presented their recommendations.

"No, that will not be necessary. They just completed a thorough evaluation of me anyway. I can manage myself."

The psychiatrist strode forth. "Xavier, you know the whole department is aware of your exploits and claims.

This self-blinding only supports those who feel you have a serious post-accident PTSD or Bipolar Disorder. Please come voluntarily to the psychiatric unit, or I will be forced to commit you there."

Xavier knew what the psychiatrist had said was true, but he was not contemplating his options. Instead he was feeling himself lose control, with rage coming over him like a tsunami of blood fury. He leapt off the table and attempted to flee, but the three physicians tried to intervene. Xavier successfully fought them off, as just a few well-thrown fists made the doctors back off quickly. The policemen then got into the act, and although both of them were large and well-trained in physical takedowns, they found Xavier difficult to subdue.   Xavier was consumed with maniacal fury, and lashed out at every life form that came within striking distance of him. Nevertheless, he was finally subdued as eventually the entire male ER staff got into the act, corralling Xavier and giving the policemen the opportunity to handcuff him. At the prompting of the psychiatrist, he was also injected with a large dose of a tranquilizer, Thorazine. He was then dragged, still kicking and screaming, up to the eighth floor and committed to the psychiatry unit, that same unit which he had failed to show up for that day, his last on the psych rotation.

CHAPTER FOURTEEN

Though he could not actually see the astonished faces of those staff members with whom he had just worked side by side, Xavier could nonetheless perceive their sorrow and shock. He was led into a single patient room, and unhandcuffed by the policemen, who subsequently completed their documentation and departed. Xavier was then seen by his Chief Resident, Will Samperton, who simply asked Xavier, "What happened?"

Xavier had finally regained his composure and, although groggy from the Thorazine, was already trying to figure out the best approach to this dilemma. He figured that the lie of the flame accident was not going to work, yet he realized that probably no one would see him as sane if he told the full truth. However, he remembered that in Florida, the commitment law, known as the Baker Act, allowed initial commitment of three days. After that point, a judge must determine competency. Therefore,

Xavier felt that when that time came, he would be able to demonstrate a good mental status and thus be released. So he concluded he would tell the truth, but leave out the more mystical parts, for certainly no one else would understand about Scriabin.

"OK, Will, I'll be up front with you. Yes, I did stare at the sun to intentionally blind myself. You have seen my growing mental powers. My intention was to heighten them further by eliminating the distraction of sight. It was not an impulsive act, nor do I regret it. Already I find it easier to "look" inside someone. For example, as they escorted me down the hall, I felt the presence of an older man, about sixty, who was no doubt staring at me. I felt inside of him a paranoia, a morbid fear that somehow I was the devil or the Antichrist. He must be a paranoid schizophrenic, right?"

"Yes, Xavier, you are correct. But he got admitted two days ago; you could have found out his diagnosis then."

"You forgot that I was removed from the rotation three days ago for the inquisition by the psychiatry and neurology departments. Oh, by the way, I could also feel that Mrs. Simpson's depression is finally clearing; her antidepressants must be kicking in, huh?"

Dr. Samperton sat silent and dumbfounded.

"What is it, Will? I can tell that you know I am right, but there is a conflict within you, some pressure to not conclude that I am sane."

"Yes, Xavier, as usual, you are correct. I have been given the message from above to not let you leave under any circumstances."

"I see. The chairmen have anticipated that I would do something which would put me in a position to get committed. They wish to study me further, correct?"

"I don't know; they haven't told me their motives. They may genuinely think that you have a neuro-psychiatric illness. Haven't you wondered, yourself, if you do?"

"Truly. I have had a shorter fuse as of late. I am prone to certain emotional. . . excesses. But none of my powers or abilities are delusional, in case that's what you were wondering."

"No, I'm afraid I've seen too much magic to believe that. And yes, the Prozac and Desyrel combination seems to finally be working for Mrs. Simpson; we were about to send her for shock therapy. Well, I'll spare you the usual questions; just try and take a low profile while you are here, OK?"

"Yes, Will, that will be fine with me."

As Will left, Xavier knew it was not just out of sympathy that Will Samperton had not asked him further questions. He could feel the genuine anguish in him which made him not want to face Xavier any further. Xavier was not left in peace, however, as they did not spare him the usual routine of every new patient: nursing assessment, physical exam, blood work, etc. However, each person who came in to perform their required duties felt genuine concern and even despair for Xavier, and made their tasks as painless as possible for him. The hour grew late, and Xavier wanted peace, and though the staff did their best to accommodate him, some of the patients didn't. Several of them knocked on Xavier's door, and asked for help from him for their problems. Xavier normally would help, although while he was a student it was made clear that he would not "interfere" with patients who weren't assigned to him. Now these same patients, who had seen Xavier perform miracles on others, hoped that constraint no longer applied. But tonight, after all he had been through, Xavier angrily told them to go away. All except one. There was a seventeen year old girl with terminal brain cancer, who had been transferred from the neurology unit because of repeated suicide attempts. She was frail, with thinning blond hair ruined by a shaved section on the left side where they had been applying radiation therapy. She knew there was no cure for her, but she looked at Xavier with big, anguished eyes and said not a word. He knew instantly what she wanted, simply to be given peace, even if just for a few hours, or minutes. Xavier silently motioned her in, and bade her to sit down next to him. He reached out for her hand, grasping nothing but air until she realized what he wanted. He sat with her for some twenty minutes, all in silence, and mentally quieted the pain, fear, hopelessness, and despair that this unfortunate young woman was suffering. Xavier grew fatigued, finding the mental exertion required for this activity far more strenuous than his usual "readings." He released her hand, and then fell back on the bed, totally exhausted. Sleep took him in seconds, but even if it hadn't, he wouldn't have been able to see the tears of happiness flowing down the pale cheeks of this eternally grateful girl. She kissed him on his hand and whispered, "I will see you in heaven, for certainly you are sent from God."

The next day, Xavier awoke to darkness, and for a brief second panicked before recalling his reality. He calmed himself, and then prepared for what he anticipated would be a demanding and critical day. The nurses came in to help him, and they were extremely nice and gracious to him. He felt a sadness in them, but Xavier could tell that it was not because of his situation.

"Why the pain in your hearts this morning? There has been tragedy or death?"

"Yes, Xavier, death, but not tragedy. Maria, the girl you helped last night, died early this morning. She did not die in her sleep, however. She sat in bed, staring ahead, with a slight smile on her face, and seemingly waited for the end. She was clearly freed of her pain and misery. Bless you, Xavier."

"I wish I could have done more."

After breakfast, Xavier again was approached by

many of the patients, and he began helping one of them. The others all tried to get in line to talk to Xavier, totally disregarding the staff's efforts to get them to group therapy and other activities. Although the staff was very partial to Xavier, his presence was creating havoc on the unit, so they had to restrict him to his room. A staff member was stationed outside the door to deter visitors. This was acceptable to Xavier, who wanted some peace and quiet anyway. Nevertheless, he instead got a procession of professional visitors. There were eye specialists, more neurologists and psychiatrists, and even a member of the media. The reporter had snuck his way through the normal security masquerading as a doctor, and wanted Xavier's story. Xavier refused to speak with him, telling him only that tomorrow would be the hearing before the judge, and that he would speak with the media upon his anticipated release.

All of these physicians were genuinely motivated to help Xavier, but were also obviously professionally fascinated by him. The ophthalmologist said there might be a new surgical procedure that could restore partial vision, the psychiatrist again advocated treatment with Lithium, and the neurologist Carbamazepine. Xavier knew he could not be forced to do any of these, and declined.

After a day full of such visitors, he thought he would finally get some rest, as he had grown weary, both from the intensity of the consultations and his need to periodically rely on his special powers to compensate for his blindness. Thus it came with great surprise that he was about to get an even more exhausting group of visitors, his family. Xavier felt their presence before they entered the room; he was finding his mental powers could reach out slightly farther now, especially when the subjects had strong emotions. And indeed his parents did, for they came in all in tears. They had just been briefed about Xavier's condition, as the original message of his hospitalization had only indicated Xavier was hospitalized with "self-inflicted eye injury." Before they spoke or reached bedside, Xavier addressed them.

"Do not suffer for me, I am quite well. I am impressed by your coming here to support me, but in actuality, all I need is my freedom."

"Xavier, we don't understand all of this, but we do love you and want the best for you," offered Mrs. Howell.

"You will understand, in time. I have a gift, which I want to use to help people, help them in ways far more powerfully than what I could accomplish as an average physician."

Mr. Howell was not satisfied. "Son, the doctors evidently disagree on exactly what is going on inside your head, but they all agree that it is not normal. This is a far more serious situation than even your burns. Are you satisfied with these physicians? Why don't we fly you to Johns Hopkins and get a second opinion, and have you treated at the best facility possible?"

"I do not need a second opinion; I have already heard two dozen 'opinions.' I simply need to be released, which will occur tomorrow after my required hearing."

All three of the gathered Howells grew increasingly concerned. They had been told by the doctors that Xavier was not in his right mind, and that the family's help in stating that he was not the same would probably be needed in court in order to keep Xavier in treatment. Xavier started picking up on this and decided he did not want to engage in further discussion which might be used against him, so he used his remaining energies to mentally put all three of his family members' minds at ease. He could keep this up for only about five minutes, and then collapsed into sleep. This was enough to send his family away, actually feeling reasonably well about Xavier's condition, if for only the night.

The third day was much the same as the second, with the exception that Xavier asked to have Dr. Robertson drop by to take a look at his burns. The arm was now about eighty percent healed, and with a glove on, Xavier could hold things in his left palm for the first time. Xavier reminded himself how fortunate he was to have his mental abilities, because sometimes the burning and itching of the arm would be maddening. The nurses continued to be very good to Xavier, especially the two who had taken an extraordinary interest in meeting all of Xavier's needs. He detected an ulterior motive, and sensed that they, like everyone else, wanted his help. Their "illness," however, was anorgasmia, and they had hoped that Xavier could mentally stimulate them. Although Xavier himself was too tired for much actual sex, he was initially glad to drive the nurses wild with mental orgasms. Unfortunately, after a few times each, the nurses wouldn't leave Xavier alone.

Xavier eagerly waited for the three o'clock court date, and was genuinely frustrated that he frequently had to ask what time it was. At about two, he received one final visitor. It was his father, who had decided this morning that he would try to reason with Xavier himself, once and for all.

"Xavier, you fell asleep before we could really talk last night. The words you said seemed reassuring in tone but not in content. Did I get the understanding that you feel being blind is OK?"

"Being blind is a handicap for most people, but for me it is a liberation, an enhancement."

"How the hell are you going to finish medical school? I have never heard of a blind doctor!"

"Perhaps I will no longer require traditional medical training."

"That's great, son. You're just going to walk out of here today, go home to your one-bedroom apartment, and with no money, no eyesight, and an unfinished education, you're going to make it in this world? It'll never happen!"

"Just watch me."

CHAPTER FIFTEEN

"Order! I will have order in my courtroom!"

The voice was that of Judge Fletcher, and the setting was the probate court. One would not have guessed it was a courtroom by the audience, as it consisted of an assortment of doctors, nurses, students, family members and, most notably, a large and noisy group of media personnel. Usually, a competency or commitment hearing was a small, somber affair, and Judge Fletcher was not too pleased with the carnival-type atmosphere he had in his courtroom that day.

Xavier Howell sat by himself on the traditional left side of the courtroom. He had waived counsel, stating that he did not need it and feeling confident the hearing would go his way. And this was in spite of the fact that he knew that many in the audience would probably advocate his being re-committed for more psychiatric treatment.

Judge Fletcher banged his gavel down, forcefully, and after demanding order again began the proceedings.

"Let the record show that on this day, September Fifth, 1991, began the competency hearing as petitioned by one Xavier Howell to be deemed free to handle his own affairs, as stipulated by the Baker Act after seventy-two hours of involuntary commitment. Mr. Howell, do you understand that you have waived counsel, and must therefore handle the defense of your position solely by yourself or your witnesses?"

"Yes, sir."

"That being the case, we will begin with the opening statement by the prosecution. Mr. Jacobs?"

"Thank you, Judge Fletcher." The prosecuting attorney did not appear like a mean and hungry shark looking for fresh meat, but neither did he look like a man ready to give up without a fight. He was robust, dark, and spoke with a loud and articulate voice.

"Judge, our position, supported and petitioned by both family and physicians, is that Xavier Howell still remains in clear and present danger to himself, and as such should be remanded to continue receiving psychiatric treatment in a protected setting. The prosecution will show that since June 16 of this year, at which time Mr. Howell suffered a severe electrical shock, he has suffered from serious and worsening psychiatric illness, such that at present time he remains at high risk of self-harm and is not competent to handle his own affairs. The prosecution wishes to make it clear to the court that it does not wish to discredit or demean the defendant, but simply to elucidate the extent of his current mental illness and to recommend that he receive further treatment."

"Very well, Mr. Jacobs, you may call your first witness."

"Thank you, your honor. We wish to call Dr. Bream."

The prosecuting attorney went to great pains to help

convey what a serious accident Xavier had suffered, making it very clear that Xavier's brain had endured a significant insult of electricity. After Dr. Bream's testimony, a different neurologist, Dr. Mahoney, gave a second opinion. Both offered their opinion that Xavier had suffered some damage to the temporal and/or limbic regions of his brain and was suffering from a syndrome of mood instability, rage attacks, and possibly delusions of grandeur. They pointed out that damage to this region of the brain is commonly associated with either seizures or the above mentioned symptoms.

Xavier chose to use his opportunity to challenge the testimony for the first time. "Your honor, I would like to ask the first witness, Dr. Bream, some questions."

"Please proceed."

"Dr. Bream, you and Dr. Mahoney both pointed out there was damage done to the temporal and/or limbic regions of my brain. Is it not true that what was visible on the PET and BEAM scans was not necessarily "damage" but simply a visible alteration? Indeed, is it not true that the PET scan showed increased activity in that area, possibly indicating an enhanced brain function instead of a damaged one?"

"Yes, that is possible."

"And is it not true, Dr. Bream, that during my EEG and BEAM testing I demonstrated a previously never accomplished level of brain wave control?"

"Yes, that is accurate."

"Your honor, I have no further questions for this witness."

The prosecution then presented the testimony of two psychiatrists, both of whom had considerable sympathy and admiration for Xavier but did feel that he was suffering from psychiatric illness. The second, Dr. Hobari himself, was succinct in his opinion:

"Mr. Howell is a most remarkable young man, possessing superior intelligence and determination. He has a tremendous ability to empathize with psychiatric patients, and he has charisma. Nevertheless, his history of flashbacks, nightmares, rage attacks, increased sexual drive, feelings of possessing great powers, and especially the self-inflicted blinding all indicate a significant psychiatric illness. His diagnosis has shifted from more of a Post-Traumatic Stress Disorder to a Manic-Depressive type of illness. The illness may have been either triggered or caused by the accident, but the illness is there, regardless."

Xavier then chose to speak again. "Dr. Hobari, would you not consider it normal for patients who have suffered the burns and loss of hair that I have endured to experience some amount of PTSD symptoms?"

"Yes, that would be considered normal."

"Does the extent of my alleged PTSD symptoms incapacitate me to the point that I am at risk to self or others?"

"No, not by itself."

"Then a large part of your opinion that I possess a Manic-Depressive illness is based on your opinion that my `feelings of possessing great powers' is delusional in nature."

"Yes, in part."

"Dr. Hobari, how many patients does the average third year medical student have during their one-month rotation on psychiatry?"

"They start with two, and may get two or three more if their original patients get well and are discharged."

"During my three and a half weeks on your service, how many patients did I have?"

"Approximately fifteen or sixteen."

"I actually had seventeen. How do you account for the great disparity between my experience and the typical student's?"

"I am not sure. You certainly possess some extraordinary abilities to relate to patients and somehow stimulate them into apparent rapid recovery. We have no evidence that the patients that you supposedly `cured' will remain that way.  You may well have effected a placebo response, or a `charisma cure' that is often seen with certain religious leaders, medicine men, or other mystical healers."

This line of questioning obviously had not gone as well for Xavier as he had hoped, and he decided not to make matters worse, and retired to his side of the bench. The next and last witness called by the prosecution was Charles Howell III.

"Mr. Howell, please tell the court if you have seen significant changes in the personality of your son Xavier."

"For the record, I speak for myself and my family in stating that we love Xavier and wish him no harm. But I have personally seen dramatic changes in him ever since the accident. He was always a very well-controlled young man, but lately he can erupt into violent rages instantly. He was always very dedicated, and that was never more evident than in his total dedication to becoming a doctor. So his self-inflicted blinding, which makes it nearly impossible for him to become a physician, goes totally against the ambitions and dreams that Xavier Howell had for many years. Almost more alarming than all of this is that when he speaks to us, it is almost as if he is a different person than the one we knew. We only want the best for our son. . . " At that point, Mr. Howell choked up and fought off tears. "But we know that he needs help."

Xavier chose not to cross-examine his father. He wished only to offer his own defense. As the proceedings were going on, he had attempted to "read" the mindset of the judge, and had gotten mixed messages, seeing that the judge was undecided in his opinion. He knew that if worse came to worst, he would have to resort to trying to mentally affect the judge's thinking in order to receive a favorable outcome. He hoped that would be unnecessary. Just in case, Xavier walked up nearer to the judge, and faced him.

"Judge, you have heard testimony stating that I have an unclear neurologic condition which may not represent disease at all. You have heard testimony that I have suffered some Post-Traumatic Stress Disorder symptoms. That is unquestionably correct, but does not constitute a psychiatric illness which so impairs me that I need confinement for my own protection. You have also heard testimony alleging that I have delusions of possessing special powers. I would offer, as proof, that I have just caused the prosecuting attorney and Dr. Hobari to both fall asleep."

The audience gasped and collectively stared at the two mentioned individuals, who had suddenly slumped over, sound asleep. Then a clamor arose from the audience, particularly the media, who were overcome with excitement.

"Order! I will have order in my courtroom or I will throw all of you out!"

All of the commotion caused Dr. Hobari and Mr. Jacobs to jolt awake, and they both looked around in confusion. The audience laughed at this, prompting another gavel pounding.

"Bailiffs, I want everyone out of my courtroom. . . well, never mind. Xavier Howell, in my thirty years on the bar I have never had such a circus made of this honored process. You, however, have demonstrated competency under the law, and I hereby declare you free to manage your own affairs."

Before the judge could even declare "Court dismissed," the audience broke out into wild applause and cheers for Xavier. A new star had been born.

CHAPTER SIXTEEN

The media descended upon Xavier the minute he was led out of the courtroom by the nurse who had accompanied him there from the hospital, although her responsibility over him had just ended. They all began firing questions and taking pictures of Xavier. He was surprisingly startled for a second by this, as he actually could just barely detect the bright lights of the flashbulbs going off in his face. Not that it mattered anymore, but Xavier smiled inwardly upon remembering that one of his many physicians had told him he felt there had only been ninety-six percent loss of vision.

Over the past three days, although Xavier had been bombarded by doctors, nurses and others, he had used whatever free time he had to plan for his courtroom defense and for this moment. He had realized, in part courtesy of his father, that in spite of having his special powers, he had no resources or funds to speak of. It was clear that Xavier had broken off from his family, and even if he hadn't, he would not have asked them for monetary assistance. Not now, not later, not ever again. So that he wouldn't give away his story for nothing, he asked for the highest bids from both television and newspaper reporters. The bidding began like an out-of-control auction, and Xavier began hearing bids of eleven and twelve hundred dollars. He settled on the two highest bidders, representatives from the Orlando Sentinel and Channel Nine news. He also wanted two other things, a new suit of black cloth, and to be chauffeured to an Orlando hotel. There, he would give his interviews later that night at eight.

A limousine was called quickly and Xavier driven down to Orlando. During the trip, he rested by putting himself to sleep. The courtroom proceedings had tired him somewhat, and he knew he would probably have to demonstrate his powers later that night. The limo arrived at the Omni Hotel, one of the most exclusive and luxurious hotels in downtown Orlando. Xavier was escorted to his room, and once inside was given the new black suit that he had requested, a forty-six long, simple yet modern-appearing outfit. Xavier had about an hour to shower and prepare for his interviews, and he needed some valet assistance. Any fatigue he earlier had felt melted in the anticipation of a great moment.

At eight o'clock sharp the knock on the door came, and Xavier summoned in his eager guests. About fifteen people came in, many of whom were there just to set up and operate recording and video equipment. The interplay of the sounds of people and machines, coupled with the waves of excitement that Xavier felt, provided an interesting overture to the evening's activities. The lead interviewer from Channel Nine News, as well as the Sentinel people, told Xavier that they were ready as soon as he was.

Xavier came forward and asked for a chair to sit in during the interview. He was resplendent in his elegant black suit, and it provided a dramatic contrast to the gleam of his eyes and of his pale, bald head. He began the session with a monolog of his story.

"My name is Xavier. Just Xavier, now, nothing more. I was reborn, in a manner of speaking, on June Sixteenth of this year by a freak accident which poured electricity through my body and brain.

"During the past few months, I have learned that this event triggered or caused certain areas of my brain to become highly active and functional, providing me with heretofore unknown mental capacities. I have the ability to reach inside another's soul, to feel and understand the conflicts and contradictions which poison mankind. Further, I can cause temporary alterations in another person's mind, to assist them in their cleansing of psychological garbage or give them at least temporary peace. The mechanism behind these abilities is linked to my new-found capacity to alter my brain wave patterns, which I discovered and demonstrated in EEG testing at MUSC Hospital. I have subsequently postulated that I can alter my brain waves to match, or duplicate, those of another person in order to replicate their internal experience. Once this is done, I can change my own patterns to resonate with the other's, thus providing me the ability to do more than just a `reading' of the other person's psyche. This is more than the vague capacities of empathy and intuition, and is more than the presumed telepathic abilities of psychics and mind readers. It is scientifically based, demonstrable and far more comprehensive than all of the anecdotal and hocus-pocus talents claimed in various quarters.

"Even more important than the fact of this quantum leap in human neuro-psychological capacity, is the potential usefulness of it. I hope to pioneer active development of this capacity in others, for I cannot believe I am the only one in the world that had the potential for this growth. Further, I want to directly use my abilities to help people, to help as many people as I possibly can.

"I will now entertain questions."

"Xavier, your description implies that you want to be some kind of super-psychiatrist. Is that accurate?"

"Yes, but not complete. My intentions go beyond simply curing individual neuroses."

"Such as?"

"I am not sure, yet. But I feel I may help in stimulating people everywhere to relinquish their ancient resentments, jealousies, and other negative affects."

"Do you have telekinetic abilities?"

"No, I cannot move inanimate objects, nor do I believe that anyone has demonstrated the ability to. But I don't think moving a penny across a desk mentally would constitute a great hope for change in mankind."

"Can you predict the future?"

"Only so far as reading a person's subconscious desires, which might help me anticipate future events."

The media kept pressing Xavier for qualities which he did not possess, making Xavier grow frustrated. He consequently made about half the audience fall asleep, causing an immediate uproar in the others, who could not believe what had happened. The stir caused the soporific reporters to stagger upright after they had slumped down or even collapsed.

"OK, Xavier, we get the message. How about doing what you claim is really important?"

"Good. First, I need a volunteer. Someone who has struggled with some particular mental anguish and wishes to be helped."

One of the assistants to the video crew stepped forward. He was a thirty-ish, blond man of medium build and long face. "My name is Conrad Davis."

"Yes, Conrad, I understand why you have volunteered. The pain of your struggles emanates from you like a warm glow. You have never forgiven yourself for not succeeding as a professional athlete, as you fell just short of your dreams. My reading of that experience is that you gave it everything that you had, and the failure was due more to lack of genetic ability and skill. You will need to overcome this or you will continue to be plagued with the lack of drive and alcoholism that you suffer from."

The man initially was overwhelmed at Xavier's insights, then blushed in embarrassment at the latter revelations. He lowered his head and closed his eyes, as if to make everything disappear.

Xavier closed his sightless eyes and uttered, "I will help you." He then proceeded to calm this man's troubled soul and assist him in forgiving himself. Conrad Davis raised his head in triumph, wheeling around and exuberantly declaring that everything Xavier said was true, and that he absolutely felt as if he was cured. The media focused on him for a few minutes, checking his credibility, but accepting the fact that Xavier had truly helped him, at least temporarily. All of the media except one older reporter who remained skeptical. "How do we know that wasn't pre-planned?"

Xavier grew immediately angered, so he mentally caused the old man to pull his toupe off of his head and stuff it in his mouth. The collection of relatively insensitive reporters roared.

"Any other questions?"

"Xavier, is it possible that you will use your powers for purposes other than the good motives you have outlined?"

"If you mean for evil purposes, no, because I cannot do something with my mind that I would not do otherwise, such as commit a crime. I admit that you will have to accept my word on this, but I offer my lifetime history of moral and ethical behavior as support for my claim."

The media inquest continued, but on a less threatening tack, trying to obtain more background information on the man who was Xavier Howell. Xavier, however, would have no part of this.

"You have the basics of my story, you have a demonstration on videotape, you have my directions for the future. You have enough. I will retire now."

The media for once knew its boundaries, and did not try to push Xavier farther. They thanked him for the remarkable interview and departed. One man, however, remained.

"Excuse the disruption, sir, but I am the guest service agent for Omni, and we wish to extend our welcome. You can remain our guest at the hotel indefinitely. A bellman will be posted outside your door at all times for your convenience and protection. Will you be needing anything else tonight, sir?"

"Yes; please inform the media that I will be needing a manager or agent, and I would like to interview applicants tomorrow morning, if possible."

"Yes, sir, I will catch them before they leave."

Xavier barely found the strength to make it to the bed. Without needing any special powers, he collapsed into a deep sleep. In the morning, he ordered breakfast from room service. He was told by the server that his story was all over the front page of the newspaper and on every news show. The day previously, a star had been born, but on this day the star became a celebrity.

CHAPTER SEVENTEEN

After a good breakfast of the hotel's special omelet, along with a side order of grits in homage to his Charleston roots, Xavier prepared himself for the day. The guest service agent had stopped by during breakfast, apologetic for interrupting but intent on delivering the flowers and messages that his celebrity status had already attracted. Some of the notes urged Xavier to remain courageous in the face of adversity, while others asked for help. Xavier was amazed at how quickly this response had occurred, only the morning after his story broke.

All of this goodwill and admiration gave Xavier an added feeling of security and purpose. However, upon stumbling out of the shower, groping for a towel, he was struck by the strong fragrance of many roses and other flowers that populated the room. It dawned on him that he would never see the beauty of the rose again, something he had always admired. Although he didn't like to admit it, Xavier had enjoyed sitting by the backyard rose garden that his father cultivated with loving care. He had learned to tell a rose by sight, and knew the difference between a Peace and a John F. Kennedy, an Oklahoma and a Don Juan. He even had learned to appreciate their smell, and he decided that the predominant type of roses in the room were Mr. Lincolns. He fought off a surge of tears which came over him like an unexpected swell on the ocean. His emotions betrayed him sometimes of late, causing temporary doubts about his choices and dreams. They were temporary doubts only, however, as he fought them off like the grogginess of a Monday morning.

Xavier located his new black attire and prepared to entertain the expected potential agents and managers as he had requested. The first one arrived at nine a.m. sharp, prompt and eager. He was about thirty, zealous and ambitious, and arranged to be first today by virtue of hounding the hotel the minute he heard about Xavier on the eleven o'clock news. He flooded Xavier with praise and admiration, and then promised him that he could get him on Good Morning America within three days. Xavier was inexperienced with dealing with show business types, and although this one may have been typical of the breed, there was something about him which was unsettling. Upon deeper reading of him, it was clear; the man truly believed that the end justified the means, and would thus stop at nothing to further his or his clients' objectives. This was clearly unacceptable, and Xavier quickly dismissed him.

The next agent arrived at nine-thirty, as the hotel had arranged to have them come at half-hour intervals. This one was a forty-four year old woman with much experience in the field of unusual entertainers. She reportedly had worked with the likes of Kreskin, Uri Geller and others with alleged superior mental gifts. The woman was immediately honest and straightforward in her approach, and didn't try too hard to impress Xavier with grandiose claims of what she could do for him. She began rather methodically informing Xavier of the steps needed to accomplish specific goals, such as striving for wide-spread exposure rather than marketing powerful or influential individuals. She would have impressed Xavier with her professionalism, but unfortunately Xavier was mentally drifting far away, into another world.

The Smoky Mountains were always a welcome relief from the congestion of city life and its other incumbent problems. These mountains were not overpowering in their scope, as in the Rockies, but impressed more with their beauty, especially now, in the fall. Blankets of fog only served to add mystery to the explosion of colors amongst the autumnal trees. Here, civilization was ex-cluded save for those few who had the ambition and stamina to hike the Appalachia Trail. Xavier felt good that this year, for the first time since their annual family pilgrimage, he was leading the hike, with Zack and Father trailing. Somehow, this was significant, to lead and not follow. . .

"Excuse me, sir? Are you OK?"

Xavier sat, motionless.

"Can you hear me? Xavier?"

With the calling of his name, Xavier reoriented to the setting of the hotel room, and tried to collect his rambling thoughts.

"Pardon me, but I seem to have been distracted. Please continue."

"Are you sure? You seemed to black out there for a minute or two."

"Yes, please go ahead with your questions and proposals."

"Good. We were going to map out a strategy or game plan to see which market we would hit first. My recommendation . . . "

I wish they would keep up, Xavier thought to himself. He always had, when he was following. But now that he was leading, now all of a sudden Dad gets tired more quickly, and Zack asks to slow down repeatedly. Did they have to try and spoil it?! It was so exhilarating, how could he slow down? He simply wouldn't; they could just lag behind. There was only one main trail anyway, it was not like they could get lost. *Look, there ahead, a deer! Somewhat high up for him, poor thing.*

"Xavier? Are you with me?"

Again it took several seconds to reorient, and once he did, the realization of what had happened hit him again.

"I'm sorry, but you will have to leave. You are well qualified but I obviously have some problem I need to understand. I will contact you later if needed."

The woman was genuinely disappointed, but politely thanked Xavier for his audience, however brief it was. She then quickly departed, leaving Xavier to ponder the recent events. Somehow, he was rapidly shifting into a daydreaming-like state, possibly what the psychiatrists called dissociating. But why? She seemed perfect for the job, and honest and well-meaning also. Xavier did note that he had barely begun to get a reading on her prior to having mentally drifted elsewhere. Perhaps something in his reading of her triggered the dissociations. Or was this an unrelated phenomenon, a new handicap he would have to deal with? In retrospect, it probably had happened already a couple of times. Indeed while he was hospitalized recently, it occurred once, come to think of it, but at the time he had dismissed its importance. There was conceivably an individual connected with that event, as he had been accosted by a patient just prior to it. Not enough data. He would continue seeing manager applicants and contemplating this mystery.

The next applicant for the position of Xavier's manager was a thirty-five year old man, who presented himself in a much more devious manner. He initially was obsequious, and then tried to overpower Xavier with the forcefulness of his personality. This man genuinely felt that Xavier should be feeling helpless at this point, due to his blindness, and that he would be impressed with a show of power. Xavier instead grew enraged with this man within minutes and almost exploded in violence towards him. He instead just grimaced, and let out a guttural yell. The man got the picture and fled out of the room.

The next candidate arrived at ten-thirty, and this one was a twenty-three year old attractive woman named Lana Marshall. She was beautiful in spirit, Xavier noticed, although he had no clue that her exterior matched her interior. He was heartened by an initial good first reading, seeing honesty, good boundaries and professional ethics, and a warm and caring personality. Unfortunately, he detected a lack of extensive experience in the field.

"What jobs have you had in this field?"

"I have lined up engagements for many of the Orlando area sports celebrities, such as Payne Stewart and Scott Skiles. I also have connections to the Palm Beach area, and have worked with some of the movie stars out there. For example, I helped set up a roast for Burt Reynolds."

As Xavier listened to her, he simultaneously read inside her to determine her character and background. She was curiously failing to mention that she had gained much experience being married for five years to a prominent agent, who had tragically died in an automobile accident ten months ago. In that interim, this young woman had taken up her husband's job and dedicated herself to it, in some small way preserving his presence and memory.

"Why is it, Mrs. Marshall, that you fail to mention the

experience and connections you have by virtue of your deceased husband?"

Lana was obviously startled by this question, and struggled briefly to regain her composure.

"You truly are gifted, aren't you? I didn't bring that up because I feel as a manager and a woman, I need to be evaluated and judged on my merits and accomplishments alone, not on those of my husband. But it is true that I learned much from him, and that his prominence in the area has opened doors for me that otherwise might have taken much longer to get through. Yes, I am young and somewhat inexperienced, but I have garnered and executed several commissions which I feel were granted to me based on my energy and personality, not on my husband's achievements."

Xavier liked her fire, and fondly thought back to his favorite piece of Scriabin and replayed some of it in his mind. This need of hers to stand on her own two feet was healthy motivation, although it was stimulated by the grief she felt at the loss of her husband. The more he read of her, the more impressed he was with the lack of neurosis present in her. Even her grief was uncomplicated; just simple, unadulterated sadness and loss, gradually waning with time and dealt with via healthy displacement into her career. There was no secondary gain, no ulterior motives behind her ambition, no pathological strivings to undo the past or create an unrealistic future. He did detect a sense of growing security and confidence in herself which was not there when she was younger, possibly explaining her early marriage to an older man. But by all accounts this man was wonderful, talented, and treated her well, at least in her memories.

"I enjoy your candor, Mrs. Marshall."

"Please, call me Lana."

"I guess that's appropriate, especially now that I wish to be known only as Xavier."

"Can I be so bold as to ask why you are choosing to discard your last name?"

"Yes. I told the press it was only because I was now reborn, changed, and that symbolically the name change would reflect this. However it also reflects my separation from my family, who did not understand me very well to begin with and now are totally mystified and unbelieving of my powers and situation."

"I appreciate your candor, too. It will make it much easier to work with you and promote you."

With that comment, Lana had almost assumed that she had gotten the job. Xavier smiled at this, wondering if she perhaps had the gift of intuition herself. For Xavier had already decided, decided that Lana was the one to help him reach his dreams.

CHAPTER EIGHTEEN

Over the next week, Lana Marshall proved her mettle by getting Xavier interviews, first by the syndicated news networks, and then by the major ones. She also functioned as Xavier's aid and traveling companion to the various locales. The interviews went well, for the most part, but after doing about six or seven of them, Xavier realized that this endeavor was only serving to gain some level of recognition and income. Besides, during some of the interviews, there continued to be doubters and skeptics demanding further proof of his capabilities. Xavier either put the interviewer to sleep or caused him to do something foolish on camera. He found that these "parlor games" curiously impressed the media more than the actual healing of people. When he did "readings" of people, their claims of Xavier's accuracy never quite convinced the viewing public, who wondered if the events had been "rigged." Likewise, if Xavier purposefully revealed unconscious conflicts to help troubled people, their relief and gratitude were still doubted by the media and others. They questioned whether the process was genuine, and whether the supposed changes would last. By the end of the week he had one of his biggest interviews, on Larry King Live. During the call-in show he was surprised to receive several very negative callers, condemning Xavier as a "heretic," a "charlatan," a "glorified palm-reader" and other similar slanders. Although he received other favorable callers, and most people were convinced that he at least had some extraordinary powers, Xavier found the abuse intolerable. He demanded to end the interview halfway through the program. He jumped up from the table and yelled "Lana!" She was backstage and came running. The host immediately called for a commercial break.

"Yes, Xavier, I'm here."

"Let us leave this travesty. I cannot endure any more of this! We need to leave, to return to Florida and begin my true journey. We have made enough notoriety and money."

"OK, Xavier, we can go straight to the airport. But perhaps you should finish the show?"

"Here, I'll finish the show!" With that, Xavier put everyone asleep, Larry King and his entire backstage crew. Lana got the message and escorted Xavier off the stage.

Upon arriving in Orlando, they were welcomed at the Omni because of the favorable publicity Xavier had given the hotel by mentioning their hospitality during his interviews. Xavier and Lana now had adjoining penthouses, and both of them fell into their respective beds, exhausted. The following morning they shared breakfast in Xavier's room and plotted further strategy.

"Xavier, that was quite a week. I know you grew sick of it, but you did a lot. I know it was stressful, but let's face it, you earned over twenty thousand dollars and became a household name. I know these may not be your ultimate goals, but these accomplishments will allow you to begin your pursuit of other goals."

Xavier smiled at the well-intentioned Lana, whose heart remained pure gold, not swayed by Xavier's early success so much that she would deter him from his true ideals and dreams. Yet those dreams were still not clearly visualized even in Xavier's mind.

"I thank you for what you have done; do not misinterpret my disgust at the shallowness of media exploitation and harassment as any reflection of my gratitude for your managing efforts."

"I understand."

"So I see. Good. Let us look forward now, to find a way to have me work directly with people and help individuals who desperately need it. This will allow me to further my psychological growth and hone my skills."

"This may be tricky. Do you wish to open some kind of clinic? I know absolutely nothing about regulations, licenses, that kind of thing."

"Good point. No, a clinic may not be immediately feasible. Perhaps you can look to see if there are reputable facilities which would allow me to work with a minimum of interference or scrutiny."

"I will see what I can find today. Right now, I have a bagful of mail to go through; there might be some interesting offers to evaluate. Is there anything you need today?"

"No, a day of peace will be fine, as long as I have my music."

Lana walked over and got the black canvas bag which contained Xavier's portable CD player and several classical CD's. He thanked her again and she departed. Before he began his listening, he contemplated his current situation. Who was he, anymore? The media had branded him a "seer," in reference to the blind prophets of ancient civilizations. It was not totally inaccurate, but somehow people seemed to miss the point that Xavier was both healer and scientist at heart, wishing to advance the realm of human accomplishment while simultaneously using his gifts to help relieve some of mankind's suffering. He was not and never had any intention of becoming a showman or entertainer. He had rationalized over and over again how his media campaign was necessary to give him the freedom to pursue his true goals, but the experience had left him shaken, reminding him of old resentments about not being understood by his family. Further, he had still struggled with adjusting to the loss of his vision, every so often finding himself in ridiculously helpless positions, or discovering one other beauty in life that he would never again see. The combination of these two anguishes evoked a flood of tears, and for at least an hour Xavier wept.

By the time Lana returned in the evening, Xavier had recuperated and regained some spirit. He felt some excitement in Lana's heart and this in turn excited him.

"What did you find?"

"Several opportunities. I found an Institute for Parapsychological Advancement in Miami very interested in working with you, agreeing to provide a minimum of interference. They will provide patients for study, coworkers who have experience in studying ESP, telepathy and other types of mind control, and a stipend. The stipend, however, is quite low; about two thousand a month. Next, I found the University of South Florida and the University of Florida very interested in working with you, and they were flexible about arranging your work to suit you. They will pay even less, but they would be a notch higher in reputation if you wanted to use them to solidify your claims. That was about it for facilities in the state.

"But your mail was truly astounding. There must have been over a thousand letters. I even hired a couple of hotel people to help me sort them out, into three stacks; the adulation pile, the hate pile, and the offer pile. I only read through the offer pile, but in case you were wondering the adulation pile was twice as big as the hate mail pile. Of the hundred or so offers, many of them were desperate pleas for help dealing with desperate situations, including AIDS and cancer patients, incapacitated war veterans, and dying children. It was very touching but very depressing, to be honest. Then there was a group of more psychiatrically ill people, more along the lines of what you were looking for, such as victims of child abuse, suicidally depressed people, people with panic attacks and phobias, and more. And then there was one very interesting offer from a lady in Palm Beach named Samantha Trent. She apparently is a wealthy socialite who suffers from some unclear unhappiness and wants help for it. She made by far a more generous offer than anyone else: free use of an entire wing of her estate plus one hundred thousand dollars. The only two stipulations: you try to help her with her problems and you stay for at least a month."

Xavier was very impressed with Lana's efforts and with the response by the public via the mail. He was intrigued by the offers, in particular the one by the Palm Beach lady. He asked Lana if in the letter she detected any ulterior motives. She said no, but decided to read it to Xavier anyway. It appeared this woman had everything in life, but was missing something, or something was keeping her back, nagging at her. She did not sound like just another rich but bored socialite.

"It sounds almost irresistible, although once again it is a rather calculated and entrepreneurial endeavor, not exactly what I had envisioned. However, if I am going to help people, it won't hurt to help people with money first. One hundred thousand?   My God, a couple more offers like that and we could build our own Institute! Oh, Lana, I would of course require your presence there. Was that mentioned?"

"No, it wasn't."

"Will you please call her and tell her that is my only stipulation, if that is acceptable to you?"

"I guess I could handle it." Lana smiled.   She immediately went to the phone and tried to reach Mrs. Trent. Mrs. Trent happened to be home, and had no problem with the added house guest. They arranged for a meeting the following morning at her estate. Xavier was pleased at her acceptance of Lana, because he could not help but wonder if Mrs. Trent's underlying motives had something to do with hidden hopes of developing a sexual or romantic relationship with him. He checked himself mid-thought, however, laughing to himself at how anyone would be immediately attracted to a bald, blind man who was extremely weird to boot!

So the next day, Lana and Xavier departed from Orlando and navigated the three-hour drive to Palm Beach. Xavier had never been there before. Lana described it to him as they slowly entered the town after crossing the bridge over the intracoastal waterway. The main drive was lined with impossibly tall and slender palm trees, and the city streets and yards were immaculate.

They arrived at the ocean boulevard and turned south. Lana described the pretty blue-green water to the left, and the old but majestic mansions lining the right, almost not visible due to the Palm Beach trademark hedges. The hedges were boxwood, pruned into an eight foot high living wall with perfect angles and corners. They soon came to the Trent estate, located on the ocean and as majestic as any home in the city except for possibly the Mar-A-Lago Estate. They pulled into the long driveway through gates clearly opened for them, and were greeted at the entrance by a butler. He escorted them inside, into the living room where awaited Mrs. Trent. She was a woman already in her fifties, although she looked younger than that due to either good living or plastic surgery. She was elegantly though not extravagantly dressed, and was entirely proper and distinguished. As Lana escorted Xavier near her, she stood to meet them.

"Hello, I'm Samantha Trent. Xavier and Lana, I presume?"

Xavier extended a hand in the direction of the voice.

"Yes, I am Xavier and this is my manager, Lana Marshall."

"Welcome to you both. Please, have a seat." Lana led Xavier to the nearest chair, and as Xavier sat down, he felt the ornate carvings on the armrests of the Victorian furniture.

"I am so glad you are interested in my offer. My problem is neither simple nor tragic, but remains a problem in spite of everything I have tried to do to eliminate it. That includes going to the best psychiatrists money can buy, improving all areas of my lifestyle, trying hypnosis and whatever else came along. To be direct with you, I am convinced I have some unconscious conflict or problem which affects me periodically as unexplained sadness or a feeling of being ill at ease. This makes no sense to me, as I am a woman who has set many goals for my life and accomplished every one of them. The psychiatrists have postulated that I still miss my divorced husband, or that I am too hung up on staying young. I have a happy social life, have many male suitors and do not miss my ex-husband. I may put too much energy into fighting off the effects of getting older, but I cannot believe that is the cause of my distress."

Xavier was delighted. Here was a woman, being very

direct and open, with no pretense and no ulterior motives that he could detect. He also found her to have a very complex and intriguing psychological make-up, not easily readable and very challenging. He knew immediately that he would accept her offer. Nevertheless, he would enjoy leaving her in suspense a bit longer. "Please, Mrs. Trent, please sit next to me for a moment."

She complied.

"I feel in you a genuine conflict of deep origin, along with the more superficial concern of staying young. Can I touch your face?"

Xavier did not see the startled reaction on Mrs. Trent's face, but after a pause she said yes. Xavier ran his fingers around her jaw, up around her mouth, nose and then eyes. He felt taut skin, stretched over very classical features. It was skin obviously well-taken care of, and showed little evidence of Mrs. Trent's five decades of life.

"How many surgeries have you had to your face?"

"Four, and don't ask me about my figure!"

Xavier laughed with her, and after she teased him a bit by asking to feel his bald head, he agreed to accept her offer.

CHAPTER NINETEEN

The background sounds of water falling from various fountains and waterfalls provided a soothing accompaniment to Samantha Trent's narrative about the estate's gardens. The gardens sounded impressive enough, but Xavier wanted even more details, especially when they got to the rose garden. With Samantha's help, he leaned over and correctly identified the aroma of the first rose as that of a Double Delight. It was characterized by large red and white petals with a strong, perfume-like fragrance. He asked for help locating the second rose bush, but couldn't place the rose's faint fragrance. Samantha gave him a hint by describing the rose as a pinkish-orange, medium-sized bloom. He then recalled the rose, a Tropicana, one he had seen in his neighbor's garden. He remembered how his father had disapproved of the rose, stating that its fragrance was too wimpy to earn placement in his garden.

Samantha then continued the tour for Xavier, describing the brightly colored koi which swam in the Oriental garden's pond. Xavier was alone with her, as Lana had left the day previously to go back to Gainesville to collect both her things and Xavier's. Xavier was using the tour as an opportunity to begin probing Samantha's mind for deeper experiences and feelings. There came into recognition an ancient feeling, long carried unconsciously, a feeling most aptly described as guilt. But it was a guilt without remorse, an apparent contradiction in terms. This guilt had been carried for years and emerged periodically as another feeling, thus possibly explaining Samantha's complaints of unexplained fatigue, irritability, and sadness. When the outdoors tour ended at a park-type bench at the far end of the gardens, Xavier asked Samantha to sit with him for a while.

"I feel a deep and ancient guilt in you, well-disguised and kept out of your awareness. Have you knowingly felt guilty about some action or behavior on your part?"

"I honestly can say no, other than childhood pranks that didn't really hurt anyone. I have always tried to be ethically sound and decent in life, particularly in business, and I am known for it. This is in contrast, however, to some of my well-to-do peers in this community."

"Then it is of significance that you cherish decency and hold to high values and principals."

"I don't understand."

"Well, if one places extraordinary value on a particular ideal, that added energy must come from either internal motivations or external, like the strongly emphasized importance of such values by parents."

"That's very interesting. My parents did stress proper values and principles. But there's nothing wrong with that."

"Not at all, unless they did it excessively, or did it out of guilt over their failures in that area. Did your family ever get involved in illegal or unethical activities?"

"Not that I know of. But there have always been rumors, rumors which I always considered mud-slinging slander. This is common with the rich. Jealousy breeds it. Are you suggesting these rumors may have been true?"

"I do not know. It would just be one possible explanation for the peculiar guilt that you have. I meant no insult to your family name."

"No insult taken. I'll have to ponder this. You have already given me new ideas and possibilities, ones that no one else has been able to suggest. I'm grateful for even your guesses. Now then, you need to meet Garth."

"Garth" was the name of a majestic beast which was Samantha's main companion and pet. He was a Harlequin Great Dane, weighing close to two hundred pounds and illustrating the best of coats in the breed. He had the highly prized coloring of being mostly white with several well-spaced, irregular but pure black patches. Garth was six years old, well past mid-life for the breed, but a perfect specimen who could have won any dog show in the country. Mrs. Trent did not "show" him, however, as she felt she had nothing to prove nor anything to gain. She cherished his presence beyond words, and he was absolutely loyal to her. Xavier felt a surge of emotion well up in her as they obviously neared the dog. He ran to her side and then growled softly in Xavier's direction.

"Garth, this is Xavier. He is my friend. Here, Xavier, let me let you pet Garth."

Xavier extended his hand and felt it placed on top of a massive head with a soft and short coat. As he moved his hand back in a petting motion, he came across the trademark clipped ears of the Dane, standing staunchly upright. Not knowing if it had any effect on the canine brain, Xavier tried to communicate the message that he was indeed a friend. The dog stopped growling and

seemed to relax a bit. Xavier then ran his hand across his
back, and gauged the immensity of the dog, far larger
than any he had encountered before. The dog seemed
willing to allow this exploration of his body, and Xavier
proceeded to feel the muscular yet lithe limbs of this
giant. As he squatted down and finished his exploration
at the dog's massive chest, Garth planted a big, sloppy
tongue right on Xavier's face.

"Well, congratulations, Xavier. You just received
Garth's stamp of approval."

Over the next several days, Xavier actually spent
more time with Garth than with Samantha. Xavier had
mistakenly assumed that Mrs. Trent would be around
most of the day, eager to receive analysis and treatment.
She in fact was an extremely busy lady, actively pursuing
a wide variety of endeavors, all of which she enjoyed
considerably. She was a woman of taste, intellect, and
good work ethics despite her "spoiled child" upbringing.
He now understood better why she initially had requested a month of his time; not only was she very
complex, she simply was not around that much.

Garth, however, was always home and had free reign
of the premises. Xavier had taken to Garth very quickly,
and Garth had responded to his messages of friendship.
Samantha was amazed at how much Garth had be-
friended Xavier, as this had never happened before with
anyone else. Xavier thought that he would need the
expected help getting from bedroom to living room and
the like, but instead would call Garth, who would walk
him to the main living area. The cook, butler, gardener
and maid all helped when needed, but Xavier preferred
the company of the dog, growing to understand
Samantha's passion for him more every day.

Xavier had come to the realization that he had become
sadly out of shape, losing nearly all of his muscular tone.
He knew he needed exercise, and his arm was now

healed to the point that he could do most exercises save ones that involved direct contact with the skin. Although Xavier had preferred swimming to jogging in the past, he now found jogging with Garth a most pleasurable and mutually beneficial experience. Xavier only needed to hold the leash, and Garth would guide him on a safe journey around the perimeter of the estate. Slowly, Xavier began to pick up on Garth's primitive emotions, feeling the anger upon hearing a noisy car go by, or the excitement of hearing another dog's bark. Xavier experimented with seeing if he could impact these emotions mentally, and found that to some degree he could.

Following one of his now standard morning runs with Garth, Xavier emerged from his shower and began toweling off. He was surprised to feel a presence in the room, and identified it as Samantha's just as she began speaking to him.

"I see that Garth is helping you regain your wonderful physique. Now that you need frequent showers, I felt you could use this."

She handed Xavier a plush bath robe which she had just purchased for him. He unabashedly dropped his towel and slipped into the robe. He was feeling something different emanating from Samantha this morning, something more than a desire for his intellectual input.

"I find it very appealing that you and my dog have become such close companions. It speaks highly of you. There has been no man of consequence in this home since Garth was just a puppy."

"I share in the joy of my friendships with both you and your magnificent animal. Garth has made my visual loss nearly inconsequential, at least as far as my mobility. By the way, Samantha, there is one aspect of my blindness which still troubles me greatly."

"What is that, Xavier?"

"That I do not have the pleasure of seeing your figure,

which I assume is as well-formed and nurtured as your face."

Silently, Samantha walked toward Xavier and dropped the robe she herself was wearing. She gently grabbed Xavier's right hand and placed it just above her left breast, and started moving it down. Xavier then followed her contours southward, finding the breast of medium size, very firm and youthfully upright. He then followed the flat stomach over to the small of her waist, and then continued down to lean hips and long legs. He found her to be on the thin side, but surprisingly firm and youthful in her tone and shape. He knew that much of this youthfulness was the artwork of skilled plastic surgeons, but it didn't seem to matter. He found her sexy. And apparently, despite his burns and his blindness, she found him likewise. Xavier was finding that adding someone else's passion coupled with his was as erotic as the act of love itself. He found it irresistible. His hand was still around her ankle, small, delicate ankles he noticed, and he pulled himself closer to her and brought his face near. He began kissing her on her ankle, worked up the inside of her leg and then between her thighs. As he continued his lovemaking, he thought briefly how wonderful it was that sex was something that didn't require light or vision anyway. After several minutes of foreplay, Samantha grabbed Xavier by his broad shoulders and pulled him upward and into her. As Xavier stood fully erect, he grabbed Samantha by her small, firm cheeks and lifted her off the ground. As she straddled him, they moaned in shared ecstasy and completed this rite of passion.

Suddenly afterward, Samantha quickly found her robe and covered herself. There was no shame or guilt, just a sense of propriety. Xavier could feel this, and thought how wonderfully well adjusted this woman was in so many aspects of her life; even the act of making love to a man half her age, whom she had known only just over a week, was somehow "correct" and devoid of neurotic doubts and worries. It was passion, pure and simple, and clearly mutual. There was simply no need for her to contemplate it further.

Samantha then kissed Xavier on his smooth head and told him she was off to her business interests for the day. She asked if she could get him anything, and after a short hesitation, he answered yes, that he actually could use a lighter suit of clothing. He still desired black, but something cut of light cloth, more like a linen summer suit. She stated she knew great tailors on Worth Avenue and that she would send one to the house for a proper fitting. Then she was off.

Xavier followed the mid-morning romantic pleasure with another pleasure he had grown fond of, sitting out by the gardens. There was a chair on a swing midway between the rose garden and the Oriental garden, which served in part as a divider between the two different settings. From that chair, Xavier could hear the gentle sounds of the waterfalls and catch occasional whiffs of perfume from the garden. Here he would rest for a while after his jog, mostly in a meditative state. Garth would often join him, lying down next to him quietly and not stirring except when he heard an intruding noise.

On this morning, however, Xavier chose not to meditate and instead enjoyed replaying the sensations of the morning's lovemaking in his mind. He then contemplated the fact that life could get very easy here, perhaps too easy, robbing him of the drive to reach his ultimate goals. He realized in the past several days, outside of some small amount of continued study of Samantha, he had not challenged himself intellectually at all.

Finding this realization slightly distasteful, he decided he should try harder to comprehend the mind of his canine friend, in order to keep his mind active. Xavier's original discovery was that he could match brain wave states with other people and then reach the area of the brain responsible for emotions and thus emotional conflict. That seemed to come easily for him right from the start. It was over time that he was learning that he could "read" other areas of the brain, including the memory centers. He had realized how important it was to develop this capacity if he was to truly help people such as Samantha, whose conscious memory offered few clues for solving her riddle.

Xavier worked on pulling in Garth's primitive memories, and slowly was actually able to do so. There was Samantha, figuring prominently in most of them, along with scattered bits of adventures with other dogs and strangers. Xavier then tried to extend himself further, looking elsewhere in Garth's brain. He then made a most startling discovery, one he should have thought of previously! Garth's visual cortex! He could tap into it, and "see" in his mind what Garth was currently seeing. This picture of sight came into his mind like an out of focus television reception, and he struggled a bit to bring it into focus. He decided he needed a common frame of reference, and called Garth to come and face him. He cradled Garth's angular head and pointed it directly at his own face, and then began tuning in the image he was so familiar with. Slowly, it came into view. There! It worked! Xavier could see his own countenance beaming with joy! What had started off as a wonderful day had now become a miraculous one; sight once lost had become sight regained.

CHAPTER TWENTY

Lana returned in a van loaded down with her personal belongings and Xavier's. It had taken her longer than anticipated to extract both of them from their prior lives, as she had to get rid of much old furniture and clothing, and settle both of their leases. She had also spent some time with friends, feeling a need to share her excitement about her new job with someone. Upon arriving at the Trent mansion, she found Xavier in a state of euphoria about his new discovery.

"Lana! Lana! I can see again! I have learned to see through the eyes of the dog! Garth! Come here, boy. I'm dying to see you, Lana, through him."

Garth was already nearby and was scrutinizing the unfamiliar figure of Lana. He came closer, and stared intently at her. Xavier looked through Garth's eyes and focused the image. Although the view was from an upward angle, Xavier got his first look at Lana's face and

figure. She was beautiful! Strikingly beautiful, in fact.
She had long, flowing brown hair framing a smiling,
perfect face. Her features were finely carved, simultaneously capturing her intelligence and her sexuality. She
was wearing white shorts with an orange top, both
revealing her hourglass physique to good advantage.
Her figure was athletic, but not to the point of losing her
distinctive curves. Garth's eyes started scanning, moving the image around, but Xavier had seen what he
wanted to.

"My god, Lana, you're beautiful. Why didn't you tell
me you were so beautiful?"

"Thank you, Xavier, but I didn't think my appearance
mattered to you. I am amazed about your vision, though!
When did you discover this?"

"Just today."

Xavier then briefed Lana on the current state of
affairs, as they had not spoken for several days due to
Lana's absence. The work with Mrs. Trent had gone well
but slowly. Lana was actually surprised at this, as she
assumed Xavier would "read" her problems within a
couple of days and then have the remaining few weeks as
a vacation. In fact, Lana had subsequently received other
offers from affluent members of the Palm Beach and
Jupiter area, and had managed to set up some tentative
appointments for Xavier, if he wanted them. Each of the
offers was on the order of twenty thousand dollars for just
a few hours with Xavier. Xavier thought these were good
opportunities and felt he could do these in the late
morning when Samantha was almost always gone. He
told Lana to set one up for the next day, and she was able
to.

The appointment was with one of Samantha's neigh-
bors, actually, and it was a man who had avidly followed
Xavier's saga. He had also caught a glimpse of Xavier and
Garth jogging. His name was E. L. Mitchell, a man of

some notoriety for international business dealings in diamonds and other gemstones. He was an older gentleman, perhaps sixty, and had a medium frame with broad shoulders shown to good advantage by well-tailored clothes. His face was powerful and rugged, and highlighted by thick silver hair. He strode up to Xavier and Lana and eagerly greeted them.

"I feel very fortunate to make your acquaintance, Xavier. Errol Mitchell is my name."

Xavier felt a firm handshake, then piqued by curiosity, tried his new discovery out on Lana, attempting to tap into her visual cortex. He stood awkwardly for several seconds without responding, as he was attempting to duplicate the feat. He did, finally getting a glimpse of Mr. Mitchell at about the time Lana was beginning to shake him.

"Pardon the pause, Mr. Mitchell, I was just observing your appearance."

The man frowned in confusion but decided to press on, and invited them in. They went into a luxuriantly appointed living room with thirty-foot ceilings, and were seated in chairs arranged for this visit. Xavier had to relinquish his sight by proxy for the time that he would do his readings, as he found "viewing" required his total concentration. This man's psyche was filled with many layers, but they were relatively easy to comprehend. Mr. Mitchell was a man born into money, and was by nature aggressive and competitive. He struggled with a strong need to prove himself. This need had been instilled in him at a young age, and continued on despite there being nothing more to prove. He had distinguished himself internationally and had made his own fortune. Yet this childhood drive pushed him relentlessly, creating restlessness and a sense of degrading his every accomplishment as not being enough. Xavier interpreted this lucidly to the man, who was overcome with amazement and relief. After discussing this for awhile, Mr. Mitchell asked Xavier if there were other conflicts he could see. Xavier briefly smiled, then asked Lana to step outside for a minute so he and Errol could have some privacy.

"Mr. Mitchell, with all due respect, you should quit worrying about the size of your penis. After all these years of serving you well, after fathering three children, after countless wonderful orgasms, you still insist on fretting over it. It is apparently within the normal range of five to seven inches, but I detect memories of you trying various devices to. . . "

"That's enough, young man, you have made your point. I believe you have satisfied my curiosity. If you will wait here for a moment, I will get the cash for your payment. Is cash OK with you?"

"That will be fine."

And so Xavier and Lana returned to the Trent estate, laughing the entire short trip over the closing events with Mr. Mitchell. Upon their return to the mansion, they were greeted by Samantha, home quite early for her.

"Hello, Xavier, Lana. Where have you been?" The question was laced with a touch of jealousy.

"Out, running an errand. Are you ready for more work?"

"Why yes, actually. That's why I was wondering."

"Very well. Let's go out to the gardens again."

The pair left Lana on her own to rest, or do whatever she wanted. As Xavier and Samantha sat, Xavier felt it wise not to interpret the temporary jealousy in her, as this was very understandable in light of recent events.

"Well, Xavier, I have some news to give you."

"I have some for you too. You first."

"OK. I have been doing some research on my family. It appears that the most damning rumors about them hit the press at about the time of the second world war. It was said that my father made business dealings with countries sympathetic to the Germans, and made a small fortune doing it because no one else would. He denied it fully and was never proven guilty, but the rumors popped up in the press off and on for the next ten years or so. This must be it, right?"

"That certainly could be the missing piece in this puzzle. Even if the rumors were false, the shame caused by them could have been enormous. It could have caused your parents to put an over-emphasis on correctness and proper ethics, and then transferred this onto you. This hypothesis actually fits better, because if your parents were truly unprincipled they would not have cared what other people thought. They would have only cared about being not proven guilty."

Xavier paused. Samantha did not respond, but sat mute in contemplation. Xavier offered, "You are not satisfied, are you?"

"Not really. I'm actually quite certain that you have uncovered the source of this distorted guilt I have carried through most of my life, but I'm bothered by the uncertainty of whether or not my family was truly guilty of criminal business dealings."

"We may never know what actually happened, and there is nothing that I can do to uncover the facts, as they are nowhere to be found in your memories or feelings."

"I can't accept that. Not yet. Although I feel your work with me is complete, you still have two more weeks on our agreement, and I may need you. I plan to continue researching this, and there may be individuals still alive who have the answers in their memories and feelings. Do you understand what I'm asking of you?"

"Yes. I will help, if I can."

"Good. Now, what was your news?"

Xavier called Garth, who was sitting right next to Samantha, to sit in front of them so that he could use his eyes.

"Samantha, that is a lovely turquoise dress you are wearing today. And that diamond necklace really sets off the outfit."

"Xavier! Are you getting better at mind reading, or what?"

"In a sense." Xavier went on to explain his new-found skill and used it to further advantage by using Samantha's eyes to see Garth for the first time. This sight excited him tremendously, as he was overwhelmed by the handsomeness of this massive dog. Xavier thought to himself that Scriabin himself would have liked this dog, with its cosmic display of black on white unlike that of any dog. The Dalmation looked like a poor step-child compared to him.

While Xavier was musing further about all this, Samantha excused herself, leaving Xavier with Garth. As she left, Xavier noticed the slight uneasiness in her psyche, not just because of her curiosity about her family but toward Xavier himself. She was slightly threatened by his new-found sight, perhaps allowing Xavier to truly see that Samantha was nearly old enough to be his mother. Or was the threat due to the presence of Lana? It was a hitherto quiescent neurosis which emerged from Samantha, one that Xavier did not expect.

Nevertheless, the following several days went smoothly, with Samantha gone much of the time and not demanding much of Xavier. He and Lana occupied themselves with a couple of "readings" here and there, picking up a small fortune in the process. They both realized that when the month was up, they would need to plan new living arrangements. Lana suggested they stay in Palm Beach, as the opportunities were lucrative and the climate and locale perfect for both of their tastes. Lana wondered if she should move into her own apartment, but Xavier would hear nothing of it. Indeed Xavier continued trying to give her half of everything he earned, but she would only deposit her customary fee of ten percent. Together they looked for places to live, and found a large house on the ocean which rented for "only" three thousand a month, a real bargain in Palm Beach. The house was old and needed some repair, but provided a perfect setting for Xavier to continue his work and have solitude when he needed it. After they returned from signing a rental contract, they were accosted at the door by Samantha.

"Where have you been, Xavier?"

"We have been looking for our next living quarters."

"Oh? I've heard that you've been doing some moonlighting lately with some of my neighbors." Mrs. Trent was clearly not happy.

"Yes, I have done a few readings during the last week. I did not think you would mind, as our work is essentially completed and I had so much free time."

"I most certainly do mind! Our agreement meant exclusive of all others. I consider this a breach of contract, and am most disappointed in you, considering you know how much I value proper business dealings."

Xavier felt a wave of nausea and anger pass through him and struggled to fight it off. He knew that jealousy in part motivated Mrs. Trent to feel the way she did, but she also happened to be correct.

"I have acted. . . inappropriately. I will refund your money in full."

"That will not be necessary; you have earned it. But do refrain from further business contacts while you are here. If you have too much "free time," you should have told me; I can arrange for you and Lana to get into various Palm Beach social events."

"That is most kind. I must excuse myself now."

Xavier rushed to his room, feeling his mood growing more unstable by the second and not knowing what would happen. He leapt onto the bed, rammed his face into a pillow and screamed into it. It was all that he could do to not destroy the room, but Xavier managed barely to contain himself. He spent the rest of the afternoon in his room, trying to achieve trance state, but he periodically lost it as disruptive feelings surged through him. That evening both Lana and Samantha checked on him, but he said he was all right and wished no visitors for the evening.

The next day, Xavier emerged from his room with the help of Garth. Both Lana and Samantha were present, and waited in the main living room. The two women had agreed that Xavier should be handled carefully, so they discussed some social functions that they could all attend to have some fun. Despite her stern posture of the previous day, Mrs. Trent wished no continued ill feelings. Xavier felt fairly well, and agreed to go to an afternoon house party held in honor of several Palm Beach philanthropists. Mrs. Trent had joined others in the cause of preserving the endangered elephants in Africa.

This party was the first time that Xavier had faced the "public" since being in Orlando, although this was a fairly elite segment of it. The house was another beachside mansion which illustrated the Palm Beach good life. Mrs. Trent introduced Xavier and Lana to many of her friends and associates. Xavier used Lana's eyes to negotiate his way around and to observe the surroundings. He began handling himself so well that he told Lana she could go ahead and mingle by herself for a little while. She did, but mostly because she viewed this as another great opportunity to make new business contacts. Xavier was left alone temporarily as Samantha became occupied with her role as being a co-host for the function. After he met at least the tenth person that afternoon, Xavier felt a momentary distraction.

The next thing he knew, he was staring ahead at the ocean. It was a tranquil vista, one that he had always cherished as a boy. It was a place to be rejuvenated, to feel his spirit and body cleansed. The water itself, surging and yielding, seemed to embody the course of his life and feelings. To swim again! He had not swum in the ocean in such a long time, it seemed. He took a couple of big strides toward the water, and indeed found some, although not the kind he was anticipating. He was shocked by chemically treated fresh water, and the cool water jolted him to his senses. Xavier realized immediately that he was not at the ocean, but that he had fallen into the host's pool. He also realized once again that he was quite completely blind.

CHAPTER TWENTY-ONE

Dr. Werner had a troubled look about him, with intense eyes partially obscured by thick, graying eyebrows which angled inward in consternation. He wasn't, however, feeling any differently from the twenty or so psychiatrists and psychologists gathered in his exclusive Palm Beach mansion. Though normally Dr. Werner was very private and avoided professional meetings at all costs, he was also neither ready to retire nor willing to relocate. Thus, like all of his gathered colleagues, he decided he could not just ignore the presence of a young phenomenon named Xavier.

"Gentlemen, and ladies, please be seated and let us begin formal discussion. As you all know we face a common threat to our livelihoods. First, has anyone here met this Xavier fellow first-hand?"

The room was silent.

"Well, then, has anybody had a patient meet him and

describe his tactics and techniques?"

Several people raised their hands but nobody wanted to speak, for fear of breaking patient confidentiality.

"Come on, doctors, we are going to have to bend a little. How many of you who just raised your hand still have these patients as clients?"

Not a single hand was raised.

"Exactly my point. I had a patient call me to chastise me for `all the wasted years of mental masturbation' and tell me that we are about to `witness the birth of the next savior.' These are not the words of a delusional or borderline patient, but one of my highest functioning VIP's! What else have you heard, gentlemen?"

Three doctors told similar stories of how patients had called to condemn their futile efforts and boast of how Xavier had "cured" them with almost instantaneous insight and understanding. One other told of how her patient was threatening to sue for malpractice simply because this patient had suffered from chronic depression until meeting with Xavier. Several others had received calls cancelling their appointments completely.

"The word is out. This Xavier is already being hailed as `the greatest healer since Jesus,' and he is obviously hitting our market. This is not the behavior of a complete idiot or a psychotic person. He is smart, smart enough to know that our community is rich both in money and neurotic people who are willing to part with it. My gut reaction is that we are dealing with a sociopath who knows exactly what he is doing."

This proclamation precipitated an avalanche of muttering, and one younger doctor stood up.

"Wait, wait. I disagree. I have connections in Gainesville, and it was leaked to me what their true impressions of Xavier were. Although many felt that this man has a post-accident manic-depressive disorder, there was much evidence showing that he truly possesses some genuine superior mental powers."

The group of doctors groaned at this, but Dr. Werner hushed everyone up to hear out this young psychiatrist.

"Let me finish. We have all seen the videotape of what he did in that hotel room for the media. Is this mass hypnosis by the power of suggestion? Hardly. He truly can manipulate others' brain waves!"

Another older doctor jumped up.

"Excuse me, young man, but simply because he may possess heightened mental powers does not exclude the possibility that he is a sociopathic charlatan. Does anyone here actually believe that this man genuinely wants only to further the cause of mental health in the world?"

Only three people raised their hands, one of whom, a younger female psychologist, bravely spoke forward in this den of old guard psychiatrists.

"Let me speak, please. We have to recognize the possibility that this man, who was a third year medical student, genuinely believes that he is on a mission for mankind. Even if it is delusional, for us to try to impede or disable him could cost us gravely in the eyes of the community and even the country! I can see the headlines now: `Jealous Palm Beach psychiatrists and psychologists rally to kill the rise of the most gifted healer of our time!' Is that what all of you want?"

Dr. Werner's relatively small conference room was not particularly suitable for the cacophony of human disagreement which now erupted in it. He again struggled to regain order, and finally had to stand up and raise his arm to get it.

"Gentlemen! If we cannot conduct ourselves in an orderly fashion, surely we will accomplish nothing! I can respond to that last comment myself. Our intent here is to save our professional lives, not to take someone else's. Xavier can continue his rise to fame and glory elsewhere; we simply need him to leave our city. I don't think history will be impressed with a savior who chose Palm Beach to be his ministry for truth and understanding. We are what we are, and this Xavier is more of a leech than anyone here today. At least we play by the rules! Now, I have asked my attorney to investigate legal options to block his ability to practice here. Mr. Silverman?"

"Yes, thank you, Karl. There are basically two routes to exert power against this man. The first is through litigation, the second through contacting the regulatory bodies. The first process would involve suing Xavier for unethical business practices, possibly making a case that he was stealing your patients. This route will be difficult, as his attorneys could argue that all of his clients elicited Xavier's services first. I believe the second option to be initially more favorable. This involves contacting the Department of Professional Regulations in Tallahassee. We have a better chance of showing that this man is practicing some form of psychotherapy without a license or degree! In addition, the burden of disabling Xavier, and the consequences of doing so, will then be placed on the DPR's shoulders, not ours."

Although the doctors' natural mistrust of lawyers tempered their reaction, there was general enthusiasm for this second proposal. The details of how to accomplish it were debated at length, as was the procedure necessary for the litigation route, if they decided to use it. Others in the room voiced ideas that the gathered should mount a collective media response in advance, but this was vetoed quickly because most Palm Beachers avoided the media at all costs. The meeting continued for hours, with a digression into small groups, each debating Xavier's clinical diagnosis or discussing what the effects on their practices had been.

*   *   *

The subject of all of this debate, meanwhile, was doing harm to nothing other than his bank account.

Xavier, with Lana, had just come from the tailor's, where
he had ordered five custom made suits. Interested in
setting an individualized image and in honor of Garth,
Xavier had decided to have unique suits created in velvet,
colored in the same black on white patterns of Garth's
coat. Each of the suits would have a different pattern to
the mottling. "Suits" was a loose term to describe them,
as they were to have no lapels or pockets, just a simple
style of total-body dress. Lana was particularly excited
about the change; she had secretly very much wanted
Xavier to get away from the all-black image, feeling it was
morbid and not original.   Once this task was accomplished, the duo then set out to visit some pet stores.
Xavier had decided that he needed a pet to carry with him
so that he could have, in essence, constant sight. He and
Lana went to several stores, and debated the pros and
cons of whether to buy a small dog, cat, ferret, or perhaps
even a snake. Snake! Xavier and Lana laughed at what
it would do for his "image," immediately branding him
a "satanist" in many quarters. As they shopped, Xavier
felt a closeness to Lana more than ever before. Even
though she frequently spoke in marketing terms, the
kinship she offered was priceless. Somehow she blended
consideration of business interests with genuinely helping Xavier to be happy and achieve whatever goals he
wanted. He reminded himself what a wonderful choice
of managers he had made, and was grateful that his
special powers had helped him to make it.
      After they arrived at the third pet store that day,
Xavier and Lana were struck by the wide array of unusual
pets. There were pot-bellied Vietnamese pigs, iguanas,
and de-scented skunks. The skunk would certainly fit,
color-wise, but Xavier just didn't like the idea of a skunk
at all. He quit using Lana's sight for a minute and thought
he could still smell the skunk without knowing where it
was in the room. They moved on to the back of the store,

to a huge aviary. Xavier had not been impressed with the cockatiels and love-birds of the other stores, but here he was faced with an impressive collection of various different large birds. A foot-high white cockatoo was certainly very pretty, as was a multi-colored parrot. But there, in the back corner, sat a mysterious medium-sized black bird with an orange beak, that was perched on a small tree limb. Xavier took to it immediately, although he didn't even know what species of bird it was. He learned that it was a mynah bird. Lana thought for one instant, *Here we go with black again*, but suppressed the thought before Xavier could detect it. She saw the happiness and excitement in his face, and knew that he had found his pet. Xavier purchased the bird immediately, and also bought a black forearm leather that the falcon and eagle trainers used. Xavier would put this on his left forearm, he thought, to cover and protect his tender arm. He would have the bird harnessed to the leather by a black cord.

On the way home, as Xavier was learning to understand the bird's brain and tune in to its visual network, he realized what he would call him. But the name given the bird at birth, Charley, would not do at all. Xavier decided to name him "Mahler," partly because it was similar to "mynah," but more so in deference to that composer whose music was notably dark and mysterious. Indeed, Xavier started replaying Mahler's second symphony, "The Resurrection," in his mind from memory and smiled as he saw himself through new eyes staring directly at him. The music in his mind produced chills in him even more than when he heard the music in actuality, and a tear of happiness ran down his cheek as Xavier contemplated how his own life had been resurrected from near death.

CHAPTER TWENTY-TWO

Samantha Trent had again waited for Xavier's arrival, but this time did not bother to query him. The bird sitting on his shoulder was explanation enough. On this occasion, she was eager for a different reason, as she had a guest for Xavier to meet. After she allowed Xavier a moment to brag about his new purchase, she asked if he would sit with them and perform a formal reading. The guest was an older gentleman, about eighty, and it appeared that life had weathered him deeply. Nevertheless, despite the havoc wrought by age and trauma, he still possessed clear blue eyes which gave witness that there was a sharp mind inside. Samantha's research had led her to this man, who had worked with her father during the war. All of the others she had interviewed offered nothing of historical value, or claimed they remembered nothing. This one man alone stated he recalled the events which led to the rumors, and was willing to go over them with Xavier present.

The old man first described how highly he thought of Samantha's father. The feeling was shared by nearly everyone who worked with Mr. Trent. He was full of energy and ambition, and spread his positive attitude to all of those who worked with him. Especially during the war, when everyone was getting depressed and even hopeless, Mr. Trent unyieldingly persevered and held his spirits high. He kept telling everyone that they would soon win the war and to keep working, as American business needed to stay strong.

One day, Mr. Trent approached this man and others with an idea to make a joint venture with overseas interests, dealing in silver and other precious metals. He explained that as a group, they could offer a variety of items in trade that didn't really matter to them, including such items of abundance as cotton and tobacco. He further explained that if the war carried on too long, some of the metals could be donated to the government for use in military construction and development. Everyone was excited, although somewhat surprised to hear certain countries, such as some North African states, were involved. Nevertheless, to the best of the old man's knowledge, Mr. Trent made good on the deal and even donated some rare metals to the military. Although Mr. Trent handled all the actual connections, it seemed above-board to all of those involved. Therefore, it came as a great shock when the various rumors and slanders emerged.

As Xavier listened to the old man and pieced together the story, he felt the man was trying to be truthful. However, he detected some very disturbing patterns of thought and feeling. Without asking a question he excused himself, as he wanted a minute in private with Samantha. Xavier stood up, took Samantha's hand, and with his new-found "vision" led her into the adjacent room.

"Samantha, please sit down. I know that for these past couple of weeks you have put your heart and soul into getting to the truth of the past. This has been an honorable quest, since you could have rested, knowing that the guilt you have suffered was not your own. Perhaps you yourself had an intuition that your father had crossed the boundaries of ethical behavior, despite having no evidence. I am afraid that although this man truly believes that your father was a hero in every sense, it is clear to me that he long ago rationalized your father's actions and convinced himself that there was nothing wrong with them. The old memories and feelings, however, undoubtedly point to the fact that Mr. Trent made profitable business deals with Axis countries during a time of war with them. He also kept his business partners well-shielded from the actual dealings. In spite of whatever rationalizations he made and convinced others of, he himself felt guilty. What he had committed was nothing short of treason."

The news hit Samantha like the atomic bomb which ended the war in question. She was speechless, although somewhere in that shock was silent recognition of what she had feared was true. After a time, she bravely offered to Xavier: "I thank you for your. . . assistance. Your work with me is now complete. You may go now if you choose, or stay if you like."

Xavier, however, did not enjoy seeing and feeling his friend and one-time lover in such well-controlled agony. He reached out with his mind and comforted her, taking away her pain, at least for the time being. She sat in peaceful silence, grateful and at some level cognizant of what Xavier had done. As Xavier departed to leave her in that peace, he projected a message. She would emerge from this stronger and healthier, freed from the bonds which had held her captive for fifty years.

Samantha attended to the old man, and Xavier went to his room to rest. The day full of mental activity had fatigued him greatly. Before he knew it, the next morning had come. Xavier awoke to his perpetual darkness, but this morning he brought the light of day in through the eyes of his bird Mahler sitting on the nightstand. Mahler was restricted by the thin black cord which was still connected to the leather on Xavier's arm, but the bird had made the best of it. When Xavier fell asleep, Mahler found a nice perch atop the clock on the nightstand. Upon Xavier's arousal the bird squawked a bit, but Xavier mentally sent him a tranquilizing message and he settled down, peacefully. Xavier delighted in the process of getting ready for the day, as it had been a task he found difficult without some vision. He put on his black suit after showering, and envisioned the Harlequin-colored suits that would be arriving soon.

As he confidently strode out of his room with Mahler perched on his shoulder, Xavier had the look of a conquering hero about him. He was eager for discourse with anyone that morning, finding life more exciting than ever. What he found was a disheartened-looking Lana reading over a letter.

"Good morning, Lana. Why the long face?"

"Xavier, I wish it was a good morning. This letter is an express mail certified letter by the Department of Professional Regulations. It states that you are under investigation by the department for practicing psychotherapy without a license or degree, and until an investigation is carried out you are asked to discontinue further fee for service activities."

Up until that moment, Xavier had gotten a better handle on the turbulent emotions which occasionally swelled through him. This letter, however, caught him off guard, and he immediately returned to blindness as the surging rage blocked out his ability to see through

Mahler. Soon after, he saw red, flashing brilliant red and nothing else. The rage took him and unmercifully tossed him about like a small boat on a storming sea. He began flailing around, ramming his fists into nearby bookcases and hurling whatever furniture came before his reckless path. The unfortunate Mahler was dragged along this mad ride and started shrieking loudly. Lana, initially stunned into mute horror, began screaming at Xavier to stop. It was the shrill cry of the mynah bird which penetrated Xavier's rage, however, and he almost instantaneously ceased his rampage. He fell to his knees with a sense of helplessness and confusion. Having heard the commotion, Mrs. Trent frantically came running in and discovered the carnage Xavier had wrought. Despite the sight of destruction, her concern went immediately to Xavier, who remained on the floor with his head down and his face covered by his hands.

"My God, Xavier, what's the matter?!"

Lana hustled over to Xavier's side to comfort and defend him.

"Somebody is trying to destroy Xavier's future. I'm sorry for the damages; we will pay for them. Xavier temporarily lost control."

"That's an understatement; it looks like a hurricane hit here. But never mind that; who is trying to destroy Xavier's future?"

Lana responded simply by giving Samantha the letter from the DPR. Samantha read it somberly while Xavier tried to regain a peaceful state of mind, obviously with difficulty. Mrs. Trent had her own emotional reaction to the letter, although greatly attenuated compared to Xavier's. She immediately phoned her attorney and demanded he meet with her at once. He was temporarily tied up in court but gave the message that he would come immediately afterward. The trio waited together in an un-dismantled living room near the main entrance, and discussed Xavier's situation. Xavier and Lana shared that their plans had been to move to the Palm Beach house they had rented, and then continue on with several more "celebrity readings." This plan was definitely now in jeopardy, although Xavier stated openly that he was not going to surrender without opposition. He admitted that in his zeal to move forward with his new powers, he had not considered if what he was doing was technically "psychotherapy," or whether it required a license to perform. His gift was unique, so how could he be categorized alongside the thousands of social workers and psychologists who called themselves psychotherapists? Samantha told Xavier the sagas of some of "the people who reached their dreams" in Palm Beach, and without exception they all overcame great handicaps and obstacles along the way. She was not talking about the bluebloods born into money, but rather the self-made millionaires who had founded their own companies or crawled up corporate ladders to the top. Although she herself was born into affluence, Samantha always respected those who worked hardest to achieve grand goals.

Xavier found this "pep talk" helpful but somewhat ironic, in that for once the roles of helper and recipient were reversed. Although he was now in full control and both listened and watched his two compatriots, he remained shaken by his emotional lability. Further, he worried that it could worsen again. He had noted to himself that, during his outburst, the one thing which shook him back into control was the shrill screeching of Mahler as the poor bird was dragged around the room. It occurred to him that Mahler could prove to be a greater asset than even he originally imagined. Xavier wondered if the bird could somehow warn him if he dissociated again.

Samantha's attorney then joined the group and was

briefed on the current situation. He tried to be upbeat, and explained that there were legal options to counter-attack. For example, there were possibly ways to classify Xavier's exploits as "entertainment." Notwithstanding, Xavier detected the attorney's pessimism inside. The obviously well-trained and experienced lawyer stated that this case was unprecedented and that he needed to research it. At least this, Xavier felt, was an honest statement made with some genuinely implied hope.

The attorney departed and left the threesome alone once again. It would be the last time, however, as Xavier knew that he wished to leave in the morning. He could not subject Samantha's prized personal possessions to the hazard that his emotional lability presented. He also knew that he truly wished to leave, leaving his and Lana's possession's in the rented house in Palm Beach. He wished to be on the road, somewhere, at least for a while. There would be time enough for the fight. But for now, a whole country awaited, and Xavier would not be delayed from his quest.

CHAPTER TWENTY-THREE

As they drove down the road, Xavier and Lana sat in contemplative silence for much of the first couple of hours. There was genuine excitement, not the least of which was the pleasure of riding in the new white Jaguar which Xavier had Lana buy while he was saying good-bye to Samantha. Xavier had never been overly focused on the status symbol an expensive automobile could be, and really just wanted the Jaguar because its sleek yet power-ful contours reminded him somewhat of Garth. Too bad it didn't come in Harlequin mottle. White was close enough.

Xavier's silence included contemplation of both joy and bittersweet feelings, the latter involving realization of having lost valued relationships. Lana, however, truly saw little to be sad about. She was driving a new Jaguar, escorting a man who both respected her boundaries and represented the ultimate dream client for a manager. He was a man of good heart and good intentions, and Lana had no doubt that there would be a place in history for him. She thought for a moment about how Xavier and her deceased spouse had a certain wonderful character quality in common; they both had zealous ambition but kept it confined to the limits of honesty and propriety.

Lana blushed for a second, wondering if Xavier knew what was going through her mind. She broke the silence, needing to discuss this issue. "Xavier, have you been `reading' my psyche without my knowledge?"

"At times, I must admit, I have. It has been a pleasure reading one whose psyche was so devoid of negatives or turmoil. Does this offend you?"

"In a way. Although I appreciate the compliment about my mind, I'd prefer that you always check with me first before reading me. OK?"

"I will respect your request."

Xavier's thoughts returned to reliving his termination with Samantha, one marked by tears on both of their parts. Xavier did not feel so drawn to her that he would overly grieve her loss, but upon feeling her sadness at his leaving he found himself equally pained. There were, finally, no further major neurotic struggles wrestling within Samantha's psyche. Just the pain of recognizing the truth concerning her father, and the inevitability of Xavier's leaving. There, in that wonderful personality whose demons Xavier had exorcised, were just the purer emotions now, albeit sad ones at present. All the more poignant though, for Xavier, as he felt enormous pride at what he had helped her to accomplish.

But there were new bridges to cross, and Lana was there to help him cross them. She had arranged the beginnings of a nation-wide tour for Xavier, where she hoped Xavier could first speak of his life and dreams, then do a few demonstrations and readings. The demand was there, so Lana had already set up dates in Atlanta and

Washington, D.C., with several other cities interested. Xavier agreed with Lana's plan, and felt good about it for several reasons: First, it got him away, away from all the pressure and stuffiness of Palm Beach. Second, it got him direct national exposure to real people, instead of microphones and cameras. And third, what he would be doing seemed clearly outside of the realm of "psychotherapy," thus eliminating the prospects of replaying the DPR scenario.

The first stop was Atlanta, and as Lana drove into downtown, Xavier caught a glimpse of the Peachtree Tower. He wanted to stay there, as he had a fond memory of going there as a child with his family and seeing the spectacular view from the seventy-seventh floor. Upon their arrival, Xavier was accosted by several people for an autograph, a new experience for him; plus the people of Palm Beach were not given to that particular behavior. Lana had actually made reservations elsewhere, but had no trouble getting a couple of adjacent penthouse rooms.

They had two days to prepare for the show. Xavier began contemplating and learning the drawbacks of celebrity. He had not previously thought about how noticeable he was; a bald, blind man wearing a white suit with black spots and having a bird perched on his shoulder. Those who knew of him ran to him for autographs and attention. Those who didn't, accused him of belonging in the circus, the zoo, or worse. Lana suggested an incognito approach: normal clothes with a hat or cap. Xavier, however, was not inclined to venture out anyway, as "sightseeing" through the eyes of Lana or Mahler was taxing and not particularly enjoyable. Xavier also found himself peculiarly uncomfortable, regardless of whether he was in the hotel or out.

The arrival of Friday evening was therefore greeted with great relief. Lana had arranged "An Evening With

Xavier" to be held in the Omniplex Theater, a multipurpose arena for various types of speakers and entertainers. On such short notice, Lana had been fortunate to arrange this comparatively moderate-sized venue. However she didn't expect the audience to fill up the ten thousand or so seats. It was therefore a great surprise that, when Xavier and Lana arrived an hour and a half before the show, the theater was already just about full, with more people coming. When show time came, the crowd was jam-packed with hundreds of people standing. Xavier was given a short introduction by the show's producer, and then he walked out to the wild applause of his new legion of fans.

"Let me tell you a story," Xavier began, "about a man who was touched by the hand of fate." Xavier proceeded to go into detail about his entire saga, not needing to add drama to the already dramatic story. Xavier made a strong, conscious attempt to present his current abilities as deriving from totally explainable and verifiable scientific fact. Nevertheless, toward the close of his speech, he speculated on whether what had happened was destiny or divine will. He further expounded on his greater goals and objectives. This included finding a way to utilize his gifts to motivate people to focus some of their energies on searching for ways to eliminate their psychological conflicts. To throw away the mental baggage that weighed them down with jealousy, bigotry, and other negative emotions; what a joyous quest! Part of the clue to doing this, he felt, was to help everyone develop their own innate but dormant capabilities for empathy and understanding. Xavier remained convinced that his powers did not materialize out of nowhere, but were from an uncovering or stimulation of his brain's natural yet minimally used powers.

Xavier then moved into the next phase of the "show," which was his reading of first the crowd and then a few

individuals. Xavier had of late been fascinated by feelings
he had experienced when faced by a large number of
people. He seemed to be picking up on a general "group
consciousness" which included their shared feelings and
thoughts. This concept actually had already been postulated by several great thinkers, such as Jung with his
"collective unconscious" and the whole Gestalt school.
However, Xavier was dissatisfied with all previous
conceptualizations, finding them somewhat lacking in
scope. When Xavier applied his mental gifts to read a
group, he felt that he was sensing a blend of conscious
and unconscious group experience. He also felt there was
much more to it than just a vague sense as implied by the
Gestaltists. So Xavier coined his own term, "mentaar,"
to describe the phenomenon.

As Xavier tried to read the mentaar of this crowd, he
began feeling an intensified experience of that same
discomfort he had noticed the last couple of days. It
suddenly dawned on him what he was feeling: the
unspoken but still pervasive bigotry prevalent in this part
of the country. Certainly there was much more to the
mentaar of this crowd; mass excitement, anticipation,
some skepticism and considerable curiosity. Beyond that
also was significant frustration, and a surprisingly strong
resentment toward the highway department for never-
ending road construction!

But the bigotry! This was one of the most distasteful
feelings Xavier had come across in his readings of individuals, and now he was faced with a crowded arena
infested with it. It made him nauseated and dizzy, and
for a moment he was flooded with the images of growing
up in Charleston. There, blacks were still frequently
looked at as being descendants of slaves. The crowd grew
restless as several minutes passed with Xavier silently
standing on stage, reeling. He collected himself and then
addressed the crowd.

"Forgive. . . my hesitation. It is difficult. . . for me to speak to you, for I am experiencing considerable. . . anger, and hatred, amongst many of you. I would ask that you attempt to put whatever anger and resentments you have aside, at least temporarily, so that I can be able to continue with the show. Forget about highway construction if just for an instant. . . "

Xavier's oblique attempt to soothe the negative mentaar helped only slightly, enough that he felt in sufficient control to proceed. He felt trapped, however, since he assumed that confrontation of the deep prejudice in the crowd would be a losing proposition. For some in the crowd, bigotry represented a conflict; it was a feeling which was neither dismissed nor comfortably accepted. For others, there was no conflict: these individuals were convinced in the correctness of their hatred. For Xavier, there was no conflict either; he simply despised bigotry. Xavier had to keep reminding himself of this, because he was fearful that this issue was so close to home that it could cause him to dissociate.

Xavier was clearly struggling, and the crowd's mentaar began to be tinged by the added baggage of impatience and disappointment. As Xavier took several more long pauses to collect himself, shouts of "Do something!" and "We want magic!" began to shower him. This hit Xavier at a vulnerable point and he was overcome with a surge of anger. He closed his eyes, reared his head back, and let out a loud groan. A second later, he made at least thirty people in the front rows fall over, dead asleep, one after the other like dominoes. The crowd gasped at this, and then grew quiet as if they had been reprimanded.

Xavier then tried once again to address the crowd, stating that he hoped they would be interested in the grander efforts and goals that he had to offer, instead of gimmicks or "parlor games." Nevertheless, it was apparent to him that further gimmickry was what they needed to see, at least initially. Therefore Xavier walked to the front edge of the stage, turned his back and positioned Mahler on his shoulder looking backward toward the crowd. Xavier instructed the audience to send up about a dozen volunteers to just stand at the foot of the stage. A horde of volunteers came forward, and arena attendants had to send many of them back to their seats. As they lined up, everyone was electrified with anticipation. Xavier started things off with a demonstration of his new visual abilities, sequentially describing each person's appearance exactly. He then decided to do some simple readings. He figured he would not get too deep inside these people for fear of losing control, or becoming further sickened by their prejudice.

He cautiously began with the first person, a twenty-four year old woman who had severe self-esteem problems and other insecurities. Xavier read in her the negativity and constant criticisms she had grown up with from her family. She had continued to play these over and over again in her mind like a never-ending recording. He urged her to mentally pull the plug on that endless CD player, and to separate herself from those who spread negativity. This woman had unconsciously chosen negative people for friends in a desperate attempt to learn how to deal with it, once and for all. Nevertheless, this was not working, as she was caught in an ongoing re-creation of her childhood dynamics, where she played the part of a helpless, powerless little girl.

The now full-grown woman burst into tears at this reading, and ran back into the crowd yelling, "He knows! Somehow he knows!"

After a rippling of audience reaction, Xavier set about reading the second individual. It was a black man, about thirty, and as soon as the eyes of the crowd focused on him, Xavier was dealt a flood of unspoken hate from many in the crowd. This time, the feelings were more

focused, and thus more powerful.   They staggered
Xavier, and he fell to his knees overcome with sickening
anguish and weakness. Lana came running out on stage
to help, totally unprepared for this turn of events. As she
talked to him, he focused on her words, making it easier
for him to decrease the effect of the crowd's mentaar. He
regained his composure, and angrily denounced the
audience.

"Your bigotry sickens me. You live, side by side,
white and black, yet you cannot put aside the animosities
from generations ago. As long as this hatred lives, there
is little hope that I or anyone else can effect change in your
psyche, at least for the good. I cannot help you."

With that, Xavier walked off stage, and was escorted
by a chorus of boos, along with chants of "Xavier Sucks!"
The nationwide tour for the new superstar Xavier was off
to a very inauspicious start.

CHAPTER TWENTY-FOUR

"Do you believe in destiny, in divine purpose?"

The question was directed at a surprised Lana, while she and Xavier ate an airplane dinner in first class on the way to Washington, D.C. Despite the joy of driving in the new Jaguar, they simply had too much traveling to do on this multi-city tour. "That's quite a question," she replied. "Is something on your mind?"

"Yes. This concept of divine purpose is very critical in trying to gain a greater understanding of my goals. If there is such a thing, then surely all of what I have been through must have a higher purpose than being a stage entertainer. I value your beliefs, Lana; what do you think?"

"I believe in God, and I do think that we each have a destiny, a role in this world. I have doubted it at times. But lately, I have rationalized many unexplainable events as being part of fate. For instance, if my husband hadn't died, I wouldn't be here with you."

"I myself have always doubted it, and felt very strongly in the concept of free will, man's capacity to make of life whatever he chooses. But of late I cannot help but wonder, wonder if my life's dramatic turns have been plotted out in advance and for a reason. If not, then it is up to me to make more of this than just celebrity and riches, for these things truly do not matter to me that much. Yes, I was raised in affluence and would chafe at losing the finer things in life, but affluence as an end-point is certainly a most hollow purpose. Accomplishment has always mattered to me more than recognition, even if I was the only one aware of the accomplishment. This was part of Xavier Howell, and is still part of Xavier."

"You yourself made it clear to me from the start that our `foray into the worlds of money and fame was clearly a vehicle to reach a higher purpose.' I haven't doubted that or forgotten your words. And certainly now that you are several hundred thousand dollars richer, I don't see it changing you or your dreams."

"Your insight remains clear and uncontaminated by ulterior motives. I will ask for it again."

And seemingly before Lana could even thank Xavier for the compliment, he lapsed into a self-induced trance. Xavier was obviously at least temporarily relieved at not feeling he was being led down a road of corruption and greed. Nevertheless, the plane soon landed in a city not unfamiliar to corruption and greed, Washington, D.C. Xavier had been there several times before, as a young boy, on tourist trips with his family. He had no desire to risk being spotted in order to see the sights again. He and Lana checked directly into the usual luxury hotel, and hibernated until his next show.

The second stop on this nationwide tour was held at a civic center which held about twenty thousand. Once again, the place was already packed and alive with excitement when Xavier arrived. This time, there was a more noticeable contingent of media types spread out throughout the front rows. The mayor himself actually introduced Xavier, and gave him a warm welcome. Xavier approached center stage wearing his now trademark Harlequin colored suit and sporting Mahler on his shoulder. He showed a bit more panache in delivering his opening monolog, but continued to lay heavy emphasis on the neurologic, scientific explanations and proof of his powers. He cautiously sidestepped the more metaphysical side to his story, as in reality Xavier had not worked out his own feelings on the issue himself. His story was well-received, but once again Xavier felt the eagerness in the crowd to witness demonstrations of his abilities. There were even about thirty or forty people in the front section who had brought pillows with them in a humorous honoring of what Xavier had done at his last show. As Xavier read the mentaar of the crowd, he immediately noticed that those up front with the pillows seemed eager to be put to sleep. So for the sake of getting a better reading and to the crowd's delight, Xavier gave them what they wanted.

As Xavier worked through the complex task of reading the audience's mentaar, he was struck by the bipolarity of the crowd, with many being heavily invested in the political scene but many others totally isolated or indifferent to it. The contrast was striking, as the political segment produced waves of zealous ambition, greed and corruption, while the other showed more frustration, resentment and hostility. This meshing of the negative mentaars was exquisitely distasteful to Xavier, and he was beginning to get the idea that "crowd reading" was going to become the most unpleasant of tasks for him to do. Buried underneath the negatives, Xavier found a positive element; a genuine patriotism and caring for the state of the nation. This gave Xavier an angle to address the audience, so he described the "political neurosis" he was picking up on; the conflicting mixture of zeal, dishonesty, and concern for the welfare of our country. He was hailed by boos for this, although Xavier detected little actual disagreement, simply disapproval at hearing it. The crowd got over it quickly, however, and wanted to get to the next phase of the show.

Xavier went on a bit about how curious he found it that many in the crowd were unaffected by the "political neurosis," but resented those in a position to have it. He sensed little eagerness to hear him expound on this further, so Xavier wrapped up his reading and asked for his first volunteer. Several people ran upstage, and Xavier perused them, settling on possibly the least eager of the lot. It was a middle-aged man in a business suit, with a strong sense of uneasiness that even the casual observer could see. Xavier motioned him forward, and began reading his psyche. He was amazed at the complexity of feelings this man was going through: fear, anger, faltering pride, and hope. Xavier then tried to tap into his cognitive centers to make sense of the feelings. He discovered to his shock that this man did not want to come up to the stage, but was coerced! He was forced to come up or his enemies would leak out some scandal he was involved with. What scandal. . . ah, the secretary! This man had sexually harassed his secretary into sleeping with him. He did not know how or when it got out, and was totally caught off guard tonight by the ultimatum to be read by Xavier or face the scandal.

"Who are your enemies, the Democrats?"

"Yes; I am a Republican."

"No, I mean specifically who are those who would attempt to ruin you by exposing possible inappropriate behavior?"

The man shifted uncomfortably, at first surprised and then unsure of what to say. "There are those who would have my political career ruined. I thought that they were friendly colleagues, but I guess I was wrong."

"Where are these men? Point them out to me."

The man complied, although it was difficult to see exactly who he was pointing to in the big crowd.

"Those of you out there who would have me used as a pawn for political gains: I will not have it. Take back your rival, and throw mud if you will, but I will not throw the mud for you."

Xavier turned his back to the audience in some disgust, but when he turned again to face them, he was amazed to feel their mentaar was predominantly one of amusement. They found this little political fiasco enormously entertaining, and gave Xavier a giant round of applause! Xavier shook his head slightly and mused to himself that this city truly had an unusual and somewhat perverse mentaar.

The rest of his D.C. show went reasonably well, with a couple more individual readings, and Xavier's status in the eyes of the press grew quickly. As he and Lana departed for their next tour stop, New York City, they were given a departing hero's good-bye by hundreds at the airport. These shows were in some ways exciting for Xavier, in other ways disappointing, and always draining. He often slept in between cities, especially on the plane. It also helped make him unavailable for autographs and conversation with fans. Lana tried to fend them off anyway, and in the process would get flirted with frequently. She handled all of the pressures of being Xavier's manager and confidante very well, and did not let it all go to her head. Lana knew that her ability to keep everything in perspective was critical to Xavier, and probably determined whether or not she would continue to be his manager.

New York provided an interesting backdrop for Xavier's next show. Xavier had never been there before, other than a layover in La Guardia, and had never really been eager to, either, showing a bit of the typical southern attitude about New Yorkers. It was a city too intense, and too intent on self destruction. Xavier asked to be taken to Central Park during his limousine ride to his hotel; he felt a great need to get some exercise, even if it was just a bit of walking. Xavier was surprised to find the park quite pretty, looking like an oasis in a concrete desert. As Xavier walked, he fondly thought of the runs with Garth, and a rush of sadness came over him, again unexpected in its intensity and suddenness. Xavier had to stop to collect himself, and gradually did. As he walked onward, he found it more difficult than usual to see with Mahler's eyes as the kept bird was overly distracted by the ubiquitous pigeons. He asked Lana for her eyes temporarily and she willingly agreed. After they had gone a few hundred yards, Xavier stopped dead in his tracks and asked for Lana's hand. He then relinquished his vision in order to better read the threatening feeling he had just felt. Somewhere ahead there was someone with a dangerous mentaar, eyeing them with evil in their heart. Xavier whispered to Lana to take him back out of the park quickly. She escorted him without a word until they got back to the waiting limo. Once they were safely riding toward their hotel, Xavier explained what he had experienced.

The episode in the park had given Xavier a clue as to what he might find emanating from the crowd's mentaar that night. As Xavier approached the stage of the thirty thousand seat arena, he felt his own anticipatory fear far greater than normal for him. As he prepared to deliver his opening speech, he focused on using Mahler's vision as much as possible. It helped him ignore the mentaar of the crowd until it was time for the reading.

Xavier decided to spread his wings a little on this part. After detailing the usual story of his accident and convalescence, he began discussing some of the metaphysical and philosophical ideas he was becoming more enamored with. He even mentioned how he really got the inspiration for blinding himself, and lauded Scriabin for his visionary legacy. He did not go so far as to proclaim that he indeed was part of a divine plan, but put the question to the audience instead. The crowd was unruly, but genuinely interested in what he was saying.

As Xavier finished his monolog, he shut both his eyes and the sight out from Mahler's eyes, and mentally reached out for the audience. What he found was a conflagration of fury, hostility, and pessimism. The negative feelings were so strong that he couldn't seek out the positive ones to help balance them out. The intense mentaar was so strong that it overwhelmed Xavier, throwing him into a rage like he had never experienced. He went wild, running around the stage screaming and swinging his microphone like a lasso overhead, almost strangling his frantic Mahler. Near backstage, he began pulling down curtains, throwing stage equipment and causing stage hands to flee in all directions. While this was going on, the crowd found the chaotic proceedings enormously entertaining, and began cheering Xavier on. Lana, however, ran to grab him and console him. The feeling of her body wrapping around his, coupled with Mahler's intensified shrieks, jolted Xavier back into some semblance of reality.

Lana escorted him to his dressing room and comforted him. She told him that he just needed to play Scriabin in his mind and the bad mentaar would fade away. The advice was sound, and Xavier began to calm down despite his still racing heart and heaving lungs. As he settled, Lana told him that he needed to stop the show, that this crowd was too much for him. But the crowd chanted, "Xavier! Xavier! Xavier!" and wanted more. Xavier struggled with his own intense reluctance to accept anything approaching defeat. As if by instinct, he summoned his inner strength and channeled his current disgust into regaining his resolve.

He gathered himself up and ventured back on stage, to the wild roar of the eager crowd. He explained to the audience that they had too much of an angry and violent mindset and that in order for him to continue they all had to think peaceful thoughts and restrain themselves. Most in the crowd cooperated as much as they could, although a few of the more perverse in the crowd wanted to do the exact opposite of what Xavier asked of them. Xavier stood tall, but struggled to fight off waves of sickening and threatening anguish. He stated that he wished to try to do a couple of individual readings. As usual, many volunteers came, and Xavier picked one in the pack, an older man for a change. This man was about fifty, with a rugged face and powerful hands. Xavier began reading him and was pleased to see that this was a man of good heart, strong work ethic and family values. He was an immigrant from Yugoslavia, and loved his new-found home, but was nevertheless quite sad about leaving his homeland and friends behind. Xavier dubbed this an "immigrant neurosis" and wondered aloud how many in the crowd suffered from this. He was hailed by thousands of waving arms and shouts of "He understands!" Xavier refocused on the man in front of him and decided to give him some mental peace, altering the recollection of homeland to just a dim and pleasant memory. The man's face glowed, and he graciously thanked Xavier and nearly broke his hand with a firm handshake.

Thus emboldened by a successful, relatively easy reading, Xavier proclaimed that he wished to help more of those with similar problems. He helped the audience en masse to relieve themselves of debilitating feelings of what they had lost or left behind. The crowd became quite workable, and by the end of the night they didn't want Xavier to leave. Although Xavier had achieved a great comeback, and had learned a new approach to a difficult crowd, he was totally exhausted. He needed Lana to assist him off the stage. Nevertheless, the impact of Xavier on the people of New York City was profound, and boded well for things to come.

CHAPTER TWENTY-FIVE

The crowd numbered about one hundred strong, and Zandu Hamareesch thought to himself how this was just the beginning. Surely, he thought, one hundred here gathered to begin spreading the word, the gospel of Xavier.

Zandu was a Southern California native, about forty, slightly balding and portly, who nevertheless had a look of wisdom and peace about him. His real name was Richard Johnson, but he had converted to a self-invented, Eastern, more mystical name when he cast aside his successful career as a stock broker and investor in order to pursue his great need for spiritual peace. He had been sent in the right direction, he recollected, years ago when one of the yoga instructors he frequented had told him that in time Zandu would find his cause and know it in his heart when it came. So for the past five years, he had spent all of his time and much of his money on searching for his own personal path to serenity.

He had found it. There was simply no question in
Zandu's mind. He had been intrigued by Xavier's story
from the minute it hit national attention, and had followed the course of his development and subsequent
nation-wide tour. If there was any doubt in his mind,
once Xavier's tour reached Los Angeles, Zandu had a
front row seat and was mesmerized by him. He felt a joy
and clarity of purpose unlike that of anything he had
experienced in his entire life. He knew, without question, that Xavier was the new Messiah and that Zandu
would help lead the people in appropriate worship of
him.

So it was that Zandu looked over the new "people of
Xavier," or at least those who had responded to his
personal calls to friends and philosophical brethren.
These were people deeply interested in Xavier's message
of hope and peace. They were willing to dedicate their
time and money, even their lives in some cases, to further
what they felt was a righteous cause. It was up to Zandu
to give them structure, organization, and direction until
such time as Xavier could relinquish his tour and lead his
people. Zandu preached to the gathering that soon that
time would come, as Xavier was undoubtedly growing
physically and emotionally fatigued by the demands
placed upon him by his country-wide tour. Moreover,
the tour was clearly designed for purposes of gaining
national understanding, and funds to pursue his lofty
goals, not as a stepping stone for more celebrity and
stardom.

Zandu had prepared for this moment. Drawing from
his years of dedicated study of religion, philosophy, and
history, he had organized a systematic process for understanding Xavier's path to peace and making it happen for
each individual. The process was to be called "The
Ascension," and involved five steps. The first was called

"The Recreation," and consisted of symbolically re-enact-
ing the accident in which Xavier was electrocuted. Zandu
showed the proper lifting of the head skyward, with first
the right hand being raised as if holding a light bulb,
followed by the left, reaching even higher. Zandu
explained how the bulb was symbolic for the light of
truth. He explained how the reaching heaven-ward for
the power to bring in the light of truth was clearly a
reflection of Xavier reaching to the omnipotence of God
to grant him the power to give new meaning and truth to
the world. As the left hand reached just above the cradled
palm of the right, Zandu demonstrated the convulsions
which followed as God gave Xavier His supernatural
powers. Following the convulsions, one fell limp to the
ground, indicating that the path of holiness began from
the soil of the earth.

Thus the first step was completed, and the gathered
were stunned by the simplicity of explanation and the
ease of credulity. No one even questioned what they had
heard so far, and all were eager to hear more. Zandu
proceeded, and detailed the second step, "The Learning." In this stage, anywhere from minutes to hours were
spent in developing the powers of empathy, telepathy,
and other mental powers, or "reading mentaar," as
Xavier himself described it. Zandu showed how this
could be done symbolically, sitting in a lotus position
with open, scanning eyes and outstretched, reaching
hands conveying the message of desire and hope for
understanding. Xavier had postulated that within each
of us lay dormant at least some of the capabilities that God
had made obvious in Xavier. So eventually, during this
second step, actual learning and growth should occur.

Again the audience had nothing but positive response to this second aspect of Zandu's proclamation.
Some doubted their own capacity to learn, especially
since they had spent much of their lifetimes trying to

learn even basic mental techniques such as transcenden-
tal meditation, and had found them difficult to master.
Yet there was such optimism that again they begged
Zandu to proceed.

The third step was called "The Blinding," and was a
re-enactment of Xavier's self-induced blinding by staring
at the sun. Zandu instructed them to rise from the lotus
position, similar to Xavier when he rose from his chair
while listening to Scriabin's "Toward the Flame." They
would then walk a few steps and turn to face the sun,
stare at it directly for an instant before then closing their
eyes. Zandu made it clear that this was a symbolic
blinding, and the few seconds of scotomata caused by the
glance at the sun was enough to give homage to the
blinding. Zandu stated that each person could continue
to stare at the sun with eyes closed for a few extra
minutes. This was so they could exult in the joy Xavier
felt at feeling that the distractions of shape and color had
been removed. As Zandu explained this process, one of
the gathered asked: "Zandu, why not go ahead and fully
blind oneself, if one is to truly be cleansed?"

Zandu replied, "Even Xavier, with his God-given
powers, was barely able to go on at first without his
eyesight, and we are comparatively far too weak to
handle it, at least now."

As everyone was aware, Xavier had mastered the art
of seeing through the eyes of anyone around him, and
used the eyes of his pet mynah bird to see more acutely
than any human eye. Yet even so, Xavier did not use his
new-found vision when he needed to use his higher
powers, thus implying the relative unimportance and
even distraction of sight.

The next step would prove the most controversial. It
was called "The Revelry," and involved actual or symbolic sex and violence. Revelry represented the ceremonial purging of one's base drives, and constituted the

necessary cleansing prior to the final step of reaching "The Serenity." Xavier himself had gone through this purging process, and although efforts had been made to hide it, Zandu estimated that the sex and violence he had experienced were far beyond that known to the public. Much of the sex, however, was not so much forced by Xavier's actions, but came in response to rumors about his "talent" with women. As Zandu told his followers about this, he was questioned on it:

"Zandu, how could Xavier be the Messiah if he acted in such an unholy way, and continued to, according to what we have heard." "A fair question. First, Xavier has to purge his own sexual and aggressive drives, and his overt behavior represents the release of these drives. Gradually, the sex and violence will hopefully be eliminated and Xavier will become pure. However, Xavier keeps encountering the "trash" mentaar of his audiences, and it is their negative emotions and thoughts that have infected Xavier. Since he is attaining purity, he has been forced to cast out that which is impure; hence the continued displays of violence, in particular.

"Nevertheless, Xavier has the utmost respect for life, and has not sacrificed any in his purging behaviors. Further, Xavier is still continuing the process of 'The Ascension,' developing greater powers and getting closer to ultimate serenity every day. What joy, what honor everyone should feel at being witness to the evolution of a savior!"

Zandu understood that due to physical limitations, fear of sexually transmitted diseases, and other reasons, there was concern that an actual Revelry was not always going to be feasible. In order to get more people exposed to the message of Xavier, Zandu made it clear that one could start out with symbolically portrayed sex and violence. Ultimately, if one could find a significant other at a similar level of Ascension, and if one was placed in an area with suitable breakables, the actual revelry could be carried out. In spite of the awkwardness of this concept, the necessity and power of it was absolute, according to Zandu. Xavier had borrowed from many great thinkers, especially Freud and Jung, in postulating that the sexual and aggressive drives pushed man into various conflicts and neuroses. Where Xavier stepped beyond any of them, however, was in his belief that ultimately man could be freed completely of these drives, instead of channeling or controlling them through various means. If the fear of losing the pleasure of sex was intimidating, Zandu pledged that the exhilaration and ecstasy of reaching true serenity was far greater than the momentary pleasure of orgasm. Once men and women were pure and holy, sex would return to being what God intended for it to be, simply and only the act of love designed to produce progeny.

This was met with much greater approval, and all begged to hear more about the final phase, "The Serenity." This represented the state of mankind closest to Godliness. The concept was not totally new, as many others had postulated an ultimate state of heaven on earth, or nirvana. But what had been an ultimate dream could now become a reality for everyone. If the message sent from God through Xavier could capture the souls and spirit of the world, there would yet be hope that the human race could survive. If he was not heard, or was rebelled against by those who were afraid, the world might not avoid its apparent destiny of self-destruction and oblivion.

Despite the closing threat, Zandu had left the gathering in a state of wonderment, and many were crying tears of joy. Shouts of "Xavier is our Savior!" and "Glory be to Xavier and Zandu!" rang out. Little did Zandu know how soon his words would become prophetic, for at that very moment Xavier was going through a major turning point.

                    *   *   *

Xavier and Lana were driving northward in a rented Mercedes, heading for the next tour stop in San Francisco. Since leaving the Jaguar in storage in Atlanta, they had preferred flying, but they both wanted to see the California coastline from Highway One. Xavier had been sitting in total silence for the first hour of the trip, but then unexpectedly began screaming at the top of his lungs, uncontrollably. He was immediately joined by one incredibly startled, screeching mynah bird.

"Xavier! What in the world?! What's wrong?"

Xavier dropped his head down as if to signify defeat.

"I cannot tolerate this anymore! The vulgar, hostile crowd mentaars, the media suffocation, and having no sense of being grounded. I need to be done with all of this, to get on with my life and my dreams, to be in a place called home."

"Xavier, are you sure? We just have one stop left, one more show to do in San Francisco. It's not 'til tomorrow; do you want to wait and see how you feel then?"

"No, Lana. No. Take me home. Take me back to Florida."

CHAPTER TWENTY-SIX

The smell of the new leather interior was a very welcome one for Xavier as he and Lana got into their Jaguar. They were both relieved to find that nothing adverse had happened to their new car while it was parked at the Atlanta airport garage. The Jaguar was not just another luxury automobile; they had ridden in several rented ones lately, but this car was a piece of home. Xavier had missed Florida, as it had been his home for the past seven years and was becoming the place he wanted to truly call home. It dawned on Xavier that the Florida they left in Palm Beach had turned hostile, and had made Xavier very aware that he was not welcome there. Conveniently he had pushed those problems totally out of awareness during his road trip.

"Lana, I am trying not to read your mind, but I cannot help but feel that you have sheltered me from the turmoil we left behind in Palm Beach. What has transpired since?"

"There has been a lot of activity by everyone, especially Mrs. Trent's attorney. It is clear that you cannot practice "psychotherapy" per se, but no final ruling has been passed. Whether you can do what you have been doing, or want to do, is still possible, given certain stipulations at this point. One thing is clear, however: that even if you do avoid the DPR, the psychiatric community in Palm Beach will continue to wage war against you."

"Why did you wait to tell me this?"

"I was afraid of upsetting you more. After all, you have been really drained by this tour already."

"You were probably correct in doing so, as admittedly I have been pushed to my limits on several occasions lately. Nevertheless, it is not fair for you to carry this kind of burden for me by yourself; I would not even ask a wife to do this for me. Is there anything else you are holding back?"

"No, Xavier, except I have not gone into detail with you about the negative mail we have received. As a whole, we get few critical letters, and most of these are from skeptics who don't believe in your abilities. There was one letter, however, which troubled me. It stated: `Abraham Lincoln, Martin Luther King, Xavier. We will help you become history.' There was no signature, and the words were typed. I'm sure this was just an idle threat, but it did upset me."

"Understandably. I am learning to expect opposition and adversity; they are inextricably connected to the road that I am traveling on."

And so the two continued on down the road, and Xavier lapsed into a semi-trance as he listened to the car's CD player playing Scriabin's piano concerto. It was a piece that Lana herself liked and, unlike the later Scriabin works, it was very romantic and melodic. By the time

Xavier fully awoke, they were cruising down the Sunshine State Parkway and were minutes away from Palm
Beach. Xavier became a bit agitated, and as soon as they
saw the sign for Okeechobee Boulevard, their turnoff,
Xavier firmly announced to Lana, "Drive on."

"What? Where?"

"Drive on, south, toward the equator, toward the
sun, toward the flame. Palm Beach will not be my home.
I feel bad mentaar, even from here. Just as I have had my
fill of glittering paparrazzi and capacity-filled crowds, I
have also had my fill of stuffy aristocrats and threatened
psychiatrists. I could fight them, and win, but it would
be a fight for ego and pride, nothing more. It came to me
in my dreams just now, the need to go south, to find my
new home, the center of my universe. South, to the Keys!
To the closest point to the equator, Key West! Home of
Ernest Hemingway. Do you know his works? He was a
great man, a great man, and wrote of great men. I
suppose women might have found him offensive, but
clearly he like Scriabin was searching for something in
life, something he never quite found. I would have loved
to have read his psyche; he was a man of great conflicts,
too! Did you know he committed suicide? I wonder if
that was his last effort to find peace in his troubled life,
to reach a place where there is no inner conflict, no battles
with great fish in the sea or snow-capped mountains."

"Xavier, are you feeling OK?"

"Not entirely; the aroma of the Palm Beach mentaar
wafts through me like the stench of entrails hanging from
a vulture's mouth. But make no mistake; my mind is
clear, my direction likewise. I hear the call from Scriabin
once again to follow the flame, as Ernest did himself."

Xavier's words did little to comfort Lana, who nevertheless continued driving south, as she herself had no
great desire to fight the powers that be in Palm Beach.
There was no further discussion of it, although Xavier

continued to wax poetic about Hemingway. Xavier's dialogue, and at times monolog, concerned Lana in that she wondered if he was simply too strange, and getting stranger.

The twosome passed Miami in the afternoon sunshine and, once past that concrete megalopolis, entered that long stretch of islands known as the Keys. They passed through Key Largo, the first major town on the way, and then neared Islamorada. As they did, Lana spotted a sign which read, "Come to Islamorada and swim with the dolphins," and pointed it out to Xavier. Lana had thought it only worth noting, but Xavier found the concept irresistible and implored Lana to stop. Lana advised against it, due to risks of publicity and even the dangers of swimming without direct eyesight. Xavier would have no part in these fears, and insisted on going. Lana knew when her cause was lost, and pulled into the small tourist trap. It was laden with conch shells for sale and other South Florida memorabilia, and had the somewhat shabby look common to the beach communities. They also had cheap bathing suits for sale, so Lana purchased one of these for Xavier. He then asked Lana to babysit Mahler as he unstrapped his arm leather and handed it to her. An attendant, who was also a lifeguard, escorted Xavier into the water. It was cool despite the warm autumnal climate. Xavier looked for a moment through the attendant's eyes and saw that they were in a cove-like area off the ocean, and there were several dolphins swimming around nearby. The attendant first explained what he was going to do, and then helped Xavier grab hold of the dorsal fin of one of the passing and apparently very friendly dolphins. Xavier was immediately pulled forward, not unlike starting off water skiing. The ride was quite a thrill, and faster than he expected. Xavier had to be careful to catch air and not water in his mouth. His swimming background made it slightly easier, however, and he felt very much at ease in the water without actual vision.   After a period of pure enjoyment, Xavier thought about trying to tap into the dolphin's brain for eyesight.

As he entered the dolphin's mind, he was struck at once how sophisticated the dolphin's brain waves were in comparison to the bird's or the dog's. In fact, Xavier detected the makings of a primitive neurosis!   The dolphin enjoyed the benevolent care and feeding provided by its owners, yet it did not enjoy being held captive. It yearned, no. . . "she" yearned for freedom, something she had known in her lifetime before being captured. Xavier then tapped into the dolphin's visual cortex and was thrillingly entitled to view the sight of onrushing ocean through the eyes of one not-so-happy dolphin. Despite the novelty of the ride, and the joy of the visual experience, Xavier could not help but empathize with the unfortunate dolphin. He decided to try to help, by mentally tranquilizing the dolphin just enough for her to forget about her unmet desires, at least temporarily.

The dolphin responded to this not by slowing down, as Xavier expected, but instead by leaping with joy, literally leaping out of the water with Xavier barely hanging on.   The attendant screamed, "Let Go!" and swam out in Xavier's direction. Xavier felt his worried presence and decided to let go anyway. The attendant quickly grabbed Xavier's arm, fearing that he was helpless and frightened, neither of which was true. Xavier reassured the man that all was well and allowed this worried lifeguard to escort him back to shore. Lana was there, waiting with a towel and holding Mahler. She likewise was worried, but was less concerned after seeing Xavier's smiling face as he emerged from the water. Xavier informed her that it was quite an experience, and suggested she try it. Lana initially declined, stating that they probably should check into a hotel so that he could shower up and rest. Xavier persisted, however, and she relented. Lana got on a bathing suit and entered the water. She demonstrated that she, too, had a fine swimming ability, and easily swam with the dolphins. She did not stay long, being more concerned with their tasks at hand. She emerged from the water glistening, and Xavier took note of her very shapely form. She reminded Xavier that they needed to get a hotel, but when she suggested that they find a nicer one than the one just across the street, Xavier disagreed. He expressed that he was fatigued and wanted to rest immediately. Lana complied, and shook her head slightly in mild dismay over Xavier's occasional fickleness.

Once inside the hotel, Xavier showered and prepared for a good rest. The efforts expended with the dolphin after a day-long car ride had taxed him. Lana checked into a room immediately next door, as had been their custom, and made sure Xavier was fine before she retired for the night. She watched some television on a small set just for a bit, then read herself to sleep.

Several hours later, Xavier arose from what had actually been a "resting" trance, for he had no intention whatsoever of sleeping. He arose and clothed himself with just his bathing suit and the black arm leather which connected him to Mahler. He tip-toed past Lana's room, casting messages of "sleep deeply" into her room. He also calmed Mahler's somewhat agitated spirit as the bird was not accustomed to this nocturnal behavior. Xavier surreptitiously snuck across the highway and went over to the "Swim with the dolphins" area. He left Mahler sitting on a dock near the water, entranced. Xavier used Mahler's eyes to direct him into the water, but once well inside he was essentially blind again. He swam a bit on his own, and then surprisingly had several dolphins join him as if to welcome their unusual guest.

Xavier scanned for the familiar female mind which he had encountered earlier in the day, and felt her presence in the group.   He mentally called her to come, not knowing if she would understand, but was pleasantly surprised to find the dolphin swimming right beside him within a few moments. He borrowed her eyes and gently led her to the perimeter of the enclosed area.   There was a metal cage, extending from sea floor to well above water level.   There were gaps in the cage that allowed water and small fish to pass through, but they were not big enough for even a baby dolphin to squeeze through.   Xavier scanned the cage as best he could, but it was too dark, even with the sharp eyes of the dolphin. He swam down to the bottom, and felt along the interface of cage and sand for a weak spot. After having to go up for air several times, he came across a section which was slightly loose but still intact.   He furiously dug underneath it, little by little working his way to the bottom of the buried pilings to which the cage was anchored.   Indeed, one of the connectors was broken, and after considerable tugging and pulling Xavier expanded the opening between cage and piling to about a foot square.   Xavier's new-found friend had been swimming playfully nearby, and again responded to Xavier's call. As the dolphin approached, Xavier reached out into the darkness with his left hand, and felt the slick body of the dolphin glide against it. He gently grabbed her dorsal fin and, with his air about to give out, ushered her through the opening he had created.   As the happy dolphin passed through, Xavier called out to her with the message "Free!" She was indeed free, and swam off into the night with blissful abandon.

The next day, on the road south to Key West, Xavier was contemplating his actions privately when Lana surprised him.

"Did you set her free?"

"What?"

"You know, did you set the dolphin free?"

"Yes. How did you know?"

"Either I'm getting better at predicting your behavior, or I just read your mind."

Xavier smiled and asked, "Would you have wanted to help?"

"Yes, actually. I was genuinely bothered by the whole idea of captive dolphins, and had hoped you might do something. Perhaps I should let you read my psyche once in a while."

"Or perhaps I should get to know you better, Lana Marshall."

CHAPTER TWENTY-SEVEN

The road to Key West was a most beautiful sight, regardless of whether it was seen through human or bird eyes. The translucent blue-green water, the white sands, and the scattered tropical foliage combined to provide continued entertainment during the three hour drive down the length of the Keys. Three hours if one was not in a hurry, which was usually the case in the Keys.

That was not the case with Xavier, who was eager to get to Key West in hope of finding his new home. Even so, he was content to allow Lana to take her time on the drive down, as this was a first time in the area for her. Xavier had been here before, as part of a "getaway" weekend for tired first year med students. He had little recollection of the event, only recalling that in good Hemingway tradition they all went to a local tavern and got thoroughly intoxicated. This was an uncommon event for Xavier, as he tended to respond poorly to

206

alcohol. He usually got irritable or euphoric initially, and then soon after either ill or uncharacteristically angry. Although the remembrance of his former trip to Key West was a pleasant recollection of male bonding, everything else was a blurry and miserable fragment of a memory.

As Xavier pondered the upcoming visit, and grew slightly impatient, he decided to have some fun with his dear pet Mahler. He tried sending messages into Mahler's brain commanding him to speak. The bird indeed would "speak" when ordered, although the result at first was little more than his standard shriek. Xavier next tried programming him to say "Lana." Little by little, the bird was able to form a reasonable facsimile of her name. Xavier would hold the bird facing directly at Lana when he sent the message for him to speak. He hoped to teach the bird the connection between the name and the person. This was of questionable value, as Mahler's eyes would not necessarily focus on Lana at the moment he said the name. While Xavier was doing this, he did get several good looks at Lana, and was again struck at how beautiful his companion was. Xavier had been no stranger to beautiful women, and most of his girlfriends had been quite attractive, but few if any possessed the combination of classically featured beauty coupled with intelligence and maturity. And all this in her mid-twenties! How was it that he had not fallen in love with her? He rationalized that he didn't want to spoil a great working relationship, or that he had other things on his mind. More to the point, she herself was not eager to get involved, at least not so soon after her husband's death. Was there more to her reservations? Did Xavier frighten her, or intimidate her? He could read her psyche to find out, but he had made a promise not to. Anyway, Xavier was beginning to believe that she could tell when he did it anyway. He decided to do a little test. Xavier began reading a relatively "non-private" part of her psyche, her current experience of viewing the beautiful scenery. Lana's eyes diverted off the scenery for just an instant, ever so slightly paused and then returned to her driving.

"Did you just feel something, Lana?"

"Maybe. Was I supposed to?"

"Lana, if you could have some of my powers, would you want them?"

"That's quite a question. I'm not sure; I don't know if I could handle everything that goes along with having those powers. Your life hasn't been easier as a result of them, yet having some extra abilities, especially in controlling one's own mind, would be a good thing."

"I hoped you would feel that way. As you know, I have speculated whether the capacity for these powers lies dormant in us all. I have sensed that you yourself have some capacity for extra-sensory perception. Just a moment ago, I tried to get your attention by reading your visual experience for a second. You seemed to sense something, something ever so slight. Can I do this again? I will continue to refrain from reading your private thoughts or feelings."

"Well, OK. You've piqued my curiosity."

Xavier proceeded to repeat the experiment, and each time he did it Lana could increasingly hone in on the very subtle sensation she felt. She was excited at her new-found skill.

"Lana, I wanted you to have this ability so that you never fear that I may be intruding on your privacy without your consent."

"Why, Xavier, I trusted your word anyway. Nevertheless, it was very thoughtful of you to teach me this ability."

During the remaining few miles of the trip, Xavier spent some of his seemingly abundant mental energy that day on teaching Mahler to say "Xavier." It was more difficult than teaching him "Lana," and more difficult than teaching Lana that she was being read. Lana admitted to herself that she wished she had Xavier's powers of total concentration and self-induced trances, for this bird's screeches of "Zayerr!" and "Zayveeer!" grew increasingly irritating. Thus it was with considerable relief that she saw that they were entering the city limits of Key West.

It was definitely not a metropolis, with no skyscrapers ruining the beautiful horizon, but it certainly was congested. It was a relatively small island, jam-packed with crowded streets and ocean-lined hotels. Everything was tight; the streets were narrow and the corners sharp. And people! People were everywhere, crossing the streets, riding old bicycles, shopping at the multitude of quaint stores. Many just sat or stood and watched everyone else. There was much to look at, for the people themselves were very interesting; people of all shapes and sizes, of widely varying clothing and hair styles, of all races and colors. It was a melting pot of vacationers, natives, bums, low-profile affluents, high-profile narcissists, free spirits, and generally every sort of idiosyncratic personality imaginable. This was a place to escape to, and by the looks of many of the people, a place where differences were easily tolerated.

Thus it was that when Xavier and Lana stepped out of the car to check into an oceanside hotel, hardly anyone gave them a second glance. Despite the good feeling this produced in Xavier, it was countered by an inexplicable underlying sensation of uneasiness and tension. After checking in, Xavier was eager to scout out the island for a desirable home, but first there was one bit of sightseeing that had to be done. He had to see the Hemingway home. As if directed by a homing beacon, Xavier directed Lana to the location of the home without difficulty. Once there, Xavier decided to leave Mahler in the car and tour the Hemingway home through the eyes of one of the many cats still inhabiting the home. "Ernest would have liked it that way," Xavier explained to Lana.

In spite of wishing that he could read a mentaar from the house itself, imagining what it could tell about the great man himself, Xavier was reminded of his limitations. He could not detect a presence in this house, nor could he from any other inanimate object. It certainly led no credence to the concept of ghosts, but Xavier never believed in them anyway. He remained a scientist, even though some of his psychic capacities were beyond what science could adequately explain. Xavier allowed himself to hear the tour guide tell stories about Hemingway's life, especially the years in Key West. The home was dear to him as he gloried in the ocean and the fishing. Xavier questioned the tour guide about Hemingway's demise, but the guide preferred to defer this question, claiming ignorance of the details. The cat whose eyes Xavier borrowed grew restless and easily distracted by the other cats, so Xavier had to periodically mentally assuage her agitation. At the end of the tour, he graciously thanked the cat, producing more than a few odd looks from fellow tourists in the process.

Following the Hemingway house visit, Xavier asked Lana to tour the island, keeping an eye on houses for sale or rent, or for a good empty lot. There were actually more than a few available homes, but most were too small or decrepit looking to even entertain the notion that they could be viable homesites. They finally found a couple of places with good potential on the northwest part of the island, away from the jam of tourists and tourist traps along the southernmost border. One was a rare empty lot, overlooking the inland waters. The other possibility was a large, white house not too far from the empty lot, a house which projected a certain majesty and uniqueness. There was a "for sale" sign out front and Lana took down the number.

Although they came up with these two possibilities, Xavier continued to feel strangely unmoved, even disheartened. He couldn't quite put his finger on why, either, something which aggravated him considerably. He asked Lana to take him to do the mandatory Key West stops, the first of which was seeing the southernmost point with its renowned brightly colored marker and sign saying "Ninety Miles to Cuba." The next obligatory stop was Sloppy Joe's, a tavern made famous by none other than Ernest Hemingway, and sadly the site of a recent large fire. The third required attraction was watching the sunset off the southwestern tip of the island. This was a routinely wonderful display of nature, as the setting sun disappearing over the near equatorial waters of the entrance to the gulf splattered vibrant colors through the atmosphere like an artist's palette.

As Xavier absorbed the beautiful view, it dawned on him: the immediately painful answer to what was troubling him. Bad mentaar! It should have been more obvious, but perhaps he was psychologically not prepared to accept the notion that Key West would have an unsuitable mentaar. But there it was, stronger than ever, as he was surrounded by at least a hundred people all trying to get the same view of the twilight horizon. These were not "bad" people, but simply very neurotic people, most of whom had not fit into conventional society for a variety of reasons. There was simply so much unresolved psychological baggage around that Xavier felt weighed down by it. Of course, it should have even been predictable; people came to Key West to escape their problems, not to resolve them. If this was their way of dealing with them, they were harmless enough, but Xavier could not bear to live there, day after day feeling the air ripe with old conflict and anguish. Yes, he could probably help them, in time, but they were not asking for help; all these people wanted was anonymity, fun, and to be left in peace.

Xavier was perplexed by this turn of events, as it left him with a piece of the puzzle which didn't fit. "Toward the flame" was perhaps not connected with going toward the equator, or was it? Would he have to move to the Bahamas? Cuba? Or was this all sheer folly on his part to over-interpret Scriabin's message?

He turned to Lana, and sadly pronounced: "Take me back to Palm Beach. This is not the place that I could ultimately call home. Neither will be Palm Beach, but it will do, until I can discover my new direction. I need time to think, time to jog, and time to listen to more Scriabin."

CHAPTER TWENTY-EIGHT

Several days passed uneventfully in the rented Palm Beach house where a mildly troubled Xavier contemplated his future. Word of his return got around town, and he was again flooded with requests for help and threats of lawsuit. Xavier did not use the time as well as he characteristically had in the past. He moped around a lot, did not exercise, and listened endlessly to the music of Scriabin, Mahler, and Rachmaninoff. He did put some time and effort into "advanced" training of his mynah bird. Xavier learned that his soothing mental messages lasted only for a short while, but he discovered a way to use this. He taught Mahler to say "Xavier!" whenever the bird did not receive one of these messages every minute or so. Xavier hoped to use this one day as protection against mental lapses such as excessive daydreaming or dissociating. The bird's shrill voice would be an effective counter to these unwelcome phenomena. The idea was intriguing, but it was difficult to make it practical. Initially, Xavier failed to realize that if he was in a trance state or asleep, and Mahler was awake, the bird would jolt him out of his peace. A partial solution to this problem was to put Mahler to sleep prior to retiring himself, and this worked well. Except for when Mahler awoke first! Xavier was determined to teach this bird to respect his sleep and trance states, and gradually trained Mahler not to shriek while he was in bed. He still faced the problem of having to send soothing messages to the bird all day long, but he found that he could teach the bird to keep quiet with any conscious mental activity.

Lana had been doing her best trying to help, fighting off all the would-be clients as well as all of the "enemies," including lawyers, angry psychiatrists, town officials and others. She tried to get Xavier mobilized, offering to drive him around in search of a new home, but he declined, stating that he had "not unraveled the mystery" and "had no direction yet." So one day, she got an idea and eagerly informed Xavier that she was going out to get him a surprise.

Several hours later, she returned, driving a new cherry red Jeep Cherokee with gold trim. Following behind was the Jaguar with a hired driver, who dropped off the car and waited for a cab. Lana ran in and fetched Xavier, who was not impressed with the new automobile.

"What purpose does a Jeep serve for us?"

"If you'd get your beady bird eyes on and go look in the Jeep, you'd find out."

Suitably chastised, an unemotional Xavier strode forward and discovered that inside the back of the Jeep, barely fitting, was a magnificent beast. At first glance, Xavier's heart leapt, as he thought it was Garth. But as he looked closer, he could tell it was a different dog, with similar but distinct markings.

"Who is this? Whose is this?"

"He's yours. I named him Scriabin. He is Garth's cousin; Samantha helped get me the connections to find him."

It was love at first sight. Xavier was overwhelmed, and tears trickled out of his blind eyes as he moved closer to the animal and opened the Jeep's hatch door. Scriabin greeted Xavier with a messy wet lick over his face. There was a leash, but Xavier was not worried about physically controlling this dog, as he was mentally communicating peace and friendliness to him. The dog responded immediately, and took to Xavier even faster than Garth had earlier. Xavier asked Lana to take Mahler from him so that he could get better acquainted with Scriabin. The bird was not happy with this, and began squawking "Xavier! Xavier!" Xavier gave him a deep trance message and soon the bird entered a never-never land of aviary dreams and desires.

Xavier thanked Lana graciously, and gave her a hug. He then took a walk with his new Great Dane, holding the leash only as a formality. He quickly mastered the use of Scriabin's eyes, interrupting his sight every few moments to continue giving the dog relaxing and friendly messages. Before long this procedure would be unnecessary, Xavier thought to himself. As he walked, his spirit returned, coming back like the sun after a cold, dark night. Soon he found himself jogging, then running as the vibrancy of life that had been his became his once again. Scriabin enjoyed the run, and began opening up his stride like a cheetah cruising over the Serengeti. Xavier rapidly discovered that he could not keep up with the dog, and had to reign him in like a runaway horse. Xavier had to stop, breathless, placing his hands on his knees and leaning over. Scriabin reached up with his head and gave him another kiss of approval.

And so it was that Xavier became emboldened and re-energized. Over the next several days, he revolved his

life around the dog, going for two runs a day, "teaching"
him about the music of his namesake, and feeding him,
which was no minor task. Lana had hired a housekeeper
and house-sitter, one Serena Valdez, to take care of the
estate prior to their cross-country tour. She had done a
good job, and now continued to tend to "Master Xavier's"
needs as they arose.

Seeing that everything was going smoothly, Lana
approached Xavier one day while he was in his study.
She timed her entrance carefully, waiting until the Scriabin
CD of the last five piano sonatas had finished playing.
"Excuse me, Xavier, could I have a moment with you?"

"Why, of course. What is on your mind?"

"I'm pleased to see that you and Scriabin get along so
well. I'm also glad to see that Serena is working out OK.
The last thing I want to do is push you, but since you
haven't decided which direction you want to take as far
as your career, I would like to take some time off until you
do."

"Are you sick of me? Will you let me read your
thoughts?"

"No, Xavier, don't read my mentaar! Just listen to me!
I need some time for myself. I have been with you every
day for the past four or five weeks, waited on you hand
and foot, battled off your enemies, arranged all your
appointments, been a chauffeur, companion, and errand
runner. You are a very special person and this has been
the most exciting time of my life, but I need a break."

"Will you be coming back?"

"Xavier! For someone who can understand the entire
world's neuroses, you're doing a lousy job understanding this one woman. Get a new direction, decide where
you want to live, then give me a call. I'll be in Orlando
with friends, the number's there next to the phone. If
you'll let me, I would like to borrow the Jaguar."

"It's yours already; you don't need to `borrow' it. I

have. . . been comfortable the last couple of days, and have not really put my heart and soul into figuring out what to do next. It has been pleasurable being alone with the company of a loyal dog, unmolested by bad mentaar, fans, enemies, and media. You are correct, however; I must face some realities soon. Forgive my. . . insensitivity."

"You have nothing to apologize for. Just call me when you are ready to get on with your dreams."

With that, Lana left Xavier there and soon departed in the Jaguar. Having spent an enormous amount of energy controlling his emotions during his brief interchange with Lana, Xavier now let down his defenses and felt a surge of painful affect. He felt loss, fear, doubt, and ultimately, rage. Within a few moments he was recklessly running around, breaking his own furniture this time. As he progressed around the living room, destroying much of what lay in his path, he approached Mahler. The bird was nervously perched on a metal stand that he had been leashed to. As Xavier approached in his fury, the frightened bird screeched out a distorted "Xavier!" jolting the wild man back to his senses. He crumbled in a heap, and began to weep. Even the gentle nudging of his concerned dog did not slow down the tears, for Xavier was overcome with feelings that didn't make a lot of sense to him. Yes, he would miss Lana, and was worried if she would return or not. But it wasn't as if he loved her, at least he didn't think he did. Xavier genuinely felt badly that he had taken Lana for granted, being oblivious to the fact that she may have had her own needs unmet during their time together. Yet, Xavier had brought her fame and fortune, allowed her to see the country, meet many important people in her industry; and he had treated her with respect. . . This was very confusing.

Xavier had a couple of days of peace in which to contemplate Lana's actions and, even more importantly, what he would do next. Lana's temporary departure did spur him on to more intensely consider his options. He interspersed his thought sessions with frequent jogs with Scriabin, which helped him regain and sharpen his occasionally faltering mental clarity. He was disturbed by several unwanted visitors; town officials either spying on him or trying to scare him into leaving, messengers from anonymous Palm Beach professionals saying that Xavier was unwelcome in their community, and even a local church leader who informed Xavier that several community churches were concerned that Xavier's activities were unholy.

Xavier was prepared for all of this, as Lana had warned him that these people would come, and had made efforts to pacify them prior to her departure. But Xavier was not prepared for the group of visitors that arrived the morning of the next day. He was sitting in his study, listening peculiarly to music he had nearly given up, Mozart. Serena approached and apologized for interrupting, but informed Xavier that a large group of visitors had come to see him. Xavier declined to see them, so Serena was forced to identify them; it was his family.

Xavier arose and strode out to meet them, with Mahler on his shoulder and Scriabin at his side. There waiting in the living room stood Mr. and Mrs. Howell, Zack, two cousins, and one unidentified man. Despite their last meeting, Xavier attempted to be cordial.

"Welcome, family. Please, have a seat. You are looking well, Mother, looks like a new dress. Buy it here in Palm Beach, perchance?"

"Why yes, Xavier, and thank you."

"Well, you didn't come down here to shop, I gather."

Mr. Howell took his cue, and explained the purpose of their visit. They had all been following Xavier's "career," watching every clip of media coverage they could, and getting every available newspaper and magazine article covering his story. They were all very concerned that Xavier had undergone a significant personality change, to the point that he seemed unrecognizable. Mr. Howell pointed out how the "old" Xavier Howell would never have been caught up in a whirlwind of media hype and celebrity. The old Xavier did not focus on the acquisition of power and money. Among the things which set Xavier Howell apart was his dedication to helping others, his clear-minded nobility and his moral fiber. Now that seemed lost, lost to the effects caused by an unfortunate accident. There were other worrisome changes, including Xavier's progressively odd speech patterns. Most alarming to the family was the scattered but increasingly frequent reports of Xavier's new penchant for violent outbursts.

"But we have not come all the way down here to criticize you," Mr. Howell went on, "but to try to offer you some help. We have a world renowned physician here with us who has also been following your career with a personal interest. Dr. Browning?"

Dr. Browning was a middle-aged man who, when seated, looked the part of the stereotypical "shrink," with beard, balding head and glasses. When he stood, however, one was overpowered by his physical presence; he stood a couple of inches taller than Xavier and weighed about fifty pounds more. He spoke with a deep, clear voice and chose his words carefully.

"Xavier, I am a neuro-psychiatrist, having originally been a neurosurgeon prior to my development of interest in psychiatry. Much of my bias in psychiatry still lies in the study of organic or biochemical causes of psychiatric disturbances. I have little use for the analytic model. During my years as a neurosurgeon, I was acquainted with many patients who had intractable temporal lobe epilepsy, caused by tumors or other lesions in this area of the brain. I was fascinated by how many of them had full blown "psychiatric" illnesses, including manic-depression, delusions, split personalities, and other exotic problems. I have dedicated the last decade of my professional life to the study and treatment of patients with these types of problems, looking for treatments that don't involve using a scalpel."

Dr. Browning continued on, going into even more technical detail about "limbic area dysfunction" and the newly discovered phenomenon of "kindling," whereby the diseased area worsens progressively, not unlike a fire given more lumber. The mention of fire intrigued Xavier, and frightened him as he wondered if Scriabin's musical message was no more than a prediction of his own demise. Veritably, there were many, including the great Horowitz himself, who thought that Scriabin was in fact crazy. He was described as a very moody individual, prone to wild extremes of passion and fury, and was also thought to be quite convinced of his own greatness. Toward the Flame? Toward burning up in one's own ambition and delusions of grandeur? It made too much sense to casually disregard.

Dr. Browning noticed Xavier's loss of concentration and brought him back with a firm grasp on Xavier's upper arm.

"Xavier, I can tell your mind is racing; this is one of the symptoms of disease. Quickly, let me just tell you there is a good medicine that will control this condition. It is Carbamazepine, also known as Tegretol. It is the only proven anti-kindling drug we know of."

Xavier raised his hand as if to silence Dr. Browning.

"I will. . . consider what you have told me today."

This was not nearly a good enough reply for Mr. Howell, who immediately launched a counter-attack. "Xavier! What the hell do you need, the president to tell you that you are sick? I don't care if you can read Shirley MacClaine's past lives' minds, you are slowly losing it!

Take the doctor's help!"

Xavier did not hear more than the first couple words of what his father was saying. The process of enduring another speech by Mr. Howell, informing Xavier of "what was wrong" with him, brought back horrid memories of resentment from throughout his childhood. Xavier immediately found himself somewhere else, somewhere peaceful, without people or problems. The ocean! It was light blue-green, clear enough to see the ocean floor. So clear that you could see the fish! The horizon was an undisturbed blue line, and the sky a cloudless background of perfection. There were sea gulls overhead, calling out. Wait! They called my. . .

Xavier returned to himself and realized that Mahler had alerted him out of a dissociation. As soon as he fully recognized what had happened, and in particular what old neurosis had been activated, he immediately had to act.

"Everyone out! I cannot tolerate this anymore! Go!"

Everyone protested, but Xavier would have none of it. He shouted them down and threatened to sick his large dog on them if they didn't leave. The family left first, and Dr. Browning lingered for just a moment. He pulled out a bottle of pills and placed it on the coffee table. "Here, take one three times a day. Just try it."

Before the doctor could explain the need for blood tests and other necessary monitoring, Xavier threw him out too. Soon after they had departed, Xavier found himself not calming down, but getting even more angry and hostile. He figured a brisk run with his dog would help quell this veritable tidal wave of re-surfaced fury. He called Scriabin and, as soon as he could put on his running gear, they were out the door.

Almost immediately, a next door neighbor's Dachshund made his presence known with his characteristic yippy bark. As it was, Xavier was barely containing his fury.   When he felt his dog's anger at this intrusive Dachshund's bark, it was too much for him and tipped him over the edge. He released the leash on Scriabin, and with it released all of his fury into the Great Dane. The powerful beast growled a lion's roar and bounded off directly toward the offending dog's bark. There was an eight-foot-tall, neatly trimmed boxwood hedge separating the two yards, but Scriabin leaped over it like a deer hurdling a brush-lined creek. Shortly thereafter, Xavier heard a murderous scream coupled with more roars, and then there was silence. Scriabin reappeared with blood all over his face and mouth. He trotted over and lay down at Xavier's feet, looking up at his very shocked and sickened master.

CHAPTER TWENTY-NINE

"Please, Lana, please come back as soon as possible."

"What's going on, Xavier?"

"I have encountered. . . problems. I have missed your help and advice. I have missed you."

"Have you come to any decisions about your professional life?"

"Yes and no. I haven't decided where I should live, but I know I should continue to find a way to help people. I would very much cherish your input and presence here. I need your professional advice, but I also want you here as a friend."

"Xavier, I'll be glad to come and talk with you. But you must understand, I can't put my life on hold indefinitely while you contemplate your future. We need to get a direction soon, and I'll help in whatever way I can. I'll be there tomorrow."

And so the pain in Xavier's heart was lessened

somewhat, and he was truly hopeful that Lana could give him support and help in deciding his future plans. Lana had such a clear mind, not brilliant in an intellectual sense, but wonderfully uncluttered by various cognitive distortions or underlying neuroses. She had a healing effect on Xavier just by the proximity of her healthy psyche. He had not realized how much she meant to him until she was gone.

Xavier had been shaken by the episode with his family and Dr. Browning. Doubts had been raised in his mind about his emotional status, for there was certainly no denying that he had been on an emotional roller-coaster complete with poorly controlled surges of sadness, aggression and sexual fantasies. Particularly violence; the displacement of his hostility onto his treasured new Dane had left him feeling extremely remorseful and frightened at what he was capable of. Most disturbing of all was Dr. Browning's discussion of "kindling," and the possibility of his misinterpretation of Scriabin's "Vers La Flamme." Xavier was genuinely afraid of his emotions at this point, and the depression he was feeling added to the confusion, as he didn't know if it was due to missing Lana, fighting with the city of Palm Beach, rejecting his family, having no clear direction, or possibly this "temporal lobe dysfunction" Dr. Browning described. The one part of this confusing picture which Xavier held on to for strength was his conviction in his special powers; after all, who else could see the world through the eyes of their pets?

The next day finally arrived for an impatient Xavier, and he greeted Lana with a powerful hug. The two sat down together in the living room and began to discuss what had happened recently.

"Lana, I know that being with me can be draining. Certainly my road of discovery and achievement has met with many pressures and obstacles. You have been so invaluable in helping me that I didn't really appreciate you until you were gone. But it is more than just your helpfulness as a manager. I have also realized that I find you to be a very special woman. You are warm and caring, and have a freshness of spirit reminiscent of a gust of cool spring air. Ironically, despite finding myself gifted now in reading and discussing feelings, I have not been very adept in the past in discussing my own feelings, particularly with women."

"Well, you're doing a pretty good job now. Xavier, I've had a few days to rest, and I'm fine. I can get burned out just like anyone else, and I still do feel you need to clarify your goals. I must admit to you that I've become somewhat worried about your emotional state, particularly your rages, even though I know it is usually due to somebody's "bad mentaar." I also think that you are a great man, with a great gift that will find you a big place in history. It has been very exciting helping you achieve that place, and I want to continue helping you with that. I would have problems with you doing nothing except just living comfortably with the money you've made already, or adding an odd reading here or there. You have to use your talent, develop it, refine it, help our world with it. I can't be a part of your life if you squander it."

While Lana spoke, Xavier unintentionally read some of the feelings she was having, in such a subtle way that Lana didn't notice. What Xavier accidentally discovered excited him beyond words. Lana was attracted to him, wanted to be with him, and cared very deeply about his welfare. Xavier's passion was stirred, and his heart started thundering within his chest. He paused for a moment in silence, then mentally directed Scriabin to approach Lana. He tricked the dog into thinking there was food in between Lana's legs, and Scriabin stuck his big, angular snout up Lana's loose summer dress. The dog took his cue and began licking around Lana's vagina. She pushed the dog gently but firmly away, only to have him return immediately, eagerly and playfully whipping his tongue out with big, slobbery swipes. She tolerated it this time for a moment, as a broad and slightly embarrassed grin came over her face. "My, what an amorous dog you have here."

Almost before Lana had finished her comment, Xavier approached beside Scriabin and got into the act, kissing the inside of Lana's left thigh. He whispered, "Scriabin and I think alike," and proceeded to work his way up Lana's thigh, eventually pushing the dog out of the way. He slipped his right hand up and hooked the edge of her panties, pulling it over to expose her already wet vagina. He found her clitoris with his tongue, and began caressing it and massaging it, driving Lana into a frenzy of passion. He reached with both hands to first stroke the insides of both thighs, then worked up the slender contours of her hips and waist. His hands approached and found her fairly large yet firm and natural breasts. His fingertips slipped underneath the lower edge of her bra and he kneaded her fleshy breasts roughly while he also intensified his tongue's action below. Lana tilted her head back, moaning in joy. Xavier quickly swung his hands down to pull off Lana's panties, and seemingly in the same motion took his own pants and underwear off. Lana's eyes were softly closed as she was mesmerized in ecstasy, but she opened them abruptly as she felt Xavier's strong hands reach back to grab her firm buttocks and pull her onto his hard and ready manhood. Xavier lifted her up off the chair and, while still standing, began making passionate love to her. He cradled her body effortlessly while she held her arms around his neck. She rode him passionately for several intense yet exquisitely sensual minutes, before Xavier carried her off into his bedroom. There was a wildness in Xavier's eyes, despite the blindness, and Xavier roughly threw Lana down on the bed. He ripped off all of her clothing, exposing her magnificently voluptuous yet lean body. Although Xavier had the benefit of both Mahler and Scriabin's eyes, since they each had followed the lusty pair into the bedroom, he didn't need to see. His hands and his passion guided him. He ripped off the remainder of his clothes, and aggressively mounted Lana to continue his lovemaking. After several more minutes of hard, frenzied sex, with Xavier pounding his pelvis on Lana's in such a way as to simultaneously stimulate her clitoris, she began screaming in delight as several ripples of orgasmic exhilaration came over her. This seemed to trigger an even more animalistic passion in Xavier, and he forcefully hoisted Lana's legs up over his shoulders and continued thrusting aggressively. Xavier reached down and clutched Lana's breasts, squeezing them so hard that she moaned in pain. At this point Xavier was nearly out of control, sweating profusely while beginning to let loose with screams of mad joy. Lana grew frightened, and was relieved to hear the spasmodic moans of ecstasy signifying his coming.

During the afterglow, or for Lana what might have been better described as aftermath, there was a ruckus outside, prompting Scriabin to growl and run out of the bedroom. Xavier was not interested, being immersed in an enraptured state. But after Scriabin continued barking menacingly, Lana nudged Xavier to attend to the situation. Xavier called for Mahler, who flew to his shoulder and perched himself. Acting instinctively, Xavier put on his robe and strode to the window of the living room overlooking the front of the small estate. Through Mahler's eyes, Xavier saw the cause of the commotion. Ahead, dangling off the top of the front gate, was a dummy of Xavier hanging in effigy. A hand-made sign nearby read, "Go to Hell, Xavier!" The perpetrators of this deed were nowhere to be found. A torrent of rage came over Xavier and he exploded, thrusting his fist through the window, shattering the glass and spraying the pieces everywhere. He yelled out through the hole, "Come, Scriabin!" and turned to join him at the door. The dog obeyed, and once reunited, Xavier went back into the bedroom, where a shaken Lana had not moved.

"Lana, I have made my decision. It is time to leave this place. Take me south, south to Islamorada, site of the liberation of the dolphin. That will be my home. I will not tolerate any more of this Palm Beach nonsense."

"Good, Xavier. When do you want to leave?"

"Immediately."

Xavier meant immediately, too, as he began packing his own suitcase. Lana was shocked that he appeared oblivious to the fact that his hand was seriously cut and bleeding. She ran and got a bandage for it, there fortunately being plenty left over. Xavier's arm had not completely healed from the burns, but he had decided that a few minutes a day of healing meditation was all he needed anymore. Lana simply handed the dressing to Xavier, knowing that he would prefer to do the dressing himself. Once done, Xavier went to find Serena, and asked her if she would join them in his new home in the Keys. Serena agreed to go, for she had felt in her heart that Xavier was a good man who had treated her with kindness and generosity. Further, Serena was a very religious woman, and she had assumed that Xavier's accident and subsequent ups and downs were all God's will. Thus she had ultimate faith that if Xavier remained of good heart and spirit, God would see him through his difficulties. Xavier was glad she agreed to come, for not only was she a good housekeeper, she was quiet and minded her own business.

Xavier hurried the preparations and instructed Lana and Serena to leave much in the house, taking only necessities and valuables. They packed the two vehicles, but left enough space in the back of the Jeep for Scriabin. Xavier asked Serena to drive the Jeep with Scriabin, and told her he would help the dog to sleep during the trip if he got unruly. She agreed, and soon the entourage was off.

The trip down was uneventful, as Xavier went into one of his "resting trances" for much of it. He had asked Lana to arouse him at Key Largo if he was oblivious when they passed it. This town of movie fame signified the beginning of the Keys. After passing it, they neared the small town of Islamorada, and they began their search for a home. In contrast to his recent behavior, Xavier was not indecisive about what he wanted; he spotted a home southwest of the town which was secluded and over-looked the gulf. It was a relatively small, old home, but sat on a large plot of land. A "For Sale" sign sat in the sandy front yard, and Lana took down the number. The group returned to the town and checked into the same hotel that Xavier and Lana had stayed in on their previous trip down. Xavier had to put a couple of hotel people asleep so that they could sneak Scriabin up into their room.

Once inside, Xavier had Lana call the number to inquire about the house. An older gentleman answered, and informed Lana that the asking price was two hundred thousand dollars, but that he was desperate and would take one hundred and seventy in cash. For a house on a couple of acres on the gulf, this was a steal. Lana informed the man that they were interested, and would like to discuss terms for financing the next day. When Xavier overheard this, he became furious and tried to grab the phone from Lana, but she was already in the act of hanging up.

"What are you doing? I said I wanted that house! We will buy it, cash, right now."

"Xavier, we can bargain him down. We can probably get the financed cost down to one hundred seventy thousand, maybe less."

Xavier grabbed Lana strongly at the shoulders and shook her. "You don't understand. I said I want it. Now. Cash."

"Get your hands off me! I've been handling your money, and you only have one hundred and sixty thousand dollars left in the bank anyway! You want to dig your own financial grave, you go right ahead!"

Lana stormed out of the room, and went down to the beach to take a walk. After a while, the setting sun sitting on a blue-green horizon helped to take away her distress. Xavier meanwhile had fallen into a heap on the hotel room bed, and was overcome with guilt and shame. How could he have acted so immaturely, so impulsively, so unlike Xavier as he knew him. He tried to mentally calm himself, but could not, uncontrollably breaking into tears.

After about an hour of this misery, he decided he couldn't take it anymore and took Mahler with him outside. He walked to a nearby tavern, which was just starting to fill with customers. Xavier was in general a stranger to alcohol, but at this moment it seemed a good alternative to the pain he was feeling. Besides, he rationalized, if it was good enough for Hemingway, it was good enough for Xavier. In fact, when Xavier straddled a bar stool and was asked what he wanted to drink, he asked, "What did Hemingway used to drink?" The bartender said, "I think he was a vodka and tonic man," so Xavier said that was what he wanted.

A few drinks later, Xavier was already getting a substantial buzz, and began being more aware or suspicious of the locals looking at him. The locals were generally not nosy, as people in these parts minded their own business and were not impressed by much. Xavier was drowning in self-pity and doubt, and thought back to the episode with Dr. Browning.

"Sometimes temporal lobe dysfunction is associated with delusions and grandiosity," thought Xavier, repeating the words of Dr. Browning. "I'll show him delusions," he mumbled to himself, and tried one of his "parlor games" on his closest fellow drinker. He caused him to spill his drink on his lap. The man did not suspect foul play and simply cursed and cleaned up the mess. Xavier got a kick out of this and proceeded to cause similar minor accidents throughout the room. With each one, he would laugh a little bit louder, until one time, when the victim was a rather large, bearded truck driver. This angry man approached Xavier and scolded him.

"Just what do you think is so goddamn funny?"

"Nothing, really."

"Well, you better keep your fat mouth shut! Who the fuck are you, anyway, Long John Silver?"

"No, just a drunk blind man with a bird."

The angry man looked puzzled at the comment about being blind, but upon looking at Xavier's eyes realized it could be true. He therefore put aside his thoughts of vengeance and returned to his seat. The crowd had grown progressively irritated with these little accidents, although surprisingly no one had realized who Xavier was; therefore no one ascribed the blame to him. The growing ugliness of the tavern's mentaar started wearing on Xavier, prompting even more drinking and more minor demonstrations of his powers. One of the newer customers then figured out who Xavier was and identified him to the rest. The truck driver and others rushed up to him, and threateningly demanded to know if he had caused all of their accidents. Xavier began absorbing some of their anger and lost his own temper, starting to swing wildly at whoever was nearest. The bouncer of the tavern came running in, and grabbed Xavier from behind with a choke hold. The poor mynah bird tried to avoid the scuffle, flapping his wings and screeching "Xavier! Lana! Xavier!" repeatedly. Xavier soon found himself sitting on the sand of the beach outside the back of the tavern, and his head was spinning.

He gathered himself up the best he could and, with Mahler in tow, staggered back to the hotel. By the time he got there, Lana had returned and was in Xavier's room changing her clothes. The sight of the nearly naked Lana ignited Xavier's passion, and he lurched forward, reaching for her waist. Lana pushed back, saying "Xavier! You're drunk!" He did not stop, however, and wrestled Lana down to the ground, mumbling something about "needing to fuck your brains out." She screamed and resisted, but Xavier had leverage over her and was very forceful. Lana began beating on Xavier's shoulders and begged him to stop, but he slapped her across the face, dropped his pants, and uncontrollably raped her.

CHAPTER THIRTY

Winston Churchill. William Styron. Vincent Van Gogh. Sergei Rachmaninoff. These were great men, with great depressions, thought a thoroughly depressed and guilt-ridden Xavier. Rachmaninoff worked through his depressions by writing great music, so perhaps it was time to listen to his music for some direction, some purpose, or maybe just some solace.

Xavier was barely able to get up and load one of his Rachmaninoff CD's, and fittingly chose the Russian's most somber and melancholy piece, "The Isle of the Dead." As this lonely symphony of ebbing and flowing anguish worked its way to a gut-wrenching climax, Xavier's emotions followed a similar path. He found himself gripping the sides of his chair with white-knuckled intensity, and grimaced as if the hand of death had clutched his heart. Likewise, as the piece dwindled away into oblivion, so Xavier felt his lifeblood seeping away, leaving him so weak and lethargic that he collapsed into another several hours of sleep.

And so Xavier's life had deteriorated into several of these listening-sleeping sessions each day, with little else in between. He would not eat, for the most part, except every second day or so. He found himself devouring a far greater than normal amount of one particular food, such as dry cereal. Serena remained a faithful housekeeper, and for the most part allowed Xavier his privacy, other than occasionally asking Xavier if he would like her to fix him something to eat. Serena was not so blind as to not realize that Xavier was deeply troubled, but in her good-hearted way decided she would just pray for him. When Xavier felt that Serena was somewhat frightened in his presence, he would mentally tranquilize her, since he did not want to lose her. Something in his hazy conscious-ness informed him to not totally give up on humanity, and she was currently his only link to it. He had lost Lana, been driven out of Palm Beach, forsaken his parents, sacrificed his medical student friends along with his career, and secluded himself in one of the most isolated parts of the country. Worse than that, he had shown that the doctors must have been correct, in that his brain had been affected, disturbed, or in some way impaired so that he was not in full control of his emotions.

What did he do to Lana? Xavier could hardly even remember what happened. It seemed as if it was someone else in his body doing something horrible to a woman he truly loved and cared for. Was it the alcohol which made it all so fuzzy? It couldn't have just been a dissociation; Mahler would have cried out. It was the act of Xavier; he could not displace responsibility. When he came to this inexorable conclusion, Xavier fell deeper into his pit of despair. He contemplated whether he could live with this act on his conscience, even if Lana did not go to the police. Yes, he could probably live most of his life in a trance state, blissfully removed from the penetrating guilt and anguish, but also numbingly sheltered from any worthwhile quality of life.   Was death perhaps now a reasonable solution?

Xavier had never considered suicide an honorable act, but the list of greats who had ended their lives by their own hands had always intrigued him.   In addition to Hemingway, there were Descartes, Tchaikovsky, even Marilyn Monroe.   Another more recent suicide had hit Xavier quite hard: The famed psychiatrist Bruno Bettleheim took his life at the same time Xavier had been reading and cherishing his book on childhood fantasies.   Yes, he was aging, but especially in old age Xavier figured a great man should have come to terms with his life and found a way to enjoy it until the hand of death snatched it away. Unless, once again, there was a vision of a better place awaiting, something Xavier had not fully been able to put faith into.   It was something he would contemplate further.

The one entity which did not allow Xavier total concentration was his loyal Harlequin Scriabin.   The dog sensed Xavier's despair and often lay at his feet in quiet sympathy.   Occasionally he would grow restless, and stick his large wet snout directly into Xavier's face and beg him to take him outside.   Scriabin wanted to run, needed to run, but Xavier's near comatose state had disabled him far more than the loss of direct sight ever did.   One day, however, after listening to one of Rachmaninoff's more energizing pieces, the Third Piano Concerto, Xavier decided he would take Scriabin for a walk on the beach. He felt too lethargic to try jogging, but the walk almost became a jog as the exuberant dog dragged Xavier along at a fast pace.   The splash of the salt air coming off the gulf was invigorating, as was the near-equatorial sunshine. All of this served to keep Xavier alive, to give him enough strength to persevere in search of a viable way to lead his

life. Xavier granted himself a respite from his pain and
remorse each day with these walks with Scriabin, mentally forcing the dysphoria out while allowing just enough
consciousness to absorb the joy of the moment. Xavier
had also trained Mahler to always stay near him without
a connecting cord. So when they went outside, Mahler
spread his wings and flew circles overhead. For the first
time in many days, Xavier tried expanding his mental
powers. He learned how far away Mahler could be before
Xavier no longer was able to use his vision. Xavier found
he could gradually extend the distance, so that a limiting
distance of initially ten feet became a hundred. It was
quite a thrill, viewing himself and Scriabin from overhead, an in vivo astral projection of sorts. One day,
following a particularly long walk, Xavier found himself
perspiring greatly and decided to take a dip in the ocean.
Using Mahler's eyes for orientation, he was able to swim
again, returning to the pastime that had always provided
him serenity. Scriabin apparently was not accustomed to
the ocean and was disturbed by Xavier's swim. The dog
ran alongside on the beach and barked furiously. Upon
Xavier's emergence from the water, the worried dog's
reaction was closer to a mugging than a welcome greet-
ing.

Once home, Xavier unfortunately lost his newly-
regained peace of mind. His reality came crashing back
on top of him, as Serena's worried psyche reminded him
of his problems. His temper continued to be a problem,
and as the walks and swims re-energized him, the energy
was used to progressively destroy much of the furniture
in the home. Fortunately, there was not that much to
destroy, as Xavier had simply not bothered to shop for
any. There was, however, a growing number of holes in
the walls.

Xavier could have displaced his rage onto Serena, or
Scriabin, or even Mahler, but some thread of decency and

respect kept him from doing this. Xavier was also afflicted with an increasing sexual drive, and again the trauma of what had occurred with Lana had so affected him that he could not even consider satisfying his sexual needs with Serena. He kept himself under control by masturbating frequently, sometimes five or six times a day. Xavier had at least learned how to mentally stimulate himself into orgasm, so that the usual method became unnecessary. Nevertheless, he found that there was still a limit to how often he could do this in a given day. He found the oral gratification of bingeing on sweets a second-best solution to the urges that plagued him. What amazed Xavier about these sexual urges was that they were not often connected with stimulating fantasies, but emerged rather like an unwanted strong gust of wind during a summer picnic. There was no joy in it, not because he was embarrassed or ashamed, but simply because it was devoid of anything pleasurable other than the few seconds of attenuated orgasm.

One day, while taking one of his now routine swims alongside the beach, Xavier felt a feeling akin to deja vu. As he swam, he recognized the feeling as more of a familiarity with a life form rather than a place. He wondered if someone was on the beach, but scanning with Mahler's eyes revealed only the excited and anxious form of Scriabin. Then it dawned on Xavier, what he sensed was the life essence of the dolphin he had liberated! He called out to her in all directions, hoping somehow she would come. Xavier's heart started beating even faster than it already was due to the swimming, and it nearly skipped a beat when he felt the smooth, slippery skin of a dolphin graze up against him. He reached out and grabbed the familiar dorsal fin and held on as the dolphin took him for a ride. Xavier had to hold on with both hands, as the dolphin was excited and swam a bit too fast. Nevertheless, Xavier felt more alive than he had felt in weeks, and it seemed as if the dolphin could sense his exhilaration.   She dove down for an instant before surging upward out of the sea, incredibly pulling Xavier completely out of the water. Scriabin nearly went berserk witnessing this awesome spectacle, and the Dane gamely tried going into the water to reach his master. The waves were too new and too scary for the young dog, and he backed out and continued barking.   Xavier, despite having a memorable experience, grew fatigued and gasped for air. He knew he had to let go of the dolphin and make his way to shore. He released her, but as he did he mentally sent his appreciation to his departing friend. Xavier gave her a parting gift by naming her "Free." He smiled to himself at not only how appropriate it was, but also how similar the name sounded to the high pitched squeals of the dolphin's native language.

Although he was totally exhausted, there remained plenty of spirit in Xavier's water-logged body, certainly enough to get him back to the house. He wore a smile, rare for him of late, as he entered the house which he hoped to call home. His new-found enthusiasm was immediately quelled as he saw that Serena was nowhere to be found and had left a note on the table. It was extremely difficult for Xavier to "read" the note, as the brains of Scriabin or Mahler did not focus well on small human handwriting. Doing the best he could, Xavier thought he saw the words "sorry" and "unholy," and more importantly, the word "good-bye." Xavier crumpled up the piece of paper and threw it against the wall, and followed that action with a fist against the same wall.

In his fatigued state there wasn't enough force to break through the wall, but there was a surprisingly sharp pain which instantly rippled up his arm. Though Xavier had wrought havoc throughout the house over the past several weeks, he had never felt quite the same pain in his hand as he did this time. He was able to block the pain mentally, but knew down deep that he had probably broken something in his hand. Seconds later a wave of despair followed the immediate rage outburst, like the slightly delayed thunder which follows distant lightning. This time, the despair was far more acute than that deadening melancholy he had suffered from recently; this was an anguish which demanded action. Xavier felt intensely suicidal, and frantically looked for a weapon of self-destruction. The first thing which occurred to him was to take the pills from Dr. Browning, and he rushed to the bedroom where they still remained in an unpacked suitcase. He grabbed the large prescription bottle filled with at least one hundred pills, and ran to the sink to get some water. He proceeded to gulp down as many of the pills as he could tolerate. Xavier's knees were shaking, and in his fatigued state he slumped to the floor, powerless. He tried to put himself in a trance, in order to not wait anxiously for the drug to take effect, but could not. Soon, however, the first wave of overdosed medication started clouding Xavier's mind. Soon thereafter there was nothing.

CHAPTER THIRTY-ONE

"Have you seen Xavier?"

The question was one Zandu Hamareesch had asked many times in the past several days. It was one he had needed to explain to many, for despite Xavier's national attention, many people in southern Florida had not cared to remember who he was. Especially in the Keys, where namelessness was a virtue. Zandu had reached a Key Largo restaurant in pursuit of Xavier, having learned that he had left Palm Beach and headed south. Zandu assumed that Xavier would be heading south for the Keys, not only just to get away, but also because he guessed that Xavier was still driven by a "Toward the Flame" quest. In all likelihood, Zandu alone understood how important that piece was to Xavier, and how he was certain it contained a message of destiny. Zandu guessed that Xavier's interpretation of that message included finding a home which was hotter, thus farther south.

Perhaps Key West. Hopefully not out of the country, for tracking Xavier in Central America would be most difficult.

"Xavier who?" The restaurant owner who responded looked at Zandu with bewilderment and a slight edge of hostility.

"A great man, a blind and bald man dressed like myself."

"No, buddy, and we don't like your kind in these parts."

Zandu wondered to himself what 'kind' this man was referring to, but simply nodded a thank you for answering his question and proceeded on. He walked out of the restaurant and shook his head as if to say no to his waiting followers. There was an incredibly long line of white trucks which had pulled off to the side of the road. "The People of Xavier," or "Xavierists," had grown to one thousand strong and had followed Zandu across the country in pursuit of their savior. Zandu had not begun the search until they had reached Palm Beach, but since that point he had stopped many times on the road south, frustratingly gaining no clue as to Xavier's whereabouts. At this point, Zandu told his messengers to spread the word to make camp a few miles north and inland, where there were open spaces large enough to hold the multitude. Zandu would carry the search onward himself, and come back to his people when he had located Xavier. Some of the others protested, wanting to continue with Zandu, but he was convinced he needed to go alone, without the added burden of other similarly odd-looking people. The others complied, reluctantly, and Zandu headed south alone.

As Zandu headed south he felt a momentary twang of doubt spring into his mind, but he pushed it away. He had to recall his own words to Xavier's people, his words of faith and perseverance, of patience and strength. He would find Xavier, and when he did, Xavier would lead his people, the chosen ones, into a higher state of consciousness. Zandu knew this would be true; it had to be true, for he and the thousand others had risked nearly everything on this venture. Most had taken all of their money, some had sold their homes, if they could, and all had left their jobs. Those with families had either taken them along or given small children to relatives for the time being. All had purchased white trucks and loaded them up with furniture which was used in "The Revelry." At each of the several stops along the way in their cross-country trek, Zandu had led the people in the five-step Ascension, which included the fourth step involving orgiastic sex and violence. The Xavierists used the furniture to vent their anger, and after destroying it would nail it back together to use for another Revelry. After several Revelries, the furniture was beginning to become unusable as furniture itself, but that didn't matter. They didn't really need it for that, as they were living in white tents and sleeping bags whenever they made camp along the way.

Zandu had started with the hundred strong or so in California, and had picked up many converts along the way. News of the Xavierists had spread, but in general they were dismissed as just another California-originated mind cult destined to burn itself out or come to some other useless demise. However, what had attracted attention was the caliber of people who had joined the ranks of Zandu. Some of these people were millionaires, and many were professional people. Very few were the burned-out hippies or drunks that the country as a whole expected them to be. This was also not just a "weekend cult," but a complete and total commitment. Word of the Ascension, in particular the Revelry, had also been newsworthy and had prompted an early negative response by some church groups who had found this unacceptable. They had also had a few run-ins with local police who did not want "their kind" making camp in their neighborhoods.

Zandu had predicted all of this and warned his fellow followers in advance, so all of these obstacles were met with no undue consternation. Zandu in fact expressed how their journey would in some ways parallel Xavier's troubled journey, in that they each would experience many tests of their fortitude. Only the strong of spirit could overcome these challenges and survive to work on true ascension. As Zandu gave his strength and courage to the multitude, they gave theirs back to him, mutually fortifying their resolve. The ever-growing camp of Xavierists was brimming with optimism, hope, and zeal. They were all convinced they were going to find the first true savior since Jesus Christ.

Zandu, or The Guru Hamareesch as some called him, was capable of some impressive feats of mental control himself. He had become a skilled meditator and self-hypnotist, as well as being able to teach these skills. He had hoped to some day do even more than this, hoping to develop Xavier-like psychic abilities. But as yet, he had not been able to go beyond his well-developed sense of deducing people's motives and probable choices based on scant clues. The same intelligence and charisma that had led to his immensely successful career in business was not lost in his ability to lead people or strive for personal development. Zandu was a man on a mission, and he would simply not be denied. He would not let down the people he had personally convinced to leave behind their lives to share in his dream of ultimate personal fulfillment through the powers of Xavier. Zandu continued his drive south and searched for something, anything, that might have caught Xavier's "eye" enough to make him and his companion stop. He tried a few more restaurants, a couple of motels, and also a couple of gas stations. Finally, when he emerged from his white truck to ask the attendant of an Exxon station if he had seen Xavier, the attendant said yes. He informed Zandu that a young woman had stopped by in a white Jaguar. With her was a bald man dressed in a white and black outfit similar to the one Zandu had. The bald one had a bird on his shoulder. He didn't have much to say, and only got out to use the rest room. The pretty woman simply paid for the gas and the two departed, heading south. South! Yes, Zandu must be on the right track. Toward the flame! He must be headed for Key West. Zandu thanked the attendant gratefully, who asked in parting who this man was. Zandu replied, "Soon, the whole world will know who that man is," and left.

*   *   *

As Zandu eagerly sped southward, passing Islamorada, he would never have guessed that the object of his quest was nearby, lying unconscious on the floor, alone in his new seaside home. Xavier was prodded awake, after some thirty hours of oblivion, by the incessant shrill calling of his name by Mahler and the slobbery swipes of a large Great Dane tongue. Xavier's first awareness was mediated through the senses of touch and hearing; there was no visual input whatsoever. His mind felt clouded and heavy, and at first there was no memory, no recollection of what this sensory information which had prompted his awakening meant to him. Comprehension of his identity returned to him first, and for a moment that felt good. But that brief feeling was obliterated when he realized he had taken a massive overdose. At that instant, he pondered if in fact he was still alive, or if he was in some other place, a place after death.

He tried to use what he thought was his body, and found his extremities also weighed down as if he were living on the planet Jupiter. He squeezed his right fist and felt a twinge of pain, allowing him to recall his recent injury. He must still be alive! His movement caused a redoubled effort by Scriabin and Mahler to revive him, and Xavier now was able to joyously recall who these were: They were friends! Xavier's mental cloud began lifting somewhat and he remembered that he could use the dog's or bird's vision for his own. He tried to capture Scriabin's visual cortex first, but incredibly found that he could not! He tried again, more determined than before, but again remained blind. He tried the same with Mahler, and again, nothing. Blackness. Total blindness. He tried to feel their primitive emotions, knowing certainly that they must be afraid for their master but also pleased to see him moving around. Nothing. Not one shred of an empathic feeling. Not one fragment of a concerned thought. Xavier was truly bewildered. He had either lost his powers completely, or truly was dead. Was this to be his fate in the afterworld, to exist without sight or other mental gifts? Perhaps this was to be his hell, lying nearly paralyzed, blind, and except for two caring but primitive beasts, utterly alone.

CHAPTER THIRTY-TWO

After a day of total misery and hopelessness, unaware of what time it was and unable to find out, Xavier stumbled out towards his kitchen in search of his first meal in two days. He was not truly hungry, but he was so weak and lethargic that he thought some food would help. He heard his dog come running in, and was then struck by something: He could sense that Scriabin was hungry! The poor dog was starving. More importantly, Xavier actually experienced the feeling that Scriabin was starving. The feeling was faint, but it was definitely there, and it wasn't just a logical deduction based on the fact that the normally voracious Great Dane hadn't eaten in two days. Xavier knew that the feeling emanated from the dog's psyche. His powers were not dead! Xavier tried then to regain his sight, and found to his dismay that it was very difficult to do. He was able to find the general area of the brain he needed to read, but the images that came into his mind were fuzzy and dim. It reminded him of trying to keep Mahler's sight while the bird spiraled upward, flying beyond one hundred feet above Xavier. This reminded him of his trusty bird, and he called out to him. The bird was nearby and flew to the familiar perch of Xavier's left shoulder. Xavier shifted his concentration to reading the bird's visual cortex, and again discovered he could only bring in significantly deteriorated images. Fortunately, there was enough of an image that Xavier was able to feed both the dog and the bird, and then himself. The knowledge of having some power return to him lifted his spirit slightly, and quelled his anxieties enough that he could finally lie down and rest.

Following what turned out to be a ten-hour sleep, Xavier arose and projected his mind out to the nearest life form for sight. He found Mahler, as usual, sitting on the nightstand next to the head of the bed. As Xavier brought in the first image of his new day, he was nearly overcome by the fairly crisp image of the morning sunshine beaming through his bedroom window. His ability to see had fully returned! Without looking for him, Xavier was also able to feel Scriabin's presence at the foot of the bed, still sleeping. He mentally called him, and the dog happily sprang to life, coming quickly to give his master a tongue-licking like never before. Xavier got to his feet, showered, and embraced the day. The recollection of all that had transpired over the last few days came back to him, however, and propelled him back into a melancholy mood.

After an hour of darkened mood, Xavier grew frustrated and briefly lost his temper, striking out at the nearest wall. A few moments after the pain in his hand wore off, it occurred to Xavier that the previous day, while he was psychically blind, he had also been emotionally numb. Could there be a connection between the return of his powers and the return of his moodiness and temper? The logical explanation was that the medication had been responsible, robbing him of his powers while somehow tranquilizing the disturbed beast within him. But that seemed too amazing to believe. The alternate explanation was that the shock of having attempted suicide was the real determinant; being in shock meant being temporarily shut off from normal emotional and cognitive functioning. Or at least what was normal functioning for him. Anyway, it probably didn't matter, since his powers were back to nearly full strength. Xavier knew he was still a little dulled, not as sharp as during his road trip when he was able to accurately read the mentaar of a crowd of fifty thousand. But he was as sharp as he needed to be for the moment, at least enough to function.

But what was left of his life and dreams? What kind of life was this, holed up in an Islamorada escape isolated from humanity? What kind of life could he lead, carrying the remorse of his actions toward Lana like a ton of bricks on his shoulders? What had happened to his dream of using his powers to bring to mankind a new serenity and mental peace? Was this all just a delusion, as Dr. Browning had suggested?

Over the next several days, Xavier pondered these and other existential questions endlessly, although his contemplation was often interrupted by surges of rage or waves of anguish. He had also rediscovered his libido, and had to renew his periodic catharsis via ejaculation. The reality of his emotional disturbance was beginning to become inescapable, and the prospects of a life filled with rage outbursts, depressive plagues, and unyielding sexual drive was nearly too much to bear. It dawned on him, however, that if indeed the good Doctor Browning had been correct, and that he was "kindling" into oblivion, that a clinical dosage of the medication might keep him under control. Xavier decided to experiment with the Carbamazepine, taking one pill twice a day at first. He found that indeed after a couple of days his emotional lability began to stabilize, but at the same time his ability to capture the eyesight of his pets gradually diminished. What a cruel trade-off! At three pills a day, Xavier was totally emotionally controlled, but also quite totally blind. At one pill a day, Xavier suffered perhaps only half the violent outbursts and sexual urges that he had without anything, but also could barely see, looking at the world as if through cataracts. At two pills a day, there seemed to be a balance of relatively minor mood fluctuations along with enough vision to get around adequately, although not much more than that. The medication seemed to have one other oddly distasteful side effect: It appeared to dull Xavier's passionate enjoyment of music, including even his beloved Scriabin.

It was during a frustrating listening of Scriabin's Prometheus Symphony that Xavier's dog first detected an intruder. Xavier then heard a knock on the door and proceeded to answer it. When he opened the door, there before him stood an unfamiliar presence, but clearly someone aware of Xavier, due to the copycat outfit of Harlequin mottle that he was wearing. It was the Guru Zandu Hamareesch.

"Xavier! Praise God, I have found you!"

"Who are you?"

"I am nothing, nobody; an ant standing next to a colossus of greatness such as you. I am called Zandu, Zandu Hamareesch."

"You have. . . goodness in your heart; this much I can tell. But what is the purpose of your quest to find me?"

"Surely you can tell, master, that I am sent to bring you to your people. They have come, one thousand strong, to worship you, to learn from you, to heal with you. They await you, not far from here."

"You will have to forgive me; my reading abilities are somewhat dulled. Please come inside. I have questions."

And so the two similarly clothed men sat down in Xavier's barren living room and began to exchange information. Zandu started, telling the wonderful saga of how so many had been so moved by Xavier's exploits that they were willing to sacrifice nearly everything in search of serenity. Zandu was modest, and underplayed his significant role in organizing the mass movement. Xavier was clearly moved by this story, finding it incredible but knowing that Zandu was telling the truth. The feeling of hearing that a whole following of worshipers had come to be with him was overpowering but also bittersweet, for Xavier knew that he was not quite the man they had come in search of. He felt he owed this man at least the truth, and proceeded to tell of his loss of impulse control with Lana, and then his suicide attempt, followed by his discovery of the effects of the medication. Upon hearing the former, Zandu was bewildered, but upon hearing the latter, he was furious.

"No! No! This is false, blaspheming science! This is corruption of your striving for purity! You are casting away your base drives in your upward evolution, and must not feel badly for what God is putting you through. God touched you with His power when you reached upward for that light socket. Can you honestly believe that sheer man-made electricity could instill upon you such supernatural abilities? All that has to do with you is divine, whereas the medication is hell-spawned, a Mephistophelian elixir designed to throw darkness on your light. Forgive my insolence, master, but I cannot stand by while that which is holy and good is corrupted by evil."

"Your faith in me is most impressive, but I am nearly overwhelmed with rage and sexual drive without this medicine. How am I to keep from hurting many lives unless I take this medication?"

"Fear not. Let your people help you heal and regain

your strength, as you in turn heal them. They will accommodate you, and allow you the opportunities you need to purge your base drives. Soon you will rise above us all in a pure state, freed from the bondage of lust and aggression and all that results from them. They will do this for you without question, and if some of them fall, the rest will understand."

Once again, Xavier was struck by the well-thought-out logic of Zandu's arguments, although he was not convinced that everyone in this camp of followers would share Zandu's unbridled zeal.

"Zandu, these followers; by what name are they called?"

"Why, of course they are called The People of Xavier, or Xavierists for short."

"Well, then, have these Xavierists faced tests of their will and resolve in their journey here?"

"Truly, though none have been insurmountable. There have been several attacks on us by threatened religious groups, police and other authorities along the way. Most were content to see that we would simply leave their community. Some would have us undone altogether. But the spirit of Xavier breathes within the heart of each and every Xavierist, and this spirit is indomitable. As is yours, although the hand of Satan has reached out to steal you away and capture your soul. You have survived, and clearly once again it is God's will that you persevere, onward to holiness and serenity."

"Well, then, Zandu, take me to my people."

Zandu eagerly escorted Xavier to his white truck, and Xavier in turn helped Scriabin into the back of the pickup. Scriabin and Mahler were all he needed. Zandu drove them northward for a couple of hours, going inland after they reached south Miami and passed by the famed Metro Zoo. Xavier recalled a visit there years ago, and how much he had enjoyed it. He supposed he had always loved animals. Especially happy and handsome ones, such as giraffes, gazelles, and tigers. He recalled how the Miami zoo kept the animals contained within natural boundaries, which was a good thing, since Xavier detested cages of any kind. Xavier reached out his mind to see if he could catch a fragment of the mentaar of the animals as they passed by the zoo, but could not.

The camp was not much farther, in a stretch of dry land close to the Everglades. The Xavierists had learned to camp on the boundaries of uninhabitable lands, the safest bets for privacy.

The sight of hundreds of white tents and white trucks was truly awesome, and in its own way celestial and pure. But Xavier was not prepared for the next sight, that of the announcement that Zandu had returned with Xavier. The cry went out and was quickly echoed throughout the camp, followed by a mad rush of black-on-white-clothed fanatics rushing forward to greet Xavier. As Xavier emerged from the developing crowd, a gasp momentarily rippled through the growing ranks, followed by more jostling for position to get closer to see him. Xavier was overcome with exhilaration and exultation, and purposefully mounted the front hood of Zandu's truck. He stood fully erect, faced the throng of people, and raised his arms heavenward. As chants of "Xavier!" rang loudly throughout the multitudes, the man of apparent destiny absorbed and cherished their love. Despite all of the fatalism of the previous day, Xavier knew there would be a tomorrow, and by all accounts it would be a very good one indeed.

CHAPTER THIRTY-THREE

"Let us hold a joyous celebration in honor of our savior!" proclaimed an exhilarated Zandu. "And let us remember this day forever, naming it `The Uniting.'" The guru Zandu was fond of naming things, having already officially named his journey over much of the United States in pursuit of Xavier "The Searching." While Zandu had conducted the last leg of "The Searching" by himself, the remainder of the Xavierists had done their best to fend for themselves. They performed the five steps of "The Ascension" on a daily basis, and used the remaining time to clean up camp and repair furniture. The younger children and teenagers present in camp at times grew very restless and were bewildered by concepts they could not quite comprehend. At first they were all quite happy to be liberated from school in order to go on a trip with their parents, but the oddness of the camp and the exposure to public sexual behaviors had disturbed many

of them. The proximity of the zoo was fortuitous but
fortunate, so the elders in the camp decided daily outings
to the zoo for the children during "The Revelry" was a
good idea. The children enjoyed the wide array of birds
and animals present at the large Metro Zoo. The mood
of the camp remained generally upbeat even before "The
Uniting," but afterwards there was an unadulterated
euphoria bordering on mass mania.

The celebration marking "The Uniting" continued for
several days, with dancing and singing the predominant
activities. Several of the camp's members were talented
musicians and had brought their instruments with them.
"The Ballad of Xavier" was the favored tune. It was a
soulful rendering of the details of Xavier's accident and
subsequent rise to power and glory. Another new
composition, "The Searching," honored Zandu's unwavering faith and determination in finding Xavier. Although at first somewhat reticent, Xavier engaged with
many in the crowd and began performing individual
readings at their request. The more of these he did, the
stronger he felt and the sharper his powers grew. Xavier
bathed himself in the glorious, healing mentaar of his
people and began to believe once again that life could
hold purpose and meaning. Perhaps Xavier could never
return to the world he knew, but for the moment,
enjoying the passionate love bestowed upon him by these
people, his people, was enough.

Occasionally Xavier would come across an individual
whose particular neurosis would cause him to dissociate.
The training of Mahler proved useful; the bird would alert
Xavier with a screech of his name, jolting him back to
reality. Upon discovering that he had just dissociated,
Xavier would become angry and quickly push away the
offending person. Others in the vicinity would see this
and drag the offending party away, often with violence.
Cries of "Heretic!" rang out, and these unfortunate

individuals were stoned, beaten, and driven out of camp with only their lives. Upon witnessing this, Xavier was struck with horrible guilt and nausea. He screamed out for them to stop this behavior but didn't wait for their response, instead fleeing the camp by foot. Zandu pursued him and overtook him, managing to intercept him.

"Xavier! Xavier, wait! They mean no harm, they simply do not understand. All they saw was their savior, their chosen one, being driven into some form of sickness by a few individuals. This naturally frightened and infuriated them. They meant only to follow your lead and drive them away. You are everything to the Xavierists; you cannot desert them because they tried to protect you!"

"Yes, Zandu, you are correct as far as it goes. But to hit them? To stone them? My god, do they think we are in biblical times? Do they think I am Jesus Christ?"

"No, neither, although certainly these are people who care not what times these are. They care only that you have been chosen by God to have special powers, to heal the masses of their twisted mentaars and to lead the devout to ultimate serenity. Those who threaten that end are enemies, and although you and I do not condone physical abuse, these offending people do need to be removed. Simply speak to the people, explain to them what form of sickness this is that you experience, and then tell them to go about removing the offending parties peacefully."

Xavier did not respond, other than dutifully nodding his head. He went back to camp and cautiously ad-dressed his people, explaining how he could not tolerate individuals with neuroses too similar to his own remain-ing ones. He told of the wonder of his bird, and explained how Mahler helped him. He also pledged to his people that he would not reject them if they acted over-zealously out of love for him. At the end of this healing reparation, Zandu called out for a group Ascension. Xavier watched in amazement as the gathered mass of people collectively went through the first step of symbolically recreating the accident. They all likewise went through "The Learning" and "The Blinding," the latter accompanied by the music of "Vers La Flamme" played through several trucks with loud stereo systems. Then followed "The Revelry," and here Xavier was struck by the combination of actual and simulated sex being performed right in front of him. Most of the sex was symbolic, and not everyone had partners, either. But the sight of over a dozen couples actively having sexual intercourse right in front of him was highly stimulating for Xavier. He felt a lust come over him which would not be denied, and called forth "Who would lay down with Xavier?!" A small horde of women came running forward, and Xavier used Mahler's eyes to great advantage to select the prettiest and most voluptuous of the younger women. She was not tall, very curvy, and still had flowing blond locks, not giving in to the head shaving that some of the Xavierists had done. Xavier took her and immediately laid her down on the ground. He proceeded to rip her Harlequin colored clothes completely off. He had no use for symbolic sex, or for foreplay at that moment, and quickly mounted her. The act drove the gathered into a wilder frenzy, and many of those who had earlier chosen not to engage in actual intercourse now could not restrain themselves. In the midst of a sea of orgasmic moans, several Xavierists began to vent their aggressiveness, and the prepared furniture soon began flying. After deliriously satisfying his lust, Xavier joined the ranks of destructors. He ran for the nearest piece of furniture and ensued with his share of the destruction. The tropical plain became a scene of carnage as everyone got into this act of wild abandon. Some in the crowd chose to vent their anger on each other, but the amount

of person-to-person violence was fairly minimal. Zandu
had effectively trained the people to displace their rage
onto inanimate objects. Following a good half hour of
demolition, Xavier joined the entire gathering in the final
step, "The Serenity," in which all sat peaceably and
experienced a quiet joy and tranquility. After this, Xavier
was besieged by worshipers, who wanted either to praise
him for bringing them new faith, or to ask for another
reading from him.

Xavier was quite fatigued, and realized it would be
difficult for him to get the rest he always needed after this
level of exertion. He looked around and spotted the girl
he had just had sex with, and asked her if she would be
his companion and chauffeur back to his home in
Islamorada. She eagerly agreed, and when asked, informed Xavier that her name was Clara. Her name
reminded Xavier of Clara Schumann, and he wondered
if somehow she was musically oriented. She was,
actually, although her voice was her instrument, not the
piano. Xavier asked her to serenade him on the way back,
but he only heard the first few bars of a popular song
before he lapsed off into a deep sleep.

Clara awoke Xavier when they arrived at the outskirts
of Islamorada, and he navigated her to his home. After
feeding Scriabin, Xavier asked Clara to prepare a meal, so
she made the best of the limited available supplies. The
food partially re-energized Xavier, as did the sight of
Clara. He witnessed her shapely form covered tightly
from head to toe. She had been forced to grab someone
else's too-small clothes after Xavier had ripped her
Harlequin robe. He felt another surge of passion, and
more gently pulled her onto the bed, this time having at
least enough control to not destroy the only clothes she
had. He blanched for a minute upon realizing how
animalistic his sexual behaviors had been of late, and took
the time to cater to Clara's needs first. The skills

developed with the nurses while Xavier was hospitalized were used to excite Clara, and Xavier threw in a new twist.   In addition to mentally stimulating her into orgasm, he simultaneously freed her from the mild apprehension she was feeling due to some old hang-ups she had about sex.   Once she had been satisfied beyond her wildest carnal dreams, he asked her to sing something classical while she sat on top of him.   She complied with a passionate rendering of the luscious Ravel's "Sheherazade." Xavier was not familiar with the piece, but it didn't matter.   The sheer pleasure of experiencing her exquisitely sexy body, plus hearing her beautiful and sensual voice, was beyond description.   Xavier's screams of ejaculatory joy coupled with those of the still climaxing soprano to create a duet of ecstasy.

The next thing Xavier knew, he sensed that time had passed. After locating his ectopic eyesight, he discovered that it was morning.   Clara had already been up and cooked breakfast. After becoming fully awake, Xavier sat down with her and ate. As he did, he more fully read her psyche and found her to be a very sheltered rich man's daughter, who was quite naive and immature.   Amazingly, there was a near-total absence of conflict in her, especially since Xavier had removed the one sexual conflict she had.   She seemed totally brainwashed in her devotion to Xavier. But it was not love, by any means. It was service. Duty. Everything done willingly, but more out of a sense of doing what one was expected to for a savior. Interesting.

Xavier felt stronger and better this morning, and went for a jog with Scriabin, followed by a brief swim. Upon his return he prepared to shower, and asked Clara to come and help him. He did not need help, but used the opportunity to invite her into the shower. They lathered each other's torsos for a long time, and then sensually progressed downward. Within a few minutes they were both again steaming with passion. As Xavier kissed Clara and lifted her onto him, he had an immediate flashback to his interlude with Lana. The memory of her, and what he ultimately did to her, instantly quelled his current libidinous surge and he nearly dropped Clara onto the shower floor. Xavier felt a flood of sadness coupled with another wave of remorse, and burst into tears. He fled out of the bathroom and dove into his bed, rolling his wet body around in the sheets. Several minutes later an equally tearful Clara tip-toed near the bed, and asked Xavier if she had done something to displease him. Xavier yelled "No!" and then instructed her to give him some privacy.

Regardless of this negative interchange, later in the day Xavier was back on his lustful ways, and spent much of the balance of the day making love to Clara. Xavier read the pain and confusion in Clara's psyche and simply made it disappear. Xavier was quite content to do nothing but rest, eat, exercise with his pets, listen to music and make love to Clara. He carried on with this for several days, and every time Clara showed a sign of creeping concern, Xavier would wipe it out and restore her contented complacency. Xavier could not wipe out his own concern about the waiting Xavierists, however, and knew he had to return to see them. One morning, after yet another passionate romantic encounter with Clara, he asked her to drive him back to the camp.

Upon their return they were greeted by an eager Zandu, who rushed out to speak with Xavier. "We have missed you."

"Indeed. I have. . . rested. Are things well here?"

"In general, yes. I have explained to the masses that you always require a period of rest after heavy mental exertion, and this seems to have quieted their concerns. They have occupied their time with repairing the broken furniture and cleaning camp. They do miss you greatly, and do not understand why you cannot rest here with them."

"Although their mentaar is a healing balm, for the most part, it is very powerful; and I doubt that I could truly rest being so alerted by it. Besides, I have a place with my dog which gives me the privacy I need."

"Very well, I believe they will comprehend and accept this. But there is one more matter. If you will excuse us, Clara." After Clara departed, the two walked off into a shady area removed from the gathering. Zandu halted first and announced, "Xavier, the people need more leadership. They are not nomads at heart; most of them left well-appointed homes and steady jobs. They have much money, and are eager to give it to you to help them build a city. Your city. They even wish to call it Xaviera. They will not live in tents the rest of their lives. We need to plan, to purchase land, to legitimize these people's existence. They are men and women of dignity and purpose, not renegades who gladly keep one step ahead of the law. We have builders, developers and construction workers amongst the ranks, even an architect. They all are grateful for your healing readings and your message of serenity, but they cannot sit idly by waiting for you to make your appearances."

"Very well. I did not ask for this, but I will accept this responsibility. Take a collection and let us see what our financial resources are for land purchase and development."

"I already have."

"What?"

"Yes, I've already taken a collection. You have two and a half million dollars to get started with."

CHAPTER THIRTY-FOUR

"This Xavier must be stopped."

The voice was that of Gunner Volkman, the leader of a small but nationwide group of right-wing fundamentalists called "People's Coalition against Cultists and Communists," or "Picks" for short. The Picks' central base was in Dallas, Texas, but this branch was located in Crystal River, Florida, not far from the nuclear power plant. Originally, they had plenty of targets, including the "communist" liberals who protested nuclear power. However, with the deterioration of the Soviet Union and its influence, the Picks had set their sights more on cultist activities. Their major goal had become to locate and help weaken any atheistic or satanic group activities. In south Florida, their spies had just reported the beginning construction of an entire new city of Xavier cult followers.

"How will we do it, Gunner? They are totally self-contained, or will be soon. We can't cut them off from important supplies, because they don't need any, other than electricity from Miami."

"That is a thought, Stan; cut off their electricity. There may be other ways, better ways. Basically their entire operation revolves around one man, this bald freak named Xavier. Assassination would certainly kill their movement, but alas, it is usually not our way. However, perhaps there is a way to psychologically assassinate this Xavier, rob him of his will, his dream. I understand that he is already somewhat emotionally unstable. Who here has studied Xavier in depth?" A thin woman with close-cropped, dark hair and severe lips strode forward. "I am Elaine, a new member of the Picks, ever since my husband was killed by Satanic cults near Ocala. I have followed Xavier since I caught wind of his story while he was still at the University of Florida. I first wondered if he was in fact a disguised Satanist himself, but I am fairly sure that he is not associated with the Satanists proper. However, the effects of his movement may be far more powerful and dangerous than the Satanists ever could be. Part of the danger lies in the fact that he truly does possess some special powers, although they appear to be nothing more than some enhanced ESP type abilities. He cannot kill people with his mind, nor can he even move a penny with it. He can, however, influence thousands of people to follow him, worship him, even give up everything for him. Also, he is not alone in the development of this movement; there are two others. The first is a woman named Lana, an agent who has been helping Xavier gain power, fame and money. Of late, she apparently has been on assignment apart from Xavier, with her last known whereabouts being in the Miami area. Perhaps she is conducting marketing or recruiting for them at this time. The second person of importance is a Southern California guru named Zandu, who has organized the masses of followers. It appears that this Zandu has assumed a role of greater importance than Lana."

"Thank you, Elaine; you will be a most valuable member of our organization. I agree that Xavier represents a grave threat, possessing the potential to threaten the fabric of organized religion. Now, I will entertain ideas about how to cripple Xavier and his organization."

And so the Picks planned and plotted, racking their brains for creative ways to sabotage Xavierism. Little did they know that theirs was not the only group of concerned citizens. In fact there were several religious, political and governmental groups who were studying the threat of Xavierism and considering whether measures needed to be taken to thwart it. Prior to her departure, Lana had known that some of this was starting, having received several death threats. Zandu had gotten the message as well, but had expected resistance and tossed it aside with the same resolve and fearlessness that he had been showing all along.

At that moment, Zandu was not worried about resistance movements. He was more concerned about the management of a growing city. Xavierism had attracted another one thousand converts in the span of a couple of weeks in South Florida. The movement was thriving, and Xavier had gotten into a new ritual of sorts, coming once daily for a speech, some therapeutic readings, and a group performance of The Ascension. He would then spend some time with Zandu and other leaders of the community in helping plan its development. He would then return with Clara to his home in Islamorada for rest and time with Scriabin. Xavier still continued to be possessed by tremendous sexual and aggressive impulses, but the combination of absorbing the healing mentaar of the Xavierists, performing The Ascension, and enjoying the privacy of his secluded home, was enough to keep his moods relatively stable. Xavier would still have bouts of intense melancholy, and could not forgive himself for his actions against Lana. In the midst of listening to some of the more painful passages of Mahler's symphonies, Xavier would cry out, "I love you, Lana, and I am sorry." Clara would come running, and comfort him, but he was inconsolable at these times. Clara remained a good housekeeper, companion, chauffeur and love slave, but Xavier had no true feelings for her other than gratitude. In fact at times of intense sex, Xavier would unconsciously cry out "Lana!" while fantasizing about making love to her.

Xavier did grow somewhat fatigued by the process of playing developer of his own community. It reminded him too much of his family heritage, and he felt like "a Howell" for a moment. It was at that moment that Xavier decided he needed to remain pure and dedicated to the task of pursuing his dreams. He discussed plans with Zandu, and saw that eventually, bringing Xavierists into Xaviera would become an unwieldy proposition. Instead, bringing Xavierism back to the masses again made more sense. Besides, the populace of Xaviera had heard his messages over and over, and for the most part possessed a very healthy mentaar. Even though Xavier had grown to detest going on a road trip, at this point it seemed the only realistic way to spread his dream. The dream itself had grown from its early version, now encompassing a broader, more lofty goal of helping show everyone in America the waste of humanity caused by neurotic conflict, prejudice, and hate. Further, he would show them how to purge themselves of these negative mind states. The only way to do this was to go out to the people, which included working with the media. However, he had learned from the errors which hampered his last tour, such as picking cities which were likely to have an overly aggressive or hostile mentaar. He was determined to not make these mistakes again.

Zandu suggested some medium-sized, benign California cities such as Berkeley or Sacramento. Xavier, however, had always been impressed with Denver hospitality, and fancied it a good place to start as it was "The Mile-High City," therefore closer to the sun. Xavier did accept Zandu's suggestion to use some furniture on stage for purging of rage if it became necessary. Xavier decided he would not only take Clara along for the ride, he would also take Scriabin. In order to avoid travel problems and unwanted public attention, they would drive. It would take at least a week to get the show arranged anyway, so they could take their time on the drive. Clara had been a continuous source of youthful energy and hope, and Xavier certainly was in need of these qualities at times. Further, she knew that Xavier periodically removed her anxieties; she not only didn't seem to mind, but was grateful. He had otherwise treated her with respect, outside of his use of her for sexual gratification. Xavier was pleased to find that she had been exposed to a fair amount of culture during her childhood, although she had not really developed a true love of fine music, art and literature.

Xavier, Clara, and the two pets loaded into the Jeep Cherokee and began their long journey. Xavier took the trip as an opportunity to be a teacher of sorts to Clara. She was close to being a tabula rasa, absorbing everything Xavier could put into her. She did not fully comprehend what Xavier saw in the music of Scriabin, although she appreciated the Chopin-like melodies of his earlier works. Clara asked that during parts of the long daily drives, she be allowed to listen to popular radio music, and Xavier accommodated this request.   He did, however, tend to put himself into a trance state during these times, since he had lost whatever taste he had for the likes of Paula Abdul and Bruce Springsteen. Clara at times would alert him to see something of beauty or importance, such as animals in the wild or impressive sunsets. She had

learned what Xavier considered important and what he
didn't. For instance, the one time she alerted him to see
an impressive building, Xavier rewarded her with a
nearly uncontrollable rage. She would not make that
mistake again. Xavier learned that Clara was not unintel-
ligent, yet she tended to play the dumb blonde role a bit
too much, perhaps in part to deter her parents from
putting heavier expectations upon her than she could
tolerate. Clara managed to navigate the entourage quite
well without any help from Xavier. Due to efficient
driving, they arrived in Denver two days earlier than
expected.

Xavier requested that they find a small, unobtrusive
motel on the outskirts of town instead of the ritzy
penthouses Lana used to put him up in. He did this in
part to avoid hassles, but more so in order to be able to
jog with Scriabin. The daily jogs with his beloved Dane
helped quell the tenuously quiescent beast inside of
Xavier. All seemed well on the eve of the big show, set
to be held in Mile High Stadium. Xavier was fortunate to
be able to get it on such short notice, but the stadium was
sold out in a matter of days despite such little advance
time. The show was being billed as "Xavier - Mind Master
for Mankind." Xavier was not particularly pleased with
the title, but did not have Lana to negotiate and simply
agreed to the terms put forth. He would earn some fifty
thousand for the show, but money seemed to be somewhat irrelevant at that point.

By show time Xavier had prepared himself well, now
knowing that vigorous exercise and sex tended to steady
him more than even his usual meditations. As he used
to, he opened by telling his story, but now had a few more
chapters to add to the saga. Xavier could tell that the
elapsed time since his last public appearance had served
to create renewed doubt, but there was also a sense of
awe that regardless, this man called Xavier was a spec-

tacle. After the telling of his history, he proceeded to talk about his dreams and his hopes for the future. The crowd was impressed, and strained to remain hushed, but periodically broke into cheers. Xavier then read the crowd's mentaar, and for the most part found it relatively healthy, with a heavier loading of hope and optimism than their negative brethren in other cities. Instead of playing parlor games and making whole sections of the audience fall asleep, Xavier informed the crowd that he would put the ones with hostility and hate in their hearts in a meditative state. Gasps of awe then echoed throughout the stadium as one by one, Xavier detected individuals who contributed severely negative mentaar and put them each in a meditative coma. The effect had a twofold purpose: to erase the doubt lingering in the audience's minds, and also to purify the mentaar as much as possible, helping Xavier keep his composure. Xavier was proud of himself, and breezed through a dozen individual therapeutic readings with only one dissociation and no violent acting out. The show was a fantastic success and the crowd did not want to let go of a new hero.

Nevertheless, Xavier grew very fatigued and nearly had to be escorted off by Clara. She took him back to the motel, where he collapsed and slept until noon of the following day. After a good breakfast in bed from Clara, Xavier felt very rested and peaceful. Through Clara's eyes he read in the newspaper about his glorious exploits. The media remained skeptical about Xavier's long-term plans and dreams, but there was no longer any doubt about Xavier's superior mental abilities or his charisma. The latter had certainly grown along with his powers. The articles energized Xavier, so he decided to take Scriabin for a jog along the mountain road they had traveled on to find the motel. Scriabin as usual was so excited that he almost knocked Xavier over by his jump-

ing. The two set out along the fairly steeply inclined road,
heading downward to start. Xavier had to calm Scriabin
a bit; he was so rambunctious that, at first, he nearly
dragged Xavier down the hill. Mahler was with Xavier
and, as had been their custom, flew overhead, providing
Xavier with an aerial view whenever he wanted it. Xavier
and company went about two miles or so before the road
leveled off, and they approached an intersection along
the way. Just as they passed it, a pickup truck loaded
with men drove past them and then turned around. Four
beefy red-neck types got out of the truck and blocked
Xavier's path. The largest, a black-bearded man with
only three fingers on his right hand, held up that deficient
hand in a message of "Stop!" Xavier felt the mentaar of
the four and knew immediately that they meant him
harm. They began to interrogate Xavier, and then
informed him that they felt he was a menace to society.
Scriabin was getting the message, too, and began to
growl. The men arrogantly demanded that Xavier give
up his nonsense and live a quiet life in private. And not
in Denver. Xavier detected venom in their hearts and
grew fearful. He decided to take no chances, and put all
four of them to sleep. As soon as the four lugs crashed
to the ground, Xavier took off for the motel, running as
fast as he could. Scriabin helped by dragging Xavier at an
even faster pace than he was normally capable of. With
the motel in sight and Xavier nearly out of breath, he
slowed to a walk and kept Scriabin on his left side. With
almost no warning a truck came barreling around the last
bend, at full speed and directly at Xavier. Xavier reacted
at the very last second, as he had caught a glimpse of the
truck through the overhead eyes of Mahler. He threw his
arms out and leapt with all of his might toward the ditch
on the side of the road. At that same instant, he heard a
loud thud, and simultaneously felt a searing pain rip
through him. As the truck sped on past, Xavier was only

aware of the hard ground he came in contact with, and an unlocalized pain within him. He called on Mahler to come closer so that he could get a look to see what the damage was. The minute Xavier surveyed the scene with the bird's eyes, he nearly vomited as he was overwhelmed with a sickening sight. It was Scriabin, not himself, who had been hit by the truck, and it was Scriabin's pain that he felt. The pain, however, soon gave way to anguish, since the poor dog lay bloody and lifeless on the road.

CHAPTER THIRTY-FIVE

The news hit Xaviera like one of the unexpected storms common to the tropics and south Florida. Zandu had gathered most of the growing city's populace and informed them that Xavier's dog Scriabin had been killed. An immediate tidal wave of mourning broke out, with many falling to their knees wailing. After the first wave of anguish, Zandu waited a bit and then held up his hand to signal that he had more to tell. The crowd quieted, and then turned their attention to their ever-diligent leader. The people of Xaviera had come to respect Zandu enormously, relied on him frequently, and almost always followed his directions. They had to, for Xavier was not always available and their love of him at times made practical matters seem unworthy of bringing to his attention. It had become the role of Zandu to handle matters of government, justice, and resolution of minor disputes. It had also become his role to be the bearer of news, good or bad.

The bad news continued. Following the murder of Scriabin, Xavier had cancelled the remainder of his tour. He was extremely depressed, and had landed himself in jail for a day for disorderly conduct. Apparently, after police failed to make significant efforts to pursue the killers of Scriabin, Xavier had gotten furious and physically assaulted one of the policemen involved. The police felt the dog's death was just an accident. They failed to believe the truth that all of the Xavierists feared, that this was a deliberate murder designed to deter Xavier from following his path of destiny and righteousness. There was no clue as to the identity of the killers, and Xavier was ill-equipped to conduct an investigation on his own. The police station had even tried to have Xavier committed to a local psychiatric hospital, but as soon as the local psychiatrists were called in they wanted no part of even examining Xavier. Clara had told Zandu this saga, and stated that Xavier was unbearable to live with, refusing to speak with her or anyone else. She promised to attempt to get him back to Xaviera as soon as possible.

The news of Xavier's instability sent further shock waves throughout the crowd, sending several into a panic. The timing for this collection of bad news couldn't have been worse, for over the past week a new unrest had arisen in Xaviera. A factionalism had developed involving different philosophies about the proper tenets and dogma of Xavierism. The majority of followers had grown to believe that in The Revelry, symbolic sex and violence actually represented a higher level of mental development, and that this was the desirable form of Xavierism. They argued that Xavier himself preached that ultimately, all base drives would be purged and that there would be no aggression, no lust, and that copulation would only be required for reproduction. By acting out the base drives symbolically, they were still continu-

ing the process of purging, while simultaneously growing closer to Xavier's ultimate state. This group was self-
dubbed the Paxavierists, in an effort to emphasize their
peace-loving orientation.

This branching off of original Xavierist protocol was
unacceptable to some of the more outspoken members of
the community. Although initially tolerant of those who
chose symbolic Revelry, these individuals who preferred
active sex and violence grew furious that the others were
presumptuous enough to proclaim that their way was
wrong. Or even more insulting, that they were somehow
developmentally more primitive than the Paxavierists.
Indeed, this small but vocal minority felt that carrying
through with actual sex and violence was the only way
that an actual catharsis of base drives could occur. They
felt that the Paxavierists were deluding themselves by
repressing the expression of these drives and were thus
actually breeding more neurosis. This was the exact
opposite of what Xavier had sought to achieve. Xavier
himself was purging and purifying himself not via symbolic acts of sex and violence but through the real thing.
This group of predominantly male Xavierists dubbed
themselves The Revelrents, and in fact began segregating
themselves into one end of the new and developing city.

Zandu had formed a city council composed of six
elders in the community who commanded widespread
respect. Zandu himself had publicly refused to accept a
need for factionalism. Only two of the seven total
councilmen were Revelrents. Negotiation on this dispute
was heated, and over the past several days, no resolution
of the dilemma had been found. Zandu had been unable,
for the first time, to come up with a good solution, or even
just a good pacification to keep his community calm and
orderly until Xavier returned. The best he could do was
to try to preach tolerance until Xavier himself could
resolve the dilemma. Therefore the delivery of news that

Xavier himself had met misfortune, and was not soon to be of help, precipitated an even greater than expected turmoil. The Revelrents were outraged at the lack of justice, and felt strongly that this was just the beginning. They worried that they would encounter more attacks on their sacred leader and on the Xavierist community. They argued that a strong defense of some kind was necessary, that a totally pacifist, liberal stance would set them up for certain doom. The Paxavierists argued back that this kind of "kill or be killed" mentality had served to start many wars and illustrated exactly the kind of hate and paranoia that Xavier was attempting to stamp out. Zandu, himself secretly Paxavierist at heart, was beginning to doubt his private position more each day, particularly after he screened the volumes of mail that he received for Xavier. There were increasing amounts of hate mail, death threats, and even a few bizarre messages. For instance, he received a package containing a dead mynah bird with the message, "Unholy use of God's animals will lead to oblivion." Another package contained a Bible and a gun with no message at all. Zandu was being forced to at least recognize that the Xavierist movement, no matter how peace-loving it could become, would threaten those who were not peace-loving and who would use violent means to thwart or destroy it. The more bold and outspoken of these people actually proclaimed the righteousness of their organizations along with their threats. This in-cluded the KKK, some fundamentalist religious organiza-tions in the Bible Belt, and some obscure outfits with odd names such as The Organization for Political Progress, The Americans for Freedom, Faith and Fairness, and The Peoples Coalition against Cultists and Communism. In general these groups sounded ill-informed and power-less, so Zandu tended to disregard their threats.

In the case of "The Peoples Coalition," Zandu was correct that they were ill-informed, for they were unaware of Lana's split from the Xavierist cause. They were not, however, powerless, for at the same time Zandu was trying to sort out the various problems with his community, the Picks were busy creating an even bigger problem.

*   *   *

Gunner Volkman congratulated his subordinates for excellent scouting and surveillance. Lana Marshall had been located. She was staying alone at a Miami Beach hotel, spending time with friends on her new boat, which was moored just out to sea. Gunner and three other Picks were housed in a fifth floor room in a relatively old and small hotel across the street. It paled in comparison to the majestic Fountainbleu that Lana was in, but it was mostly vacant and quite obscure. This provided them with the privacy and secrecy that they needed. Gunner looked through his telescope, which was focused on a hotel room at about the same level up in the Fountainbleu. As he continued surveying his prey, he was granted the unexpected pleasure of seeing Lana Marshall undress.

"Hmm. . . Nice ass. Great tits, too. This may be even more fun than I anticipated. OK, let's go."

The foursome eagerly bolted out of their room. Upon arriving at the Fountainbleu, they unobtrusively made their way inside. They all gathered at room 417, and Sancho, the Pick disguised as a bellman, knocked at the door.

"Hello, Ms. Marshall, this is a hotel representative. We need to discuss your bill, please."

Lana finished dressing in casual clothes and approached the door, but did not open it. She peered through the small lens embedded in the door and saw only the uniformed Hispanic.

"What is wrong? I left my credit card indent when I checked in. That should cover my three-day stay."

"Perhaps there is some mistake, but apparently it did

not go through. We will need you to use a different card, or another form of payment. The management is sorry for the inconvenience, but I can correct the situation here, saving you a trip to the front desk."

"Very well, I will get my purse." Lana was suspicious, and upon getting her purse she took out the can of mace she kept for emergencies. She cautiously opened the door, and immediately Sancho lunged at her. Lana fired the mace directly in his face, and he recoiled backward, crying out in misery. Yet at that same instant the three others poured into the room and all lunged for Lana as well. She had just enough time to fire the mace at one other intruder, partially disabling him, but the other two tackled her down to the ground, pinning her arms. Gunner wrestled the mace away from her hand, while the other Pick covered Lana's mouth to make her stop screaming. Gunner put his chiseled face directly in front of Lana's and firmly stated, "Do not scream; we will not harm you."

After a minute or so of futile struggling, particularly after the two gagging Picks had recovered and joined in the restraining of Lana, she ceased resisting. They lifted her onto a chair and proceeded to tie her down. While his henchmen completed this task, Gunner Volkman sat down opposite to Lana and addressed her.

"It is so nice to make your acquaintance, Lana Marshall. I am Gunner, leader of an organization that is dedicated to aiding the fight against subversive cult groups. We have temporarily detained you in order to aid our cause of thwarting the rise of a man called Xavier."

"Xavier! I no longer have anything to do with Xavier!"

"Oh, really? Our intelligence informs us that you are the key agent and companion of this demigod named Xavier."

"Your intelligence must be mentally retarded. I fled from Xavier's side several weeks ago after he raped me and proved to me that he was mentally unstable."

"Very good attempt, possibly even true. However, I tend to doubt it, as you are not far from his camp. I suspect that you are probably doing marketing and networking for him from a distance."

"You're absolutely crazy! I'm here on a vacation, to get away from that maniac and sort through my thoughts."

"Again a good try, but again doubtful. Even if what you say is true, you may have value to us anyway, as this Xavier will not allow you to come to harm because of him. Please be assured that we have no intention of killing you, for it is not our way. We are a civilized organization trying to help our beleaguered country in whatever way we can. If you remain calm, we will take good care of you while we proceed with efforts to contact Xavier."

As Sancho finished tightening the knots on Lana's hands, he reached around. He grabbed Lana's left thigh with one hand, and fondled her breasts with the other. She yelled out, "Stop it!" and Gunner walked over next to her.

"Sancho! Get your hands off the lady! My apologies, Ms. Marshall, my men are not yet fully disciplined. They definitely need further training. In fact, now is a good time to start." Gunner pulled out a knife and cut open Lana's buttoned blouse. He then pulled the large bra down under her breasts, which made them sit upright as if on display. He then reached to each thigh and sliced open Lana's skirt. Gunner stowed his knife, then reached out and put his palms on the outside of Lana's breasts. He then slowly pulled his hands back, barely touching her breasts with his fingertips. He addressed the petrified Lana.

"My men need to learn restraint. They will have to stare at your magnificent body but not touch it, or I will shoot their hands off. The same, of course, does not apply to me."

Lana shut her eyes and tried to block out the sound of the devilish laugh of this evil man standing in front of her. It seemed her suffering on account of Xavier had not completely ended. Indeed, it possibly might have only just begun.

CHAPTER THIRTY-SIX

Clara breathed a fatigued sigh of relief as she saw the now familiar sign saying "Come Swim With The Dolphins In Islamorada." She pressed on the gas pedal of the rented car just a bit harder, eager to finish the ordeal of getting Xavier home. They had actually flown from Denver to Miami, yet the trip home seemed much harder than the trip to Denver because of Xavier's state. He had lapsed into an involutional melancholia, a nearly catatonic state of muteness and lethargy. Part of it was self-induced, as Xavier used whatever self-control he still possessed to maintain a near brain-dead state of mental activity. Clara was petrified at escorting this mummy, this relic of the great man that she had allowed herself to worship and service. Since Xavier was essentially inca-pacitated, he was not able to quell any of Clara's fears. This left her in a heightened state of anxiety, magnified in comparison to her tranquilized moods of the past couple of weeks.

Clara pulled the car up into the driveway of Xavier's oceanside home and helped lead him inside. She led him directly to the bed, where he collapsed into a deep sleep. Although Mahler continued to be his never-ending companion, even the bird seemed disturbed, nestling uncomfortably on his old bedside perch. Clara herself went to bed, and tried to sleep as well, albeit somewhat unsuccessfully. She was eager for morning to come, as at least she could relieve some of her anxieties by cooking. She cooked a massive breakfast, with enough eggs, pancakes, juices and toast to feed four people. Unfortunately, after Xavier awoke he showed little interest in eating. In fact he showed little interest in anything, with the exception of going to his listening room and listening to some Rachmaninoff. After Clara heard him play "The Isle of the Dead" some seven or eight times in a row, she became so alarmed that she couldn't stand it. She called Zandu and informed him that they had arrived but that Xavier was not well. Zandu stated that he was relieved that they had arrived, and that Clara should attempt to persuade Xavier to come, as his people needed him. If she could not persuade him to come that day, Zandu promised he would come down the next day and help get him back to Xaviera.

Zandu did not tell Clara that he had his hands full dealing with the civil unrest, not to mention a new-found possible problem: Some quack organization claimed to have kidnapped Lana Marshall, and was holding her ransom for ten million dollars plus a pledge to disband Xavierism. The PCCC, as they identified themselves, demanded a response within twenty-four hours or they promised to send one of Lana's rings, with her finger attached, as proof of their seriousness. Zandu was instructed to call a certain number to respond, and was informed that the phone was a stolen cellular portable.

Therefore, tracing the number would serve no purpose other than alerting the Picks to treachery.

*   *   *

Gunner Volkman carried the small phone, being rather fond of the novelty of its compactness. He gripped it tightly for a moment, allowing his surge of anger to pass after several long moments. He had just received very unfavorable news from his head spy, Stan. The information obtained from the new Pick, Elaine, had indeed been several weeks old, and people in Xaviera seemed oblivious to the disappearance of Lana. Thus Gunner Volkman had to grapple with the likely reality that what Lana had told them was true. Nevertheless, the overall game plan remained powerful, and they would play out their hand. Gunner was extremely displeased at Elaine for not being accurate and for making him look ignorant. He chastised himself internally for allowing himself to trust a newcomer. He summoned her to their temporary hole-up in the Fountainbleu and interrogated her about the details of her surveillance. She was heartbroken at hearing the news, and ran out of the room just before Gunner was about to throw her out of the Picks.

Elaine did not give up so easily, however. She had heard rumors that Xavier was living somewhere south of Miami, and she got in her car and began a journey for redemption. She followed the same route as Zandu had weeks earlier, stopping at gas stations and restaurants asking about a bald-headed man wearing black-on-white clothing. She had more immediate success than Zandu had, and after only an hour's search discovered an oceanside villa with a white Jaguar and another car outside. She drove past and waited for nightfall, then returned to within a few hundred yards and got out of her car. She prepared herself for her mission, donning dark clothing and putting black shoe polish on her face. The night was not clear, and Elaine found it relatively easy to unobtrusively slither her way to just outside the house. She peered in the window and saw nothing but a nearly empty room. She worked her way around the house and, upon spying the third room, she found what she was looking for: a bald man sleeping with a black bird perched next to him on the nightstand. The window was not locked and a standard Florida window screen was easily cut through. Elaine climbed into the room quietly, but Mahler detected her presence and began screeching "Xavier! Xavier!" As Xavier began to awaken, the lithe woman deftly ran across the room and neatly snatched the bird into a gunny sack. Xavier gained his senses and, despite his blindness, knew what was happening. He yelled out "Intruder! Face me, you coward, instead of stealing my bird!" but he could sense her escaping presence. He then thought to reach out his mind into the night, and tried to focus on tranquilizing the fleeing villain. He connected with the woman's cortex for an instant, slowing her down, but a great surge of adrenaline in her overrode the progressively attenuated signal coming from Xavier. She fought through it like running barefoot on soft sand, and gradually regained her full stride, disappearing into the night.

Xavier was left in his blindness, and proclaimed his anguish by screaming a blood-curdling wail at the top of his lungs. A petrified Clara ran in and discovered him helplessly kneeling, defeated, on the floor. She turned on the lights and observed the open window, and realized that Mahler was gone. She gingerly tried to voice a word of comfort for Xavier, but this seemed only to precipitate a breakthrough of rage. Xavier aggressively leapt to his feet. He began swinging wildly, running around the room, breaking everything he could get his hands on. Clara stood motionless for a second, paralyzed by her fear, but then fled out of the room. She grabbed only her purse, scrambled out and started the rental car. As she frantically drove off, she fought to block out the fading screams of a helpless, defeated Xavier.

The next day, when Zandu returned to Islamorada, the Xavier he found was not the man he used to know. The maelstrom of fury that had consumed him the previous day had waned, and Xavier was again frozen in mute catatonia. The only evidence of his existence was his breathing and the fact that he was listening to music. It was somber music, Zandu noticed, with melodies created out of some composer's anguish and misery. Zandu tried to act as if nothing had changed, and greeted Xavier warmly. Xavier barely even moved. Zandu firmly grabbed him by the shoulders and addressed him more seriously.

"Xavier, you must not give in to your own emotions. I can see that you have been dealt yet another blow, with the loss of your bird and, I presume, Clara. They are replaceable; you are not. You are the one and only Xavier. You may use my eyes, you can use any living thing's eyes on this planet; you have the gift. You have many gifts, but none stronger than your gift to inspire thousands to follow your lead, worship you, believe in you, give up everything for you. You have a vision of a better world, freed from the same kinds of evil people who have caused you such recent misery. Only you can deliver our world from its ugly destiny of perpetual hate and conflict. Come now, come with me to your people; they need you and you need them. Allow their benevolent mentaar to heal your wounds, just as they did before."

Xavier raised his head up, and Zandu could see tears trickle out of his blinded eyes. Xavier borrowed Zandu's eyesight for a second, looking at his own unkempt and disheartened figure. He snapped upright, as a surge of anger seemed to chase the intense despair away. The anger was caused by Xavier's hatred of pity, either by others or by himself. He would not pity himself; he would either correct the situation, or die in the process. The proud Xavier raised up off the chair and wordlessly strode forth, and Zandu knew that this meant it was time to go. As they began to walk out the door, Xavier paused and announced, "We should take the Jaguar; I want my people to know who it is that arrives."

There was no doubt in the people's minds whose Jaguar it was as it slowly made its way up to the main arena of the new city of Xaviera. The "city" was still in its infancy, with many houses and buildings still under construction. It was quite a sight to behold, as the predominant style everywhere was simple, modern and uniform, but uniquely painted only white and black. The sight was much more uplifting than the mentaar, for as they approached, Xavier could feel that all was not well in his camp. Zandu had warned him that there had come to be divisiveness in the camp, with strong difference of opinion on what constituted the truest form of Xavierism. Xavier did not seem troubled by this at first, partly because he did not read deeper into Zandu's psyche to comprehend the magnitude of the problem. Instead, he had already begun to think about what he would say to his people, how he would precipitate a resurgence of positive, strong mentaar which would in turn help himself. Zandu had been correct in his words; only the combination of Xavier and his people could heal each other.

The news of Xavier's return spread like wildfire throughout the camp and all came running to the central arena. A stage and podium had been constructed, with an impressive array of amplifiers for speeches to the masses. Seating had not been constructed yet, as only a concrete slab denoted the seating area. Within ten minutes, over two thousand people jammed together on that slab, the tension and anticipation so tangible it seemed as if the air was electrified. As Xavier slowly

walked to the podium with Zandu's escort, the crowd
cheered "Xavier! Xavier! Xavier!" madly. He was using
Zandu's eyes; upon seeing the masses, he noticed that
many in the crowd had birds on their shoulders, some of
them mynah birds. Xavier took the podium and raised
his hand for silence.

"I have returned to my people, for we need each
other. I have need for sight; who among you would lend
me your bird so that I need not rely on Zandu?"

Several people in the front ranks rushed forward and
eagerly extended their squawking birds to Xavier. Most
of the offered birds were in fact mynahs, but Xavier was
too disheartened at the reminder of his lost friend and
chose a large white Cockatoo instead. He thanked the
woman who graciously parted with the large bird, and
placed it on his shoulder.

"Thank you. Zandu informs me that there is dissension amongst you regarding the proper steps of Ascension to Serenity. I feel the anger and frustration, the
confusion and hostility. I am sorry that I have not been
here to correct this problem, but as you know, I have been
occupied with spreading the message of Xavierism across
the land." Xavier paused for several long moments as he
fought off a wave of sickness, a familiar nausea he had
experienced before when encountering negative mentaars
during his first road trip.

"We must put down our hostilities, let go of our hate,
or certainly we are no better than the bigots and war-
mongers that threaten the future of our planet. The goal
of reaching ultimate serenity is not in question; we all
hold it to our hearts as the hope for our future and the
future of our children. How we get there is not as
important as getting there itself."

With this last sentence Xavier felt an even greater
surge of sickness, this one staggering him. He gripped
the sides of the podium for support, and Zandu jumped

forward to help him but Xavier waved him off.

"I. . . understand that there are many of you who feel that during Ascension. . . there should be only symbolic sex and violence, and others who strongly disagree. The Ascension was a construction of Zandu's to mirror the course of my own ascent to Serenity, to provide a vehicle for you to follow the same path. I truly believe that some actual expression of the base drives must occur before a true state of serenity can be achieved. However, if one chooses the course of following that path symbolically, that is still better than nothing at all. Eventually, symbolic Revelry will be one basis of the higher form of Xavierism. Unfortunately even I am not at that level yet, despite being able to easily displace my base drives onto others. We must all seek our common goal in a way that we are morally and ethically comfortable with, and we must all show tolerance for those who have somewhat different values. As such, I recommend that we put aside our differences and each follow the path to serenity as our conscience dictates."

There were murmurs among the crowd, but none dared challenge the new proclamations of Xavier. Xavier himself felt another surge of disability, and this time had to lean on Zandu for support. Zandu helped him off the stage and escorted him into his private lodging. As they walked, they could both hear renewed chants of "Xavier! Xavier! Xavier!" But both men knew in their hearts that there remained much unspoken dissension, a great tension that jeopardized the welfare of the entire city of Xaviera.

CHAPTER THIRTY-SEVEN

"Dammit, I am losing my patience with these Xavierists. It's been twenty-four hours. I promised to send them one of your fingers, Ms. Marshall, preferably with an identifying ring attached to it. Let me see your hands. . . oh, foolish me, they are tied up. Well, let me see what else we can send."

Gunner Volkman walked up to Lana and circled around her, like a predator eying its kill. He was disturbed in his scrutiny by a knock on the door. "Stan, go see who that is. Send them away."

Stan hurried up to the door and looked through the glass peephole. "It's Elaine!"

"What is she doing back? Send her away, Stan."

The burly Pick spy opened the door and conducted a brief interrogation of Elaine outside in the hall. Stan then allowed her to enter, announcing that she had something important to show Gunner.

"I have tried to redeem myself, sir. I have stolen Xavier's eyes, his bird which he calls Mahler." With that, she removed the sack covering the bird and proudly displayed him, holding on to a homemade leash she had crafted.

"Where did you get this bird?"

"I tracked Xavier down, and found him holed up in a house in Islamorada. I simply broke in and wrested the bird away while he slept."

"Very commendable, Elaine; you show considerable ingenuity. But how are we to know that this is Xavier's bird?"

"Wait just a minute, and he will speak."

"Is that a fact? Well, then, we have time. We will sit and wait for this bird to convince us that he is Xavier's." Gunner displayed his skepticism with a bone-chilling laugh. He told Elaine to sit next to him on the couch and he scrutinized both her and the bird in silence.

Several minutes went by, with not a peep from the bird. Elaine began to perspire and was quite puzzled. On the trip up, the bird had been speaking actively, saying "Xavier!" frequently, as well as many other things.

"It seems that your bird has lost his voice. Laryngitis, perhaps?"

Elaine squirmed a bit more. She then stood up quickly with an idea, and proclaimed, "Wait, he knows this woman, let me give him to her." She turned around and walked over to Lana, placing the bird on her lap. After only a few seconds had passed, the bird perkily announced, "Lana, I love you. Lana, I love you. Lana, I am sorry."

Gunner Volkman nearly fell out of the sofa in disbelief. Lana herself was stunned, and blushed with emotion. The others hooted with amazement and amusement. Gunner then stiffened and called for silence.

"Wait! This is actually an excellent situation. We have

more bargaining power now, since we have two hostages. And unless this bird learned his brief vocabulary from someone else, this bitch Lana is lying. This Xavier really cares about her. Stan, what we need is a videotape. Go get a camcorder, and we will videotape the woman and the bird together, hopefully with the bird providing sound effects. Hurry!"

Within half an hour Stan reappeared with a camcorder, and Gunner did not ask him where he got it. Gunner took it and began filming footage of Lana, who remained gagged and tied up in a chair with much of her body exposed. The mynah bird was placed in her lap, and after about five minutes of filming, cooperated again with screeching first, "Xavier! Xavier!" and then, "Lana, I love you." As soon as he got that on tape, Gunner narrated his new ultimatum that unless they received contact from the Xavierists within three hours, they would rape Lana and then kill her. And kill the bird. Gunner gave the tape to Stan, but rewarded Elaine with the joint responsibility of taking it to the Xavierists. The two departed immediately for Xaviera.

The trip to Xaviera took about forty-five minutes. The two Picks saw the growing city rising out of the tropical wastelands, and it reminded Elaine of an Emerald City in black and white. They worked their way to what seemed to be the main area, and when they asked where the city leader was, they were directed to Zandu's abode. Two Xavierists stood outside, and questioned them on their intentions. They stated that they had a tape from Lana Marshall to give to Xavier. Zandu and Xavier were busy conferring on the status of the threatening civil war, and Zandu in particular flared with anger upon being disturbed by his watchmen. A heavily packaged videotape was delivered; and upon being told what it was, Xavier eagerly insisted they watch it. Zandu grumbled something about this being another prank threat of some kind, but both of them grew immediately silent upon witnessing the image on the television.

Zandu's first reaction was to leap up and yell at his guard to go and detain the deliverer of the tape. This Xavierist ran out of the room but, upon going outside, saw the unwanted visitors already hurriedly departing in their car. Xavier, meanwhile, was desperately trying to get his untrained cockatoo to look at the television, since Zandu's eyes were with his guards. The sight of Lana, half naked and tied down, with Mahler on her lap, was more than he could tolerate. He watched the entire tape, until he heard the voice of Gunner Volkman making his demands. He stood up without saying a word, and walked straight out of the house. Zandu ran after him, breathlessly yelling, "Xavier! Where are you going?"

"I am going to solve the problem that I have created."

"Wait! What does that mean?"

"Zandu, I have caused enough pain. The world is not ready for Xavierism. I have already hurt Lana enough; I will not permit her to suffer any further. I will give my life for hers."

The normally calm and ever diplomatic Zandu lost his cool and began screaming. "You cannot give up! You owe it to the thousands who have given everything for you! We can defeat these infidels!"

"You forget, Zandu, that it is you who started "The Xavierists," you who led these people here, and even you who created "The Ascension." If this is Xavierism, then you are their leader. So lead them!"

With that, Xavier continued to march off. Zandu, totally crazed with fear and confusion, ran after him and tackled him to the ground. Xavier responded defensively and pushed him off, then mentally tranquilized him. Zandu fell to the ground in a heap. Xavier got up and groped for his eyesight, as the bird was flapping and squawking nearby. He followed the trace of its essence and gathered the bird into his arms, then took off for his Jaguar. He sped off, the car weaving back and forth as his new companion's eyes nervously darted away from the road frequently.

The argument and tussle between Xavier and Zandu had been witnessed by several Xavierists, and news of the rift spread like wildfire. Several of the more militant Revelrents saw this as an excellent opportunity to gain power, and they rallied their members to congregate and seize the moment. One of Zandu's guards was actually a Revelrent, and he spread the news that Xavier had gone to give his life to save a woman. The leader of the Revelrent faction, a fiery young man of twenty-nine named Raynaud, took a machine gun and led several of his compatriots to the main arena. He had them turn on the amplifier, and fired several rounds into the air to announce his seriousness. People began flooding out of their homes and other buildings to see what the commotion was about. A gathering mass of people formed in front of Raynaud, many of them already frightened at seeing the sight of a machine gun firing. Raynaud proclaimed triumphantly:

"Xavier is gone! But we are still here! We must survive! Zandu is weak, and the peace-loving Paxavierists mentality will not survive against a world filled with criminals and hate! The war to exterminate us has already begun, and this is just the beginning! We must defend ourselves, arm ourselves, and not delude ourselves into thinking we can forget our basic human aggressiveness! Long live the Revelrents!!"

With that, Raynaud fired another round of machine gun blasts into the air. However, instead of signaling the triumphant rise of the Revelrents, it only precipitated the beginning of all-out chaos. He was charged by a large group of frantic Paxavierists. Raynaud proceeded to open fire directly over their heads. Most of the onrushing

Paxavierists instantly checked their rush, but two of them charged forward with abandon. Raynaud lowered his gun and pumped a round of bullets directly at the legs of the two crazed Paxavierists. The salvo rippled through their thighs with little resistance, effectively amputating both of them as they crumpled to the ground in agony. The sight of blood red on the harlequin colored clothing of the stricken caused many in the crowd to erupt in a violent frenzy. Soon there was all-out pandemonium, with the more aggressive but greatly outnumbered Revelrents wielding either genuine or homemade weapons. Some of the Paxavierists immediately fled, but the majority attempted to physically subdue the Revelrents. Many were overcome, including Raynaud, who was beaten into oblivion with the same weapon of destruction he had brandished a minute ago. Although the surge of still well-meaning Paxavierists had controlled the actions of many of the upstart Revelrents, others had resorted to arson to perpetuate the confusion and chaos. Soon many of the newly constructed wooden buildings were ablaze with flames, and the fire spread rapidly with no resistance. The sight of actual fire stimulated panic even more intensely than the sound of machine gun fire, and the undamaged survivors of the melee fled out of the doomed city with only their lives.

*   *   *

By this point, Xavier was halfway to Islamorada, and not thinking about what he had left behind. Yet all of a sudden he felt the anguish of a thousand souls, and he knew that disaster had struck. It did not deter him from his task at hand, and in fact strengthened his resolve to continue onward. He hurried to his home and, once inside, called the number which had been repeated five times in the videotape. After only one ring, the voice that Xavier recognized from the tape answered.

"Yes?"

"This is Xavier, the man you seek. Xavierism is dead, the city in chaos and the people disbanding as we speak. You have no further need to detain Lana Marshall."

"Ah, but we do. As long as there lives Xavier, there lives Xavierism. We will continue to hold Lana until we receive our monetary demands, plus have proof of Xavierism's demise."

"Your ransom is not reasonable, as I have nowhere near that much money to give you. It does not matter. I am prepared to give my life for Lana's."

Gunner Volkman paused and contemplated the situation. He was genuinely frustrated at the prospect of not getting any money out of this entire proposition. He debated for a second whether Xavier could have been bluffing, and even wondered if Xavier was a poker player. But there was such a sense of despair and anguish in his voice, such a sense of finality, that Gunner concluded his offer was genuine. So, were all of his efforts for naught? Perhaps not, as getting Xavier to commit suicide would be a crowning achievement for the Picks. Yes! The People's Coalition would gain great power and prestige at having felled the Xavierist cult by precipitating a suicide of their leader. Yes, this would be a very suitable ending.

"Xavier, how do you propose to do this deed?"

"I will take an overdose of medication. You will send your spy in four hours, who will find me dead in my Islamorada home."

"How is it that you will do this, not knowing if we will keep our end of the bargain?"

"You forget, I have certain powers. Your spy was named Elaine, and she was cast out of the Picks, only to redeem herself by stealing my bird. I read beyond that to see if I could discern the Pick philosophy, and I gathered that you will do anything to meet your goals except murder. I am not sure why you draw the line there, but that is irrelevant. I cannot, however, tolerate the chances of rape or other harm befalling Lana. You will carry out your end of the bargain, and release Lana following discovery of my demise."

"You truly are skilled, Xavier, but you represent a threat to America that we cannot allow. You have a deal."

Gunner Volkman put the phone down but, surprisingly, found it difficult to rejoice at his victory. He remembered his all-important image, and then manufactured a forced yell and announced the destruction of Xavier and his followers. He told the others of the deal, and Lana overheard. She immediately screamed a muffled "No!" and began to cry. Gunner told Stan, who had returned with Elaine, to untie Lana as they were soon to travel south. Lana was hysterically weeping, sucking in air between sobs. As soon as Stan removed the last of her binds, Lana had her one and only chance. She bolted up and, before anyone could react, sprinted toward the window. To the absolute shock and surprise of everyone in the room, she hastily opened the window and leapt out.

CHAPTER THIRTY-EIGHT

"Thirty-one Tegretol left, not enough to be sure."

Xavier mumbled this to himself as he looked at the handful of pills he had spread out on the marble counter top in his bathroom. He rummaged around for other medications, and found some Tylenol and a bottle of Robaxisal, a narcotic muscle relaxer Xavier had used during his burn rehabilitation. Robaxisal, yes! At least fifty or sixty of them! That would do it; together with the Tegretol, the combined drugs would quickly drive him into a fatal coma. With no more than an instant's hesitation, Xavier began gulping pills down, one handful after another chased down with water. After he had swallowed all of the available pills, he went to his listening chair and put on Rachmaninoff's "Isle of the Dead" for the last time. He put the CD player on "Repeat" and proceeded to listen to it while he waited to begin fading away.

And as he waited, he unfortunately couldn't escape having to process some of the chaos in his mind. The cataclysm of the Xavierists had caused the horrific mentaar of a thousand anguished souls to be projected out into the ether, and only Xavier could appreciate what had happened from a distance. This created yet another wave of intolerable guilt, and Xavier prayed for the relief of the early sedative effects of the drugs. Within less than twenty minutes, the first effect did occur, but it was more a wretched wave of nausea than the hoped-for sedation. He tried to mentally silence the nausea, and attenuated the sensation somewhat, but he started to involuntarily gag and retch. He attempted to resist, but he soon began regurgitating the contents of his stomach, spitting dozens of different colored pills all over the floor. The gastric spasms continued until seemingly everything in his stomach had been ejected. After overcoming a surge of weakness and lightheadedness, Xavier was left with the inescapable conclusion that his suicide attempt had failed. How? Why? More importantly, what was he to do?

Xavier contemplated his situation intently, incredibly first thinking about Hemingway, and how he must have done it. But no! The path had been laid out for him long ago, and he had simply not been able to decipher it. The key lay not with Hemingway, or anyone else simply because they had committed suicide. It had to lie with Scriabin. How did Scriabin die? It was by infection, a silly infection from a minor sore which today would have easily treated with antibiotics. How symbolic! The ignorance of the times killed a man just reaching the secrets of the cosmos. But that gave no clue for Xavier. It must be something else from the legacy of Scriabin. Toward the Flame! Yes, Toward the Flame! Of course! Oblivion through the purification of fire! Only thus could he truly ascend, and perhaps join Scriabin in another world. Or perhaps it was simply the destiny which fate held for those struggling to solve the cosmic challenges, the mysteries which he and Scriabin had at least discovered some clues to. But mysteries not solved; no, the world was not yet ready to take advantage of the clues that were already found. Perhaps Xavier's death would lead others down that same path of discovery, enlightenment, and search for serenity.

Xavier replaced the Rachmaninoff CD with the Horowitz version of Toward the Flame, his favorite of the seven different pianists' recordings he possessed. He then went in search of means to light the fire which would carry him out of this world. He was able to locate some matches, and also some newspapers. Xavier's hands trembled, and he didn't know whether it was due to anticipatory anxiety or the effects of some medication that got into his system. He shakily spread the newspapers around the room, mostly away from the stereo, because he did not want the music to end prior to his incineration. He took a deep breath, fumbled with the matches a bit and began lighting the papers. Xavier then unceremoniously settled into his chair and cherished the electrifying sounds of his favorite piece, the piece of his destiny.

CHAPTER THIRTY-NINE

Lana Marshall's destiny was not to die along with Xavier, at least not now. She had leapt out of the window knowing that the pool lay directly below, and that it was probably her only chance at survival. She landed with a tremendous splash, with barely two feet clearance from the edge of the pool. The shock of the impact rattled through her like being electrocuted, and for a moment she felt herself losing consciousness. However, she was immediately jarred again by striking the bottom, and this actually jolted her into reflexively springing out with her legs and bounding up for air. Incredibly, there were no painful sensations indicating she had sustained serious injury, only a generalized tingling. She groped for the edge of the pool and quickly got out. Some well-meaning and concerned guests rushed up to help, but she pushed them aside and headed out, sprinting directly toward the beach.

Lana disregarded the fact that her clothes had been sliced open and her body was significantly exposed. After only a moment's pause to identify which one of the several moored boats was hers, she leapt into the ocean and began swimming vigorously straight out through the breakers. The salt water burned in several areas, alerting her that she had sustained at least a few scrapes. She kept focused on her boat, which had a distinctive black band running the length of the otherwise white thirty-foot cabin cruiser. Lana's friends were still celebrating Lana's good fortune in the agent business, and music could be heard nearly all the way to the beach. Lana swam the hundred yards or so quickly, and as soon as her friends saw her they knew she was not swimming for personal enjoyment. They hurried to gather her up and into the boat. She caught her breath for a moment, then told them that she needed the boat immediately. She implored them to swim ashore and report to the authorities that she had "escaped from cultist abductors in room 417." Her friends momentarily thought that this still might be a gag, and mocked her story by joking that they couldn't because they had "a couple of Cuban refugee stowaways they had to watch over." Lana became frantic and screamed her seriousness at them until they were convinced. The friends then begged for more details, and did not want to leave her alone. But Lana emphatically demanded they leave, and they reluctantly departed.

Lana aimed her cabin cruiser south and raced the vessel as fast as it would go. She gave a second of thanks to her deceased husband for teaching her the fundamentals of boating, and then focused her attention back on Xavier. The pain of his abuse of her was not forgotten by any means, and she definitely had some unfinished business with him on that matter. But Lana had come to realize that she really did love Xavier. In fact, she had not really fallen out of love with Xavier; she had only come to the conclusion that she could not trust him during his emotional upheavals. Lana had struggled with many complicated feelings besides love: compassion, awe, pity, and more recently, fear and rage. Nothing had been simple with Xavier, not his life, his destiny, or even his feelings for her. Lana had not overheard the word suicide from Gunner's conversation with Xavier, but she had heard enough to suspect that was what was on his mind. Perhaps it was just a bit of the sixth sense Xavier had tried to develop in her, but she was certain of what Xavier was thinking this time. Regardless of what their future together held, if they had one, she had to stop him from committing suicide to save her life!

She raced the boat at full throttle for over an hour and began to grow worried that she would be too late. To make matters worse, those "friends" of hers had used up much of the gas and the meter was running near empty. She was fortunate that she had the Islamorada "Swim With the Dolphins" contraption as a landmark to look for, to indicate that she was near her intended destination. Straining to see with the salty air stinging her eyes, she finally spotted it, and eased off the throttle. She guided the boat close to the shore, pausing only to heave the anchor overboard before she dove out. She swam the brief distance to shore, aided by the surf, and then hit the ground running.

"My god!" Lana exclaimed, as she saw that Xavier's house was in flames! She picked up her already full sprint to the limits of her physical capacity, cursed the soft sand and finally barreled in through the front door. She screamed "Xavier!" and found him exactly where she knew he would be, sitting mesmerized in his favorite chair, listening to Scriabin. The fire was engulfing him, with flames and smoke everywhere. The flames had reached his chair, and had just caught the sleeve of his left arm. Although the fire had begun to sear through flesh,

Xavier was oblivious to it. He had put himself into a deeper and deeper trance with each playing of the five-minute Vers La Flamme, and totally disregarded the growing cauldron around him. Lana ran and grabbed him, using her still-wet body to advantage by putting out the flame on his arm. She frantically dragged him out the front door, which by now itself had become encircled with fire. Xavier struggled out of his death trance, and gradually became more cognizant of the new reality which had befallen him. He reached up and gently touched Lana's face, read her psyche and knew exactly what she had in mind. Lana fondly remembered the sensation of being read by Xavier, and the same feeling she had disliked earlier was like an intangible kiss to her at this moment. For a second too long they shared the enrapturing feeling of life, and the indomitable desire to preserve it. Lana realized they had no time for this mental rendezvous, and she quickly grabbed Xavier's hand. She shouted "COME ON!" and pulled him out of the chair. Lana led the way as they ducked under the edge of the inferno and ran outside. They barely escaped a fiery death, as Xavier heard the last distinctive notes of "Toward The Flame" incinerate along with the stereo and everything else inside.

The two jubilantly sprinted toward the ocean and simultaneously dove in. They swam in tandem to the boat, with Xavier following Lana's mental presence without difficulty. Lana arrived at the boat and first guided Xavier up the hanging ladder. Once safely aboard, they faced each other and breathlessly embraced. The passion they shared at that moment was so fervid, so exhilarating that they both lifted their heads back in sheer ecstasy and howled.

A moment later, Lana experienced a wave of panic and anger as she relived the last moments of when he last touched her. The memory of his uncontrollable sexual battery of her struck her with an infuriating flashback. She stiffened, forcibly pushed him a foot away and proceeded to punch him in the face. "That's for abusing me, you crazy son of a bitch!" she yelled at him as he fell backward and haplessly tumbled in a heap. He was quite a pathetic sight; a half-unconscious, partly re-burned blind man flailing around amongst some empty beer cans in the corner of the boat.

While Xavier struggled to gain some semblance of control, Lana put her re-surfaced fury aside and put herself to the tasks at hand. She checked the throttle position and ignition, surveyed the length of the boat, and then began pulling up the anchor. It was heavy and, as she got it near the surface of the water, she struggled to get it aboard. Xavier was still dazed and smarting, but began regaining his composure. He located her presence and sensed her strain, so he got up to help her. He walked over next to her, and placed his hands next to hers on the anchor line. As they lifted the anchor together, their spirits again began to soar. Xavier's strength had always been in the art of healing, and he clutched to the hope of healing Lana's pain even more than his own. He communicated his deepest sorrow, sorrow so great he was willing to give his life, and did so without saying a word. He chose not to simply remove Lana's pain mentally, feeling that would be an abuse of his powers. After communicating his sorrow, he sent messages of gratitude and, ultimately, love. Love for her first, but also love of life. The joy of life was never more real to both of them, and although neither knew what lay in store for them, they joyously set off to sea.

EPILOGUE

No one knew where Xavier and Lana went after their last encounter in Islamorada. There were many rumors, with Xavier being placed in Cuba, Ecuador, Panama, and even Africa. One story had it that Xavier had gone to a small island in the Caribbean and had quickly converted the locals into a pacifist, happy commune with healthy mentaar. This story maintained that Lana was Xavier's "medication," helping keep his urges and surges under control.

Another story had it that Xavier and Lana quickly split apart and that Xavier immediately took to being a total recluse. Lana was rumored to have returned to the States incognito, for fear of being abducted again.

There were also scattered reports of "Xavier sightings," for any tall, bald figure with Xavieresque garb was easily noticed and assumed to be Xavier. However, in every sighting that was closely examined, the person involved was either a Xavier want-to-be or an actual Xavierist who had not given up the cause. Xavierism per se had in fact

302

not completely died with the fiery cataclysm in South Florida. Indeed, one Zandu Hamareesch had simply named it "The Purification," and convinced his few but still faithful followers that it was a necessary transitional stage. First, he explained, the Revelrents had broken off and disintegrated as a movement. Second, of the Paxavierists themselves, only the truly devout were able to emotionally survive Xavier's apparent demise, and remain committed to his cause. And last, Xavier was assumed to have deliberately removed himself from modern society, for it was too plagued with polluted, evil mentaar. Xavier would remain in hibernation until such time as his teachings were heeded by the masses; only then could he gloriously return to the Utopian world that he envisioned.

As to the official status of Xavier and Lana, little authenticated information was available. Government and Florida officials conducted a complete investigation, and found no conclusive evidence to suggest that either was still alive. They were ultimately classified as "lost at sea."

In fact the only reliable report resulted from when they were spotted the same day as when Xavier's house burned down. It occurred at another "Come Swim With The Dolphins" attraction located several miles south of Islamorada. The owner told the story often, each time remaining angry but somehow relishing his brief moment in the spotlight of fame. As he remembered, a roughly thirty-foot cabin cruiser pulled up just as the sun was setting. A tall, bald man wearing a black-on-white outfit was accompanied by a very shapely brunette as they docked their boat at his pier. The twosome initially appeared pleasant and happy, but perhaps not entirely in love, although he wasn't sure if the man was ill or maybe just odd. The woman did most of the talking, and in fact the man excused himself soon after arrival. She requested they have their boat filled with gas, plus have as much gas in portable tanks as the man could provide. She asked for food and water, and nothing else, and paid for it all with a thick gold chain. The owner asked the woman where they were headed and she only replied "South."

All seemed well as he watched them sail off, but he was immediately struck at the horde of dolphins swimming and leaping around the boat. He ran to check his pen, and in fact all of his dolphins were gone. The owner ran to the edge of his dock, screaming in vain as he watched the large boat get away. The last sight of them would remain forever etched in his mind; the two of them leading an entourage of dolphins, with a black bird flying overhead, speeding away in a boat named "Vers La Flamme."

THE END

ABOUT THE AUTHOR

Ray Dean, M.D. is a psychiatrist from Florida. He has been creative throughout his life, with talent as a pianist, composer, sculptor, cartoonist, and poet. He has distinguished himself in his career as a psychiatrist, having been medical director of a psychiatric hospital for several years. Following the path of Jonathan Kellerman, he is shifting into a career as a writer and phasing down his psychiatric practice. He uses his medical background and experience to craft novels which are based on substance and fact, but uses his artistic bent to inject the necessary sparkle and novelty.